Deception

by

Noel Primrose

ISBN: 978-1-917601-23-8

Noel was born in Glasgow but now lives in an East Sussex village with his wife Lynda.

He was a Chartered Engineer and began his career in 1954 serving an engineering apprenticeship with British Railways engaged in the maintenance of steam locomotives. He then spent 7 years on the design and construction of railway electrification before joining the National Health Service in 1966 with the United Bristol Hospitals. Subsequently he transferred to Tunbridge Wells and subsequently Eastbourne. In all he spent 34 years in the NHS most of which were at Board level before retiring in 2000.

His main interests are his family and being outdoors where walking and gardening are his main pursuits. In the past he was passionate about running, especially marathons and half marathons. Noel is a keen football and rugby fan.

Published 2024

This book is dedicated to my unforgettable and inspirational Mum, and to my Dad, who taught me to be strong in the face of adversity

Other books by the Author

A Fall to the Top

Treachery

Betrayal

PROLOGUE

There were seven of them in the room, three men, four women, gathered with a common purpose, and yet, the small talk which might have been expected amongst friends, or even business colleagues, was almost absent; such dialogue as there was, was stilted and muted. The occasional outbursts of laughter, which would usually have emerged as experiences were recounted, were missing. The atmosphere was almost one of foreboding, and added to by the fact that everyone present was wearing a black face mask; the sharing of identity was forbidden.

The formal meeting would begin shortly but there were no prior discussions or lobbying of support for proposals due to be put forward. One or two stood apart, alone with their individual thoughts, showing no interest in either the food set before them, or their colleagues, if that's what the others could be called. The atmosphere was tense, fear was ever-present at these meetings.

At the rear of the room, a table was elegantly set for a light buffet lunch; the quality of the fare provided gave a clear indication of the importance of the event and the wealth available to its provider. Amongst the offerings could be found

Beluga caviar, Dublin Bay prawns, Green Bay oysters, smoked Scottish wild salmon, white truffles, Dom Perignon champagne and a range of freshly squeezed fruit juices. Consumption of the champagne was modest; everyone wanted to retain sharp wits for the dealings that lay ahead. There was no service; those who had attended to the catering had long since departed.

The casual onlooker would have been puzzled at the layout of the room. For one thing, although it was midday, the heavy, pure silk, green curtains had been pulled across the windows hiding the beautiful views of the lake beyond. Behind the curtains, steel shutters ensured that unauthorised access would be difficult, whether for person, camera or listening device. The floors were of black marble; the walls were white and plain, relieved only by a simple pale green frieze. The matching pale green ceiling was panelled and decorated with gold gilt motifs.

Seven dark green leather armchairs had been placed in an arc facing the windows; in front of each was a small white marble-topped desk, built into it were the controls for the audio-visual equipment. In front of the arc of chairs, some distance away was a dais, rising about thirty centimetres above the floor; on this sat a white throne-like leather armchair, a clear symbol of the authority of its owner. It too was attended by a desk, larger than the others and arrayed with a panel of controls and switches. Nobody ventured near the dais; that was forbidden. Those present knew the power it represented.

The villa was registered to the ownership of a local politician, but in fact, it belonged to an organisation - an organisation without a name. A name wasn't required, names attracted attention and were open to the attribution of blame, whether justified or not; anonymity was its mantra. There were seven similar properties; one in each of the cabal's seven operational zones. These comprised: Europe, Russia and the Balkans; China and Japan; Africa and the Middle East; India, East and West Pakistan and Bangladesh; Australasia and the Pacific Rim countries; the United States and Canada; and the countries of South America. The zones were referred to by their number, one to seven. Each zone had its own designated leader who was simply addressed by their zone number, one to seven

The organisation had a strategically located base within each of its seven zones. The bases all had good road access to a major international airport, although all those involved usually travelled by a privately owned or chartered jet aircraft. All seven were set in extensive, heavily guarded, secure grounds to ensure privacy.

The organisation had been in existence for over three decades, year on year extending its influence both politically and commercially by legal or illegal methods. Those who obstructed progress were dealt with; assassination or destruction were the final arbiters.

A single low-resonating gong-tone announced that the meeting would commence in twenty seconds. Those present immediately made their way to their respective chairs. They would all be in place before their undisputed despotic Leader entered the room. He would remain their leader until he died or chose to retire. He alone would nominate his successor; even in death, his decision was unlikely to be challenged.

To safeguard against the Leader's untimely death, the name of the successor was held deep in the web and could only be activated by a code of twenty-eight digits. Each zone representative, and their undercover deputy, knew only four digits which would be entered in zone number order; only by acting together could they enter the complete code to determine their new leader. The Leader, that was how he was known, had the full code and could nominate his successor as often as he thought necessary. Some speculated from time to time, within the safe confines of their thoughts, as to what would happen if the members unanimously concluded that he had outlived his usefulness, but no-one had ever dared give voice to the idea. All were afraid that he might somehow learn of their prospective disloyalty and knew dire consequences would surely follow discovery.

The meeting would be short as were all meetings of the group; its purpose was to give direction, make reports and receive information. There were no debates, no arguments, no voting; the Leader would listen and he alone would decide on the action to be taken.

The gong sounded again, signalling the entrance of the Leader; a man of smallish stature, who could have been any age between fifty and seventy. He was dressed in a plain, white linen, immaculately tailored suit. His head, neck and face were fully covered with a red, skin-tight mask; black eyes peered through the slits in the mask. His whole countenance projected an aura of power and evil. He paid no regard to those assembled as he took his seat in the throne-like chair; they had been under his observation since their arrival. He offered no greeting or welcome. How they felt was an irrelevancy; he ruled by fear and indifference, not popularity. His bronzed fingers travelled over the keyboard as he entered a code to activate his and the other control panels.

'Your report Number One.' The language of the meeting was always English. His voice was toneless, almost resonant and without accent; they all knew it was electronically created.

Truth to tell he didn't really need the reports, he trusted no-one, and each of those present had a deputy who secretly kept him informed. The purpose of the meeting was more about exercising control over those present than listening to them report what he already knew.

The occupant of chair Number One, who represented Europe, Russia and the Balkans, remained seated, as was the custom when making reports to the Leader. What the others thought or how they received his report was of little import. 'Our infra-structure is almost complete; we have infiltrated all Government *and Opposition factions at senior level. Our intelligence network is now fully operational; we have total control of the distribution of all drugs, alcohol, tobacco and most medications. All competitive elements have been dealt with through negotiation or elimination, usually the latter. We have covertly modified local Stock Exchange computer software and can manipulate data at your direction. Current estimated annual operating profit to date is one hundred billion US dollars. I await your instructions regarding neighbouring territories.'*

The Leader received the report with a small nod of satisfaction. The occupant of Chair One relaxed for the first time since he received his invitation to the gathering.

'Your report Number Three.' All those attending, were of equal standing, and would only speak when invited to by their Leader. Number Three, who represented Africa and the Middle East, began slowly, choosing her words carefully. 'We have completed the covert installation of radio-active charges in the designated petrochemical refineries; you can issue extortion demands when you are ready. Based on current levels of oil storage, I believe an annual yield equivalent to twenty billion US dollars is possible.' The occupant of Chair Seven leant back in her seat waiting for the Leader's response.

The Leader's eyes narrowed. 'And the attacks on the temples in Iran, Number Three, what of those? War and strife in the Middle East are key elements of my plan.'

The woman licked her lips nervously, nodding as she searched for the right words. 'The attacks will take place this week-end. I have deferred them until the current Holy week concludes; I considered that the delay would not prevent achievement of our objective. The temples would have been full of worshippers during this period, the loss of innocent lives including children would have been unnecessarily high; public outrage would have been immeasurable.'

The Leader displayed no outward signs of emotion; his voice gave no hint of the anger he felt at this blatant disregard of his authority. 'I am disappointed Number Three, I chose the dates for the attacks very carefully, a high death toll was an essential element of my plan. The buildings themselves were of no account. You will not disobey my instructions again.' The Leader reached forward and pressed a button.

Almost immediately two masked men silently entered the room behind the arc of seats and walked across to Chair Three. Its occupant let out a yell of surprise and her eyes filled with fear; she knew she was doomed. The two men, sombrely dressed in black suits dragged the woman kicking and yelling across the floor and out of the room.

The Leader offered no explanation as to the woman's fate. 'I will introduce a replacement representative for Zone Three at our next gathering. Your report Number Seven.'

Number Seven was the representative for the continent of South America. He spoke neither too quickly, nor too slowly, seeking to convey confidence. 'Manufacture of biological products is proceeding to plan. We have already stockpiled the quantities of Ebola, Anthrax and Sars you require and by the end of this month, we will have completed production of your Novichok requirement, thereby meeting your instructions in full.'

The Leader nodded approvingly. 'I will announce targets at our next meeting and give details of the plans for deployment. You will all be involved; this will be our greatest ever venture.It has the potential to generate billions of dollars annually in perpetuity.' His eyes glinted as he savoured the prospect; those who knew him longest detected an uncharacteristic note of excitement.

The meeting continued, for another hour ending with a warning from the leader. 'I have learned recently that the United States and British Intelligence agencies have acquired some knowledge of the existence of our organisation and are about to launch an operation to secure our demise.

I understand that the British agent involved is a male named Jos Cole. He is resourceful, he is ruthless, he is dangerous; he should be eliminated whenever an opportunity presents. A reward of one million dollars will be given to whoever brings about the death of this agent.

As yet, I have not ascertained the identity of the United States agent involved, but hope to do so in the near future. I will keep you informed as and when I learn more. In the meantime, be on your guard.'

NATO MEETING. STOCKHOLM, SWEDEN

NATO representatives, political and military had gathered in the Rikdag to mark Sweden's membership of NATO; speeches flowed, free world rhetoric was the order of the day. By prior agreement, through diplomatic channels, there was no specific mention of Russia, nor of Ukraine. But there had been a firm commitment by members, that any territorial incursion – invasion - or so-called 'special military operation' threatening a NATO member or an ally, would lead to the introduction of worldwide sanctions against the aggressor.

Underground

Deep below the Rikdag, another meeting was about to take place away from the glare of the media. The Director of the CIA had scheduled a meeting with his British counterpart, the Head of MI6.

The American, Mitch Rosetti was being led along a corridor to a totally-shielded room. The room was carpeted and furnished with comfortable armchairs and coffee tables, but there were no wall hangings or ornamental reliefs of any kind whatsoever. Concealment of spyware however minute would be difficult.

Captain Nils Ahlman used his swipe card and pushed open the heavy metal door, then stood back inviting his two guests to enter. Rosetti motioned his Aide to go ahead; Louise Schultz nodded and went in. Ahlman realised what was happening and protested. *'I assure you there are no surveillance bugs present in the room; it is checked daily.'*

Rosetti stared at him and gave an empty smile. *'I'm sure that is the case, Captain; and I'm sure my Aide will be able to confirm your findings,'* a deliberate pause followed, *'**after** she has carried out her own checks.'*

Ahlman shrugged and stood back. Schultz made her way into the room and pushed the door closed behind her. She then began meticulously scanning the room and its furnishings. The scanner was state-of-the-art technology; if there was a bug, she would find it. Five minutes passed, then another five before the door opened and Schultz stepped out into the corridor. She nodded at Rosetti. *'All clear, sir.'* Rosetti smiled at her, *'Thank you, Louise, you can rejoin the Conference.'*

Ahlman smirked but said nothing.

Rosetti turned to the young Captain. *'Your assurances have been verified, Captain, the meeting can take place as planned. Show my British colleague in as soon as she arrives; our meeting will be brief.'*

Ahlman smiled thinly. *'Yes, sir.'*

Rosetti entered, swung the door closed behind him and sat down on the nearest armchair, putting his briefcase on an adjacent coffee table. He ignored the collection of liquor-full decanters and sat back to await his guest, the Head of MI6.

A few minutes later the door opened and Germaine Moore made her way into the room; a forty-something, smallish, *slightly-built woman with short-cropped, blonde hair. Rosetti rose, smiling broadly and took a step towards his compatriot, putting a hand on each of her shoulders. 'Great to meet face-to-face, Gerry' He studied her briefly, 'You're looking a touch tired if you don't mind me saying so.'*

The Head of MI5 smiled weakly. 'Good to see you too, Mitch, sun-tanned and lean as ever. I guess my makeup isn't as good as I thought. You're right, I am just about knackered. My political masters are so fucking unrealistic; pains in the arse, all of them.'

Rosetti smiled, 'Tell me about it. Grab a seat and relax best you can; pour yourself a drink. I had the room checked for bugs by the way, it's clear.'

Moore slumped into a chair and put her bulky briefcase on the floor; an astute observer would have noted that hers was identical to Rosetti's. She poured herself a whisky, glanced at Rosetti and raised an invitational eyebrow.

Rosetti shook his head, 'Saving myself for later; I've got to get back to my lot, soon as. Sorry I haven't got more time. You are the bearer of good news, I hope?'

Moore nodded, 'Yes, it's all systems go; I've had the nod for three zones, Europe, Oz, India etc. That leaves you with the remaining four zones; you being the bigger hitter. I've been told that my budget is unlimited, although that can change rapidly if I don't get the required results.'

Rosetti face lit up and he punched the air. 'Well done, Gerry, just what we wanted; I'm happy with the split. And who's your

Agent on this one? I guess it will be that guy...' He stopped midstream when Moore put her finger to her lips. Puzzlement furrowed his brow. 'I told you, there are no bugs in here; we can speak freely, I assure you.'

Moore sighed deeply. 'I know Mitch, but I'm just adding another layer of security; I don't want to know who your operative is and I don't want you knowing mine. We know there's a leak somewhere in one of our organisations, maybe in both of them. That's why you came down here accompanied by a specialist security aide. I'm being super-cautious, I know, maybe even paranoid, but if anything does get out, it's down to you or me.'

Rosetti shrugged, 'Sorry it has to be that way. I'd trust you with my life, Gerry'

'And I you, Mitch. But bear with me this time, this is the biggest joint mission we'll ever tackle.'

'I guess so. On reflection, you're probably right. I have one reservation though, I thought there might be occasions when our agents might work together, watch each other's backs. This is one helluva a mission they're embarking on.'

Moore smiled, a gleam in her eye, and took another sip of whisky. 'I've thought of that.' and pointed to her briefcase. 'They can communicate via mobiles; they can only tune into each other on a narrow, secure frequency; codename Deception. The details are in there. You and I and our agents are the only ones who will know of this arrangement.

Rosetti nodded, and pushed his briefcase across to Moore. As previously agreed, the duo exchanged briefcases.

'I presume this lot is as we agreed, Gerry? We're sharing everything we know about the organisation we've christened the Hydra?'

Moore nodded. 'Yes. We familiarise ourselves with the papers, then pass them on to our respective agents on a read and destroy basis. Correct?'

Rosetti nodded and glanced at his watch. 'Correct. I have to go, sorry.' He reached into his pocket and retrieved a memory stick. 'As agreed, everything on this is for your eyes only. I assume you've got one for me.'

Moore nodded. 'Of course.' She rummaged in an inside pocket and handed over a stick. 'Job done; all we have to do now is succeed in kicking the shit out of the Hydra. Good luck, Mitch.'

Rosetti bent forward and kissed her on the cheek. 'You too, Gerry, see you around.'

The meeting over, Rosetti exited the room and headed back to the main NATO gathering. Moore left five minutes later. She would be picked up outside the Rikdag and taken to a local military airport; from there an RAF flight would take her back to London.

A puzzled Nils Ahlman watched them depart, wondering why two key government officials had met in such a clandestine manner for such a brief meeting.

CHAPTER ONE

A naked man lay on the floor of a small room; a room just three metres square; the walls and ceiling painted black, harbingers of death. His movements constrained by leather straps around his wrists and ankles, writhing and straining were wasted effort. Above him an uncased fluorescent tube provided harsh soulless lighting. He was alone, but was he under surveillance? He looked around as best he could, allowing himself a small smile when he failed to detect any security cameras.

This gave him hope that he could at least try to escape and he struggled again to release himself, eventually giving up, his energy drained; the leather straps were too strong. And that was when he heard it, a low humming noise, the meshing of gears; sounds he didn't understand. The walls seemed to be moving, steadily closing in; he was going to be crushed to death, this was the end. 'Stop, stop, I'll do what you want.' He knew his pleas wouldn't be answered - he was doomed.

Jos Cole woke with a start, his heart pounding, his body bathed in sweat. It wasn't the first time he'd had this dream and he doubted if it would be the last. At least it had spared him a rude awakening by his shrieking phone alarm which was set for 6am. Over the years he had trained himself to waken on demand and, on most occasions, it was an ability that had served him well, but today was different.

He had been summoned to a meeting with the Head of MI6 at 9am and he knew better than to be late; even a couple of minutes would draw a reprimand. He had set his alarm early to allow time to fulfil the requirements of his newly self-imposed fitness programme.

A recent annual medical had seen him achieve an A1 classification in all key areas, but Dr Ogilvie, a dour officious little Scot whom Cole hadn't previously encountered, had observed. *'Aye, very good Commander, A1 all round for the most part; your SAS background has served you well, but you're not perfect. Certainly not as good as you might like to think you are. You could lose a pound or two to good effect, and while you're at it, do something to build up your stamina. Added to that, you could hardly be regarded as supple; I'd like to see you do something to loosen up those joints of yours. And, I'll be including a note in my report that you need to cut back on your alcohol intake; I wouldn't be surprised if you consume more than you claim.'*

The criticisms had nettled him but he accepted that Ogilvie was probably right. He was exactly two pounds over what he over what he regarded as his best weight; he tended for the most part to rely on his natural fitness, rather than follow any particular exercise routine. Losing a couple of pounds wouldn't be a problem, but stamina and suppleness were a different matter. He hated routine and had a tendency to do the exercises he enjoyed, rather than persevering with the broad range of physical disciplines necessary to achieve maximum benefit. Inwardly he couldn't deny he had let his fitness slip since his SAS days. There was no ruthless sergeant in the driving seat demanding 110%.

He had never been told how he had come to be head-hunted by MI6, but the thought of being a Special Agent had appealed to him; operating overseas and authorised to kill and destroy if that's what it took to achieve a result. His unarmed combat skills must have been a factor and of course his linguistic abilities; he was fluent in French, German and passable with Russian. But that probably applied to others, so why him?

Ogilvie had peered at him over his spectacles when rendering his summing up, like a headmaster addressing an errant pupil. *'It's very easy to go into decline Commander and you've taken the first step in my view. You require a good diet and regular, appropriate exercise to sustain and improve your fitness. And I stress the word appropriate. I'll be making suitable recommendations in my report.'*

Cole had groaned inwardly, knowing that Gerry Moore, MI6 Chief would undoubtedly latch on to Ogilvie's comments and require him to improve. She seemed to seize on any adverse observations and ensure that they were followed up. And, just as he had anticipated, on the occasion of his annual review she had pursued the criticisms relentlessly. Despite his protestations he had been forced to commit to his current fitness programme. From a range of options on offer he had chosen running to improve his stamina, and had elected to undertake additional martial arts sessions to improve his movement, balance and suppleness.

He swung his legs out of bed and pulled on his cobalt-blue dressing gown, a birthday present from the Chief's personal assistant, Sal Galt. *'Blue does suit you, Jos and there's nothing like silk next to the skin, don't you agree?'*

'It is very sexy Sal, but there's nothing can beat skin next to skin, it's potentially so much more rewarding. Don't you think? I could prove it to you if the opportunity came along.' His eyes had held hers, waiting for a response.

'I'll take a rain check on that, Jos.' she had replied smiling.

Cole enjoyed teasing her; they were close, and flirting was part of their ritual, but it had never led to a liaison and probably never would. *Still nothing ventured, nothing gained, I'll keep trying.*

He made his way to the bathroom and freshened up before returning to his bedroom where he pulled on his shorts and trainers, then headed to his exercise room. It had been a spare bedroom, but it never been used as such; if he did have an overnight guest, it would be a woman and it would be his intention that she ended up in his bed.

A treadmill session lay ahead, though ideally, he would have preferred to run outdoors along the Embankment and through London's central parks. But not long back from a perilous mission involving the Mafia he'd felt vulnerable. They would seek revenge and he could hardly jog round the capital equipped with a firearm in a shoulder holster hung over a running vest.

In any case the gym served all his needs; weights, rowing machine and his latest acquisition, a state-of- the-art treadmill. It sat apart from the other equipment facing a silver screen, three metres wide and two metres high. The screen continued at right angles on both sides by around two metres to form a small alley. *Now where shall we go today?*

He selected a computer disc and slotted it into the computer's control unit; the system hummed into life and the room was filled with the sound of voices chattering. Traffic noises could be heard in the distance, and somewhere nearby a band playing. Ahead, and to either side of Cole, the silver screens were filled with runners preparing for a race; he felt like he was in the centre of the action.

On this occasion he had elected to run the Hastings Half Marathon, setting himself a target time of ninety minutes for the thirteen miles. The treadmill would maintain the required speed and display the route as he progressed. It would adjust itself up and down as the road gradients changed and do everything possible to capture the atmosphere of the event itself. The installation had been expensive but he found it easier to run

5

with *company*; good fortune at the gambling tables had provided most of the funds for the purchase.

The ninety minutes target he'd set himself was demanding, but he was in control of the treadmill's speed and could gain time if running well or, more likely, slow it down if he was tiring.

As he ran. he reflected on Sal Galt's telephone call the night before. *'The Chief wants to see you Jos, nine sharp. Don't be late. She's sending Tom to pick you up at eight forty-five.'*

Cole's brow furrowed; he was invariably punctual and wondered why Galt had felt the need to issue a caution. Sending one of the car pool drivers to pick him up was itself unusual. 'What's going on, Sal?'

'I honestly don't know Jos, but whatever it is, it's worrying her; I haven't known her so touchy and grumpy for as long as I can remember.'

'You must know something, Sal, surely?'

'I said I didn't Jos. She's on edge, so watch your Ps and Qs.' Her tone had been firm, almost cross.

'Must be something big?' He had ventured, continuing to probe. 'They're not thinking of merging MI5 and MI6 again, are they?'

*'No, it's not a restructuring issue; she would share that with me. I'm pretty sure it's an assignment. Must go now, and remember, **don't be late***'.

6

Cole smiled at the thought of a mission; it had been some months since his last outing and fingers crossed it would be somewhere warm. An escape from the cold grey dreariness which prevailed in the early months of the UK year would be a bonus. On the other hand, if it was an assignment, why hadn't Bill Tanner, Moore's Chief of Staff, been in touch, or even his deputy Eddie Robinson? He regularly played golf with Bill and regarded him as his closest friend. Surely, he would have let him know if something big was on the move. *Assuming he knows about it, Jos.* Cole pursed his lips. *Strange, very strange.*

The screen showed the road beginning a steep climb; Hastings' Queensway. Cole struggled to maintain the speed the treadmill was demanding of him if he was to achieve his target time. Reluctantly he reduced his pace a fraction; hoping to regain any time lost in the final stages. The climb completed, he used runners ahead of him as pacemakers and pushed hard for the finishing line. At last, he crossed the finishing line, his half marathon completed. The computer prompted the crowd to roar and displayed his time, 90minutes 22seconds. *Damn it.* Failure always annoyed and frustrated him.

He rested for ten minutes, then finished his exercise session with some upper body weight training. Afterwards, he showered and dressed, ready for the day ahead.

Between assignments Cole visited H.Q. daily, gathering intelligence through communications extracted from the airways by GCHQ or the alliance known as the Five Eyes. This was the unglamourous aspect of being an Agent; every day brought a small mountain of paperwork. The routine bored him but he knew it was essential if he was to maintain his knowledge of the political and criminal worlds and be an effective Agent.

On the brighter side, the visits provided an opportunity to engage with Instructors and practice a wide range of hand-to hand combat training and weapons use. The facilities were state-of-the-art and there was always something new to be learned. He was aware that his performance during these sessions was routinely monitored, and would be the subject of regular reports to the Chief. His friend Bill Tanner kept him informed of any concerns or misgivings arising; forewarned was to be forearmed when you were dealing with Gerry Moore.

He searched his memory for anything he'd heard, or read, which could have triggered his urgent mobilisation. Nothing came to mind and he wondered if she was just undertaking a general review and would use the occasion to throw her weight around. *Someone has to crack the whip, Jos.* He smiled inwardly at the image of Gerry Moore this created.

Cole left his King's Road apartment shortly before 8.45am; the solid door swinging securely closed behind him. It was protected by a complex high-tech security system and access was judged to be impossible without the numeric code. At the heart of the system was a five digit electronically activated lock whose code was known only to the Chief, Bill Tanner, Sal Galt and himself. The number was randomly generated and changed regularly. The door was solid steel, clad with an oak veneer and outwardly looked like all the other doors in the apartment block, but when activated, four steel bars slid into position to prevent unauthorised access.

Cole stepped out into the chill grey of a January morning wrinkling his nose when he saw the sky. It held the threat of rain, clouds were forming and seemed to absorb each other into an ever-darkening shade of grey. *More rain ahead,* thought Cole gloomily. *I do hope this assignment sees me headed for the Tropics.*

He crossed the pavement and pulled open the door of the waiting dark-grey Rover.

'Good morning, Tom.'

'Good morning, Sir.'

'Looks like we're in for some of the wet stuff.'

'Do we need to go through the routine, Sir? We've known each other a long time.'

Cole stifled a sigh; the driver was referring to a security procedure involving an exchange of coded phrases he could never be bothered to keep abreast of.

'You're right, Tom, we can forego that charade.' He appreciated the merits of the system; every agent didn't know every driver and vice versa and it wasn't many years ago that an MI6 agent had been abducted and found later floating in the

Thames. The occurrence had led to a tightening up of security, some of it tedious in its execution but necessary nevertheless.

Most drivers chattered incessantly as they went about their duties, keen to glean whatever they could from their occupant; others remain silent only speaking when spoken to. Tom Carver was in the latter category; a stout ruddy-cheeked man in his mid-fifties and the owner of a rich Somerset accent. Not that it mattered; there wouldn't be much time available for conversation during the short journey to MI6 Headquarters. *Why had he been picked up?*

'Everything all right at home Tom? Wife keeping well these days?" Cole recalled that Mrs Carver had been ill not too long ago, although he couldn't remember what had been wrong with her.

'Oh yes Sir. Everything's just fine at the moment. The missus seems to have got over her problem; kind of you to enquire, thank you.'

This concluded their conversation and Cole settled back into the rich leather upholstery to enjoy the ride, once again contemplating his forthcoming meeting.

Arriving at their destination, both Cole and Carver had to produce identification before they were afforded access through the main gates. All the parties involved knew each other but it was too close to the Chief's watchful eye to set aside procedure. There was an abundance of CCTV on the site and every movement was caught on camera. Entrance and exit routines were rigidly observed and reflected the Chief's policy that Headquarters security was a top organisational priority. She argued, rightly, that '*any breach would be a national disgrace.*'

The Rover rolled forward the short distance to the flight of steps that led up to the entrance to the building which lay at the very heart of Cole's life.

'Perhaps I'll see you later Sir. I'll be in the car pool room if you need me."

'Thanks Tom, I'll see how things work out. I'll probably walk back if it's not raining.' A glance at his watch told him it was 8.55am; he was on time.

CHAPTER TWO

The MI6 building had undergone major repairs following the explosion of a device planted by the Mafia; the only occasion in its history that the internal security of the organisation had been seriously breached. There were no telltale signs remaining, neither internally nor externally, to give evidence to the failure in security that had caused so much damage. The media publicity that ensued had crucified MI6, turning it into a laughing stock throughout the world's spy fraternity. It had incurred the wrath of the Prime Minister and led to the resignation of the previous Head of MI6, Edgar Johnston.

Moore had overhauled the organisation from top to bottom, making it clear that heads would roll if MI6 were ever again to be subjected to a similar occurrence. The Prime Minister had made it clear to her that she would be the first to go, and that MI6 itself might not survive the aftermath.

Security had been tightened extensively following the incident, which had seen a bomb explode internally, ripping a huge hole in the external wall of the building. The restoration work, which had been carried out under Moore's personal direction, had been meticulous. *'No visible sign must remain of our failure for future visitors and staff to see every time they enter our Headquarters'*

Cole knew that his car would have been closely observed from the instant it arrived at MI6 Headquarters. At some stage, the series of security cameras would have caught his image and matched it centrally with his coded security pass which had been scanned electronically by the security guard at the entrance gate when he first entered the precinct. It was no longer sufficient for the bearer's image to match that on his identification pass; it also had to match one held on computer. Moore had insisted that security was tight but discreet. *'We don't want to look like scared rabbits, afraid of our own shadows.'*

Visitors not in possession of a valid pass were subject to alternative procedures and their vehicles were not allowed to park or wait near the building; in Cole's view the external measures were foolproof. But the biggest risk remained unchanged - infiltration by double agents. Although in that regard matters were also improving; there was far less reliance placed on the Old Boys' network as a pathway for recruitment.

The entrance to HQ had been remodelled since the explosion and although spacious and well furnished, with a feeling of informality, it too was under continuous surveillance by concealed cameras and listening devices. It was entirely self-contained, with subsequent access to other areas of the building strictly controlled. Highly sophisticated scanners could detect explosives, electronic devices or weapons and would display their existence on screen in the central control room. Subdued wall colours and numerous paintings disguised the concrete and steel enclosure, which formed the reception area to MI6. Everyone entering the building was initially restricted to this area; further progress was controlled jointly by security staff situated in reception and the central control room. A single door and two lifts provided access to the other areas of the building.

Cole crossed to the reception desk which stood like an island in the centre of the entrance area and was, as always, attended by two security staff; on this occasion a man and a woman. The man, youngish with an athletic physique, extended a welcome, 'Good morning, sir, how can I be of assistance?'

His female companion, an attractive redhead, who was relatively new to the organisation, eyed Cole with interest. He held her gaze briefly, smiled and nodded politely.

'Commander Cole to see the Chief, I have an appointment at 9 o'clock.'

The young man glanced at his watch, 'Cutting it fine sir. Can I have your security pass or other form of authorisation please?'

Cole bit on his tongue; he regarded this added layer of security as tedious and unnecessary. The appropriate checks had been undertaken; they had already ensured he was who he claimed to be, and they knew why he was present. But he knew that any protest would be futile. He produced his pass and it was duly swiped through a scanner; a display of his head and shoulders immediately filled a screen set into the counter. His security classification was recorded along with confirmation that he did have an appointment with the Chief.

The screen also showed that his firearm, a Walther PPK, had been detected by one of the metal detectors but confirmed that he was authorised to carry a weapon in the building. He had reflected from time to time that this could prove to be security's Achilles heel; if an agent such as himself defected to the other side, lives of key staff would be at risk. Moore had acknowledged his concerns but decided not to take any action, *'We have to draw the line somewhere; I have to trust my own agents, or explain why I recruited them in the first place.'*

'Thank you, Commander, please use the left-hand lift.'

As Cole crossed to the lift, its doors opened automatically, then closed immediately behind him when he entered. It then began its journey to the sixth floor, as programmed by the young man in reception. Cole began to relax knowing that the formalities of security were now over, albeit every corridor and all communal areas remained under the watchful eye of the CCTV system. *I suppose we had to move on from the old days* mused Cole *but life was so much simpler then.*

The lift had two sets of doors, and on stopping, the rear set opened onto a short corridor. This was Moore's personal kingdom, the heart of MI6. A few doors led off on either side along its length; keypads ensuring that only authorised staff could gain access. Her office was located at the far end of the corridor and could only be accessed through an outer office occupied by the delectable and redoubtable Sal Galt

Cole wondered if Moore had an alternative escape route she could use in emergencies. If there was one, it was well concealed, and he knew that any enquiry would bring a frosty and uninformative response; as was always the case when his curiosity strayed beyond what was necessary for him to fulfil his duties.

The door to Moore's outer office was open and he strolled in without knocking.

'Good morning, Jos.' A smiling Sal Galt, smartly dressed as always in a designer business suit, was genuinely pleased to see him.

'You're looking very pleased with yourself Sal, business or pleasure?' He raised an enquiring eyebrow, waiting momentarily for a reply before going on. 'I suspect a romantic interlude?' Cole smiled, 'I just hope he was very old and decrepit, I wouldn't want to see myself with a young rival.'

Galt faked a swoony expression. 'I'm sure you don't believe for one moment that anyone could rival you Jos. In any case, a rival for what exactly?'

'Your affections, what else Sal.'

'If you really want to know Jos, I enjoyed a social evening with an old school chum. And before you ask, female, and definitely not a rival for your non-existent affections.'

'One of these days…' Before Cole could finish his banter Moore's voice intruded.

'Send Cole in straight away Sal, he's already two minutes late. And perhaps you could save your socialising for your leisure hours; this isn't some kind of dating agency.'

Cole and Galt exchanged amused smiles and shrugged shoulders; both mildly surprised that Moore had deigned to listen in on an outer office conversation.

Cole made his way into Moore's office; firmly closing the door behind him. Moore was seated behind her desk, a serious look on her face.

'Sit down, Cole.' *Woof, woof, there's a good doggie.* As usual she managed to make it sound more like a command rather than an invitation. 'What do you know about the Hydra?' Moore enquired, pointedly skipping even the briefest of social preliminaries.

Cole blinked. 'As I recall, it's a mythical Greek legendary water-snakelike monster with seven heads. That's the sum of my knowledge. I didn't study the classics.' His spirits lifted, maybe a warm Mediterranean mission was on the cards.

Moore nodded appreciatively. 'I did study the Classics and you're correct, though some writings said it had nine heads one of which was immortal. But that's not the Hydra I'm alluding to.'

Cole shrugged. 'I haven't heard of any other, so which Hydra do you have in mind.'

'To be honest, I didn't expect you to have heard of it; it's a new organisation, so named courtesy of Mitch Rosetti. It's all in here.' Moore pushed a box file filled with papers across her desk. 'Read these papers before you leave the building, digest every word, remember every detail, return the box to Sal when you've finished; these are the only copies. Come back tomorrow early and read them again if needs be. Say nothing to anyone about what these papers reveal. And I do mean nothing, absolutely nothing, not even to your friend Bill Tanner, other agents, nobody. Understood?'

Cole was taken aback by the aggression in her voice. He was routinely required to read briefing papers generated by GCHQ and other Government departments, a task which he didn't really enjoy, but which he nevertheless undertook diligently. Moore clearly wasn't her usual self, there was a real edge to her voice; it was cloaked in irritation, anger almost.

Christ, she's under considerable stress. 'This sounds big, Chief, I'd value your summary of what this box contains if at all possible. It'll make it easier and quicker for me to understand the papers.'

Moore sighed and nodded. 'You're right, of course you are, I'm not thinking straight. This whole business threatens democracy and freedom throughout the world. And time is not on our side. The Hydra has infiltrated governments and government departments throughout the world. There's no doubt it's been going on for years and we didn't see it happening. We're at the eleventh hour; MI6 and the CIA, have decided to act quickly to stop it in its tracks before it's too late. What I'm about to tell you is known only to our Prime Minister, the President of the United States, Mitch Rosetti and his agent, and you and me. By choice I don't know the name of Mitch's agent. We've agreed to operate as independently as possible. The entire Cabinet is being kept in the dark and that includes the Foreign Secretary and the Home Secretary.'

Cole's eyes widened., 'Christ, you must be talking about the Holy Grail of crime and terrorism - world domination.' Cole expressed his scepticism, shaking his head. 'I don't believe it's possible; it's a fantasy world, a delusion. There are too many criminal organisations, too many vested interests in this sad old world for any single organisation to take over its entirety. It just won't happen, it's impossible!'

Moore slapped her desk in frustration with both hands. 'What do you take me for? Do you think I'm a fucking fool, think I've lost my marbles? It is fucking happening; even as we speak it's extending its influence throughout the world. What two ingredients bestow power, tell me?'

Cole sat open-mouthed at Moore's onslaught, his thoughts racing, determined to formulate a reply, 'People power, democratic support, intelligence...'His words tailed away as he saw Moore shake her head, her expression verging on pity.

'No, no and no, sadly at the end of the day only two thing matter; money and military power. Together they determine whether freedom and democracy thrive. Think about it, Cole; put those two driving forces in the wrong hands and we all become puppets.'

Cole grimaced and acquiesced grudgingly. 'I guess so but, you must admit it's highly unlikely.'

Moore sighed and shook her head, a faraway look in her eyes. 'You haven't read these papers; you'll think differently when you have. Think of a world divided into seven zones; they're all listed in your briefing notes; each with its own leadership. An organisation we've christened the Hydra; an organisation led by an evil genius whose identity is unknown. It's an organisation that has operated for thirty years or more under the radar. An organisation that has been bringing together, drug cartels, religious and militant extremists and corrupt governments. Just like global warming it's been happening for decades and we've ignored its consequences. It's an organisation out to rule the world, even our own government isn't immune from its influences.'

Cole still found it hard, impossible almost, to accept what he was hearing, but he respected the woman in front of him; she hadn't been given to exaggeration in all the time he'd known her.

'So, what do you have in mind?' His tone respectful, cautious, apprehensive; thoughts racing around his brain at break-neck speed. *Christ, what does she have in mind for me?*

'I want you to read the papers before you leave here; they must remain here overnight. I want you to come back tomorrow morning and read them again. We'll meet at 11am to discuss a way forward.

The CIA and ourselves are taking on this organisation; our plan is to chop the heads off the Hydra, one by one. We aim to destroy its money sources, fracture it irredeemably and render it impotent. We will divide the zones between us and we'll operate independently. We have to win this one Jos; have to, or democracy is finished.'

Cole smiled at the use of his first name, rarely did she address him in that way. 'I'll get started right away.'

Moore nodded, her expression grim, 'Off you go. Sal will take you to an office and see to your needs for as long as you're here. We'll meet at 11am tomorrow; don't be late.'

Cole nodded, smiled at her, then made his way to the door. He heard Moore buzz through and was greeted by Galt who sensed that their usual banter wasn't expected. 'Follow me Jos, I've temporarily vacated an adjacent office for you; buzz through if you need anything.'

She led the way and showed him into a small meeting room housing a circular cherry-wood table and four leather-bound armchairs. On the table was a silver tray bearing an array of wrapped sandwiches and vacuum flasks, presumably tea or coffee.

'Thank you, Sal, that's perfect.'

'It's serious, Jos, isn't it?

'Very serious. Can't chat, sorry. I must get on.'

CHAPTER THREE

Next morning

The following morning Cole made his way to the office for 8am; his night's sleep disturbed by a myriad of short-lived dreams. He surmised that Moore would want this mission put in hand immediately and would expect him to have at least an outline plan for its execution. For the first time since joining the Service he was truly nervous; the mission seemed too big for one agent and he was probably the least experienced currently operating.

He'd been at his desk for about half an hour when the door pushed open and Sal Galt made her way in carrying a tray.

'Good morning, Jos, I suspected you would make an early start. I've brought you a mug of black coffee and a couple of croissants.'

'Bless you Sal, I didn't sleep well last night, **and** I skipped breakfast. I need to get my head round this stuff.'

'I won't linger, I know the stakes are high on this one. I'll give you a nudge just before 11.'

'Thanks, Sal, make that 10.55, I mustn't be late and incur Gerry's wrath again. He winked at her. 'Maybe, some day, when this over we could have breakfast in bed.'

Galt smiled wistfully. 'Somehow, I don't think that's going to happen, Jos. I'll go now and leave you to it.'

As soon as she'd gone Cole grabbed a croissant, took a bite, had a long mouthful of coffee then returned his attention to the papers. He couldn't fail to be impressed by what he was reading, notwithstanding he'd read it the previous day. The Hydra was a superbly organised outfit - its tentacles extended far and wide - its membership notorious and famous in equal measure. Every area of society had been penetrated; political, financial, business, energy companies, celebrity influencers, extremists, all were represented. Not for the first time he shook his head, this was too big; he couldn't handle it working alone. He sat back, finished the remaining croissant and gave thought to what he would say to Moore.

He was reading the two-page Summary and Objectives for the umpteenth time when there was a soft knock on the door and Galt put her head round. 'It's just coming up to five to eleven, Jos.'

'Thanks, Sal, I'll join you in a moment; I need to put these papers in order.'

Moore's office seemed warmer than usual or was he literally, *feeling the heat*?

'Good morning, Cole, nice of you to get here on time for a change. Sit,' Moore motioned at a seat.

Cole was momentarily irritated. *Woof, woof, I'm back at Crufts again, there's a nice dog.* Then he caught sight of her red-rimmed eyes, her weary countenance and her sagging shoulders. He forced sympathy into his tone. 'You look like you've been up all night.'

Her eyes flashed momentarily. 'I have been up all fucking night; making sure I've gleaned every bit of intelligence I can before sending you off on this mission. You can spare me the sympathy; let's get down to business, time is short. I assume you've read the papers?'

Cole nodded. 'Several times over, the Summary and Objectives pages a dozen times. It's a big ask; I'm flattered you've chosen me, probably your least experienced agent.'

Moore waved her hands dismissively. 'You're all paid the same and the only way to be experienced is to get experience.'

'But...', Cole started to explain his view but Moore cut him off.

'No buts, Jos.' She sighed, her shoulders sinking even lower. 'I've chosen you because of your particular attributes, no other reason. And I've had enough of Mitch Rosetti discretely asking if we've got the capabilities to handle a job of this magnitude, and how quickly can we get it under way. I don't want you expressing any doubts.'

'I'm up for the job, Chief, but I do feel it merits more than one agent, super-agent that I am. I reckon each zone justifies an agent with local support to pull this off.'

'I've made that decision, Jos, it's you and you only. I know that you have your own contacts in each of your three zones and the local consul or embassy will render assistance on use of the codeword **Deception.** Everything you require, explosives, weaponry, telecoms, clothing, gadgetry etc is in the process of being assembled for shipping to whatever embassies and consuls you nominate. They will also make transport available for you on demand.' She paused briefly, holding his gaze,

'Observations?'

'Firstly, I'm ready when you give the go-ahead, all I want to know is the order in which I'm expected to tackle the three zones. And it really would be nice to know who my opposite number is.'

Moore shook her head. 'I told you yesterday that the CIA and ourselves are acting independently, albeit to the same timescale. There's a leak in one, or both, of our organisations; the fewer people involved the better.

'As for the order of attack, Australia and the Pacific Rim are first up, followed by India, the two Pakistans and Bangladesh After that you're nearly on home turf with Europe, Russia and the Balkans. The gear you'll require for your Australia op will be in place by the time you touch down in Sydney.'

Cole nodded. 'That seems logical. I don't suppose we know the order the CIA have settled on?'

'No idea and I'm not sure it matters. If necessary, you will be able to contact your opposite number using a telephone I'll give you. Knowing you, secret or otherwise, at some point you'll try to get in touch with your opposite number. At that point you can take the opportunity to find out how the CIA's programme is progressing. Personally, if I were in your position I would keep my head down. But if needs must, whoever instigates a call will identify themselves using the Deception codeword; the responder will use Eureka. Any questions?'

'The briefing papers seem to indicate that at least 80% of the content was sourced by the CIA. How come?'

Moore hesitated before replying. 'A good question, and it's one I can't answer. Let's just be thankful they have better informants than we have. Anything else?'

Cole smiled for the first time since entering Moore's office. 'Final question, when do we kick off?

It was Moore's turn to smile. 'Tonight. Dress up warm; it'll be cold on the plane. You'll be flown by RAF jet to Sydney airport where you'll be picked up and driven to your destination. Report back here at 8pm tonight; I'll accompany you to RAF Northolt. Are we done?'

Cole shook his head. 'On reflection, one more clarification if I may. Wouldn't it be better to use multiple agents, all kicking off on the same day? Surely operating sequentially is almost akin to warning the Hydra that its top echelon is at risk?'

Moore nodded. 'That's true, but we want to scare the shit out of the leadership. We're hoping the Hydra will begin to fragment when they see their top brass being eliminated. We want cartels and gangs to withdraw from the organisation; they are at their strongest when co-ordinated as a single entity. Once we've seen to the leadership, we'll involve law enforcement agencies all over the world to deal with the underlings.'

Cole shrugged. 'The theory is OK, I guess. Let's hope it works in the real world. I'll report back at 8pm sharp. I'm looking forward to landing in Sydney; it's the middle of their summer.'

Sal Galt stopped typing as her office door opened, a smile lighting up her face, 'I was just about to enquire about coffee, but looks like you're on the way out?'

Cole put a finger to his lips and dropped his voice to a whisper. 'The mission has kicked off, I'm on my way back to the flat to pack.'

'Going somewhere nice?'

'Sorry, that's on the secret list. Maybe Gerry will tell you. Look after her; she's more strained that I've ever seen her. Sorry, but I can't linger, must get a move on. When this is over, we really must go out to dinner.'

'Maybe Jos, and I do mean maybe. And it'll be for a meal only, there'll be no afters. You're not adding me to your list of acquisitions.'

Cole smiled wickedly, 'Wouldn't dream of it; though it's not a bad idea.'

Later that day

Cole chose to walk to HQ, a long flight of sitting lay ahead. He took the opportunity to appreciate the lights along the banks of the Thames and the chatter of people he passed on the way. To say this mission was dangerous was an understatement. Worst case scenario, this might be his last stroll along the embankment. He had taken Moore's advice and dressed up warm - sturdy navy-blue corduroy trousers - a heavy white roll-neck woollen sweater - and a fawn duffel jacket. His luggage consisted of a small rucksack; Moore had assured him that suitable clothes would be available for him at the local Embassy along with all the other essentials for the mission.

The usual security formalities completed he made his way to HQ's entrance portico, surprised when he saw Moore standing waiting for him. A white Land Rover Countryman stood nearby, engine running. Moore actually smiled. 'Good evening, Jos.'

Cole returned the smile and nodded. 'Chief.'

The driver got out and opened a rear door for Moore; Cole got in the other side. Belts fastened, settling in completed,

Moore instructed the driver to proceed. They drove along in silence for ten minutes or so with Moore obviously deep in thought. Cole was getting restive with a question he needed to ask; he let a few more minutes pass then finally interrupted the silence. 'Chief, something I have to ask.'

She turned to look at him, something in her expression suggested she knew what was coming.

'What is it, Jos?' The tone of her voice wary.

Christian name again, a good sign or a bad sign? Maybe she thinks this is a last goodbye. 'You haven't asked me how I'm going to tackle this mission.'

'We both know that. There was no need to pose the question.'

Cole didn't want any last-minute arguments and made sure his voice held no sense of challenge. 'I realise that, but you have to admit it's not your usual approach. Normally you want to delve into the detail, make sure as far as possible I'm on the right track. In fact, sometimes you've been a real pain-in-the-arse, but this time, zilch, not the faintest show of interest. I'm asking myself, why?'

Moore sighed loudly, her expression visibly saddening. 'I'm sending you into the lion's den, way beyond anything you've ever tackled and I'm worried; it's as simple as that. Worried about the global enormity of the situation - worried about security - worried about your safety – and dammit, worried you won't come back. There could be a security leak in our

30

department, it's more likely than not. The less anyone knows about your mission the better, and I'm including myself in that scenario. I think it best that I don't know what your plans are; if I don't know, then no-one else can get to know. I'm sorry it has to be that way, Jos, believe me.'

There was nothing to be said, Cole just nodded.

R.A.F. Northolt

Moore showed her security identity pass and was waved through without any further formalities. The guard barely glanced at Cole and the driver. In the near distance a Dassault Falcon 8X sat on the runway ready for take-off.

'Head for that plane, Mark.'

Mark Ross nodded and accelerated quickly towards the aircraft, coming to a halt just a few metres short of the wing tip.

Wants to get home, Cole thought, *can't say I blame him.*

Cole unclipped his safety belt and made to get out of the car, stopping when Moore place her hand on his arm.

'A final bit of advice, Jos. Don't make use of your Commander title at any time, even in the Embassies. You are now who your passport says you are, to all intents just an ordinary tourist. By the way, you're in for a surprise when you get on the plane. It has one other passenger, Charlie Gibb, and if you think he looks like you, you're right. He's as near your double as I could come up with and keep my search under the radar. You will not speak with him nor he with you; you are

31

seated well apart, keep it that way. When you get on the plane, you will find an RAF uniform, shoes etc on your seat; change into it before you land in Sydney. By the way, the aircrew don't know who the pair of you are though obviously they'll have their suspicions.

'When you land in Sydney, Charlie will get off first; you will stay on board for another thirty minutes. An RAF officer of your general build will board the plane; he will remain on the plane and when it's refuelled will be flown back to Northolt. After he's boarded, let a few minutes pass, then you get off the plane. A vehicle will be on station and you will be taken to another car somewhere in the city. From there, you will be driven to your next rendezvous where you will meet up with an old friend.'

'And who would that be?' Cole was resigned to the cloak-and-dagger approach Moore had adopted and made no protest.

Moore smiled, 'You'll find out in due course. Your friend will take you to a safe house where you'll find everything you require. From that point on you are in charge of your own destiny. Use the burner phone and the code word to contact me if absolutely necessary, preferably only after the job is done.'

'Does Charlie Gibb know the risk he's taking? I mean, if the Hydra do know anything of this mission, he's putting his life on the line if they think he's me.'

Moore shrugged her shoulders. 'He's aware he's at risk, but not from whom; he's been briefed how to minimise that risk.

And he's being well paid. That's it, Jos, good luck.' Moore ended the conversation abruptly, there was nothing more to be said.

Briefing complete, Cole got out and made his way over to the plane and climbed the steps, turning at the top to wave goodbye but all he got was a rear view of the departing Land Rover.

There was no crew to welcome him on board, no attractive stewardess to serve refreshments. The sole occupant, Charlie Gibb, was seated in a rear seat, sleeping soundly if appearances were anything to go by. Cole studied his so-called double for a few seconds. *Not a bad likeness I guess, but no way is he as good looking as me.* He caught sight of an RAF uniform, neatly folded, on one of the front seats and moved up the plane to sit down.

A member of the ground crew closed the door and removed the boarding ladder, at which point, the cockpit door opened and the co-pilot, emerged to carry out the final safety checks. He looked to see that Cole had fastened his safety belt but said nothing. Presumably satisfied, and without a word of greeting he returned to the cockpit.

A few minutes passed as the aircraft went through the take-off procedures with Air Traffic Control. It then taxied to the runway where it came to a halt. Cole sighed. *Get on with it, let's get this show on the way.* Minutes passed and at last the engine revs mounted, the jet rolled forward gathering speed, then finally lifted sharply into the air rapidly gaining altitude. Cole allowed himself a smile, his mission was now under way; he had a plan and his destiny was now entirely in his own hands.

CHAPTER FOUR

Day One: Sydney

The Dassault Falcon landed in Sydney shortly after 9am local time, and following a brief conversation with Air Traffic Control the pilot taxied the aircraft to an Australian Air Force hangar. The jet stopped short of the open hangar doors and a couple of ground crew staff pushed a set of steps into position.

Cole looked on as Gibb stood, and with the briefest of glances at Cole, strode towards the door. The co-pilot was waiting and opened the door for Gibb to make his exit. Cole's double muttered what sounded like a thank you, briefly took in the outdoor scenario, then made his way down the steps. Cole mentally wished Gibb luck; he was going to need it.

To his surprise the co-pilot closed the door putting Cole on full alert. He was due to get off. *What the fuck's going on? Christ, maybe the aircrew are in league with the Hydra.* He slowly reached for his carry-on bag, poised to remove his Walther. He caught the co-pilot's eye and smiled, relaxing slightly when his smile was returned.

'There's been a change of plan,' he explained, 'we've been instructed to taxi into the hangar and you can make your exit away from prying eyes. Apparently, they completed the repairs on plane they had in there earlier than expected and it's flown off on test somewhere. As it's turned out the RAF uniform hasn't been necessary; leave it behind in the office when you change. Your car and chauffer are waiting outside the far end of the hangar.'

Cole nodded, 'Sounds sensible, thank you.'

'The name's Terry Grant, by the way; don't suppose you'll give us a hint as to what's going on?'

Cole shook his head, 'I'm sure you've been briefed not to ask questions.'

The co-pilot shrugged. 'Just thought I'd try, you've aroused our curiosity, sorry.'

At that point the noise from the jet engines rose in volume and the aircraft slowly rolled forward into the hangar; the huge doors began to slide closed as soon as the tailplane was clear.

Cole's thoughts were racing. *The guy seemed genuine, but all the best crooks do. Sure, the changeover was best done behind clothes doors, but so were executions. And who gave them the authority to change plans? Could the Hydra have set this up? No, it was OK, they couldn't have had intelligence on his movements this early. Or could they? They could well do if there was a leak in MI6. But what choice do you have, Jos, you have to get off the plane.*

The co-pilot had opened the door and was looking at him expectantly, eyebrows raised. Cole nodded and pulled his bag to his chest, slipping his hand inside to find his Walther, moving across to the exit as he did so. Grant was displaying no interest in his departure; he seemed to be watching the pilot filling in some paperwork.

Meantime, a young woman, dressed in grey overalls, was completing the task of putting the steps against the plane and stepping on the footbrake to hold it in place. Job done she gave Cole a radiant smile and beckoned him to descend. Cole returned the smile. *Hmm, gorgeous, wish I had time on my hands.* As he stepped onto the tarmac, she flashed another smile. 'I've been told we mustn't converse but that's crazy. Welcome to Australia mystery man.' She pointed to a small room at the end of the hangar. 'You'll find your change of clothing in there. When you're done, go out the adjacent door; your taxi awaits you nearby.' Cole was beginning to feel more relaxed, but on his guard and his hand still on the Walther. 'Thank you, Miss...?

'My friends call me, Daisy.'

'And who wouldn't want you as a friend, Daisy, I hope we meet again.'

'I'll keep my fingers crossed, but somehow I doubt it'

Cole hurried across to the small office where he ditched the uniform then quickly changed into shorts and tee-shirt; the outside temperature was already in the low seventies and rising. 'Ah, that's better.' It was such a relief to replace his formal footwear with trainers.

His third chauffeur in twenty-four hours was a young woman of Asian descent. She greeted him with a radiant smile, then moved over to open the door for him to get into the rear seat.

'All set, sir?' Her accent was one hundred per cent Australian, 'Got any new instructions for me?'

Cole grimaced internally; he had no idea where he was due to meet his contact. 'No, just stick with your instructions, please.'

The car eased forward and headed towards a remote corner of the airport where there was a string of large maintenance sheds and warehouses. Cole went on guard when the car turned between two of the buildings and headed towards a large steel gate. A security guard was seated in a small hut with its door open and heard their approach. He looked up from his book and satisfied with what he saw pressed a button on his handheld controller; the gate began to swing open immediately and Cole was on his way to an unknown destination in Sydney.

I wonder who I'm meeting? Cole's curiosity grew with each passing minute. He was relatively new to MI6 and had never operated in Australia so who could it be? The journey had been in progress for twenty minutes, when to Cole's surprise, the driver pulled up outside a small café in Campelltown City, a suburb on the south-western outskirts of metropolitan Sydney. *What the hell. Is this a set-up. Calm down, Jos, you're becoming paranoid.*

'We're here, sir.'

Where the hell is 'here' exactly? His irritation at the cloak-and-dagger arrangements spiked again, but there was nothing he could do but get out of the car. He slid out onto the pavement and without a word the driver pulled away, made a U-turn and headed back towards central Sydney.

Cole looked around feeling very exposed. There were a few locals going about their business but no-one showed the least interest in his presence. A couple of minutes passed. *Shit. Might as well have a coffee as stand here like a lemon.* The café didn't look too inspiring but needs must, so he made his way in and was heading towards the counter when he heard a voice he recognised. 'Over here Jos, thought you was never gonna work out what to do.' He looked to his left, and there, seated at a table, was his old SAS sergeant, Jethro Watkins.

'I don't believe it!' Cole's mouth gaped, head shaking in disbelief, 'What a co-incidence bumping into you here.' He strode forward, hand extended, smiling broadly. 'I feel like I've won the lottery.'

'Chance would be a fine thing. You want to join me in a coffee or get on our way?'

'We're running late,' Cole winked, 'let's head off.'

Watkins settled up then guided Cole along a short corridor to the rear of the cafe and from there, into a small parking area, where he walked over to a red MG roadster. Cole whistled, 'Nice one.'

The two men settled in the car and Watkins accelerated out of the parking area's rear exit, headed south as far as Cole could tell. He didn't contain his curiosity for long. 'OK Jethro, now that we're mobile, pray tell me what you are doing in Australia? Last time we met, Sergeant Watkins, you were shouting orders at me, a real bastard you were.'

'I had to be with amateurs like you under my command, and anyway, I have to correct you Jos. Last time we met we were in Afghanistan, and you saved my life.'

'I was just doing what you taught me to do, Jethro, nothing more, nothing less.'

'I was cornered, out of ammo, pinned down, six of them; not one left standing by the time you finished. That done you half-dragged, half-carried me a mile to safety. I owe you my life man and still have the scars to prove it. You deserved a medal for what you did, though I don't expect you got one.'

'That's history, Jethro, you're embarrassing me. Let's set the past aside and answer my question, what are you doing in Australia?'

'I kinda took a leaf out of your book and sought a new life. Unlike you though, I wanted somewhere sunnier, somewhere warmer, and opted for Oz. I wanted some excitement in my life, one without red tape and officers. Again, I followed your lead and managed to get into ASIS, the Australian Secret Intelligence Service. Weren't easy but I done it; been in the Service for five years now and it's lived up to my hopes.'

'I'm impressed Jethro. Tell me, are you on duty now?'

'No, I aint. Don't know how your Chief got my number, but she got in touch with me and asked me to pick you up and take you back to my place. Said you had business to attend to down my way. I was only too pleased to oblige and here I am. I've got the week off and I'm at your service. She told me this was all very hush-hush and not a word to anyone; I haven't even told my partner.'

Cole's eyes widened, 'You're married?'

'Kind off, you'll get to meet him when we get to my place.'

Cole gaped. 'You're er ...'

'Got it in one; yes, I'm gay.'

Jethro Watkins was a giant of a man, 1.9metres tall and built like a grizzly bear. Born in Jamaica, a dazzling smile never far from his lips; he was gentle by nature until otherwise necessary.

'And where exactly is your place, Jethro?'

'Me and my partner got a shack on the beach down on Bateman's Bay, about 150 kilometres south of here, around 120 east of Canberra. It's a pity you're on duty, we coulda had us a helluva re-union. Now are you going to tell me what this is all about, or is it Top Secret need-to-know stuff?'

Cole sighed, it was Top Secret, by far the most secret mission he had ever been entrusted with, but Jethro was his friend; a colleague in a similar line of business. He would trust him with his life. *Fuck it, the Chief knows I'm my own man, it's my life on the line, and I need help.*

'It is Top Secret, Jethro, I mean it; the Chief will crucify me if she ever finds out I've shared what's going on with anyone. This is bigger than anything I've ever encountered, maybe even bigger than World War 2.'

'I can't believe what I'm hearing, Jos. Are you sure you're not exaggerating the hell out of this mission of yours?'

Cole searched his conscience and the promise he'd made Gerry Moore on his honour. Pros and cons swirled around in his head, there was no easy answer. There was though, one overriding fact that led to an undeniable conclusion; caution and secrecy were laudable, but all a waste of space if his mission was unsuccessful. He had a plan and he needed help to achieve it, and that help, as it turned out, could be provided by Jethro.

'OK, listen up and keep what I tell you to yourself, or I swear I'll kill you; and I mean it.'

Jethro smiled with sympathy etched in his expression; he could imagine what Cole was going through. 'I know you don't mean that buddy, but I won't argue. I promise what you'll tell me will go no further. I won't even tell my partner; I swear on my mother's grave.'

'I believe you, Jethro. First up, what I'm about to share with you is only known to Gerry Moore, Mitch Rosetti, me and my opposite number in the CIA. I'm betraying a confidence for the first time since I joined the SAS. Pin your ears back and be prepared to be shocked. Save any questions to the end.'

Cole spent over an hour explaining the global situation, his near photographic memory serving him well as he explained the extent of the Hydra's influence and its operations. He explained its alliances with terrorist groups, large and small. He chose not to identify the mission's targets, unsure if that might be a step too far.

Watkins was stunned and drove in silence as he considered the implications of what he had heard. A full five minutes elapsed before he spoke. 'You've scared the shit out of me, Jos. What the fuck are you supposed to do about this...this Armageddon? I can't see that little old Jos Cole, can handle anything this big all on his ownio. What in hell is the strategy, man?'

'We do have a plan. It might not work but we have a plan. And I'm not entirely on my own, there's my opposite number in the States. Added to that, I'm trying to recruit you, if you're willing?'

Jethro let out a large guffaw. 'I'll help in any way I can, buddy, but this business is too big even for such a fantastic team like you and me. But go on, tell me more about this plan that Moore and Rosetti have come up with'

Cole smiled; he had an ally. 'The strategy is simple enough; we divide and conquer.'

Watkins rolled his eyes, his voice loaded with scepticism as he repeated Cole's words, 'Divide...and...conquer. What the fuck does that entail? Are you going to infiltrate every fucking gang or cabal and tell tales in dark corners? Get real, Jos that'll never work.'

'I've given it a lot of thought and I think we can give the set-up a bloody nose. First off, we systematically wipe out the leadership; that's my job. If that can be done across all seven Zones it will spread uncertainty and create fear and distrust. They will be leaderless and at that point Rosetti and Moore will call in global and local law enforcement agencies to sweep up the small fry.'

Watkins shrugged. 'I'm not convinced but I suppose it might work.'

'Got any better suggestions?'

The big man sighed and shook his head. 'Not really, other than maybe an all-out attack from day one.'

'Considered that, but it's full of risk. The Hydra has people operating under the radar at the highest level of government and law enforcement; the word would probably get out before we set the ball rolling and they'd go into hiding. We weighed up all the options and came to the conclusion that the plan we have stands the best chance of success.'

'So where do I come in? And let me say straight up that I don't want a direct role in taking out the leadership of the Hydra. I'll give you all the help I can setting up, but I won't get directly involved in any gunfights or the like. Me and Billy have too good a life to put it all at risk.'

'Wouldn't expect you to, Jethro. That's my job. But I have my own take on the plan and that's where I think you can help. I need information.'

'What kind of info, Jos? I'll help all I can, maybe involve my partner too if I think it's safe. Thing is I've never heard mention of the Hydra within our intelligence agencies; not a whisper. My partner's name is Billy Austin by the way, I think you and he will get on well. So, what is it you want to know exactly?'

Cole felt secure and able to relax fully; for the first time since he landed in Australia, jet lag was taking over.

'Tell you what. I'm feeling tired so how about I take a nap and we'll discuss what I need to know with Billy present when we get to your place?'

'No problem, Bro, just don't snore.'

CHAPTER FIVE

Day Two.

'Wakey, wakey, sleepy head, we're nearly there.' Jethro reached over and gently squeezed Cole's arm.

Cole rubbed his eyes and stretched best he could. 'How long have I been asleep?'

'About three-quarters of an hour, didn't really put a timer on you. Slept like a baby, you did.'

Cole took a moment to take in the outside view, the sea on his left getting ever closer as the car approached the outskirts of what he assumed was Bateman's Bay. 'Is that Bateman's Bay I can see up ahead?'

'Sho is, Bro, can't say I know who Bateman was, must look it up sometime.'

'Can't help you. Might be the same guy, Rudyard Kipling named his place after.'

Watkins looked at him quizzingly. 'Who?'

'You've surely heard of Rudyard Kipling, he wrote Peter Pan and lived in a place called Bateman's in East Sussex, a county on the coast right down in the south of England?

Watkins shrugged, 'I know East Sussex and I've heard of Peter Pan, but that's about it.'

They were on the coastal road; the shoreline with its sandy beach and gently breaking waves looked idyllic. Cole sighed inwardly, thinking of what lay ahead and wondering if this was the last shoreline he might get to see. Watkins began slowing down and pulled in alongside a wooden lodge, no more than a good stone's throw from the sea. There was a small overgrown garden bordered by a low white picket fence to the front of the property.

A bronzed, six-packed thirty-something guy, wearing bathing trunks and loafers appeared at the side of the lodge and made his way towards the car. Watkins was first out and walked quickly towards his companion; the two men embraced each other and exchanged a conversation Cole couldn't make out.

Watkins eased out of the embrace and turned to face Cole.

'Jos, I want you to meet the man in my life, Billy Austin. And Billy, this is Jos Cole, the only reason I'm still on this planet of ours.'

Austin smiled and took a step towards Cole, hand outstretched. 'Pleased to meet you. I've heard so much about you from this man,' he nodded towards his partner. 'I've got the barbecue all set to go, but first things first. I'll show you your room and you can stow your stuff. Shouldn't take long, it looks like you're travelling light. That done, my guess is you'd like a shower before sampling my cooking?'

'Can't think of anything better. Lead the way, Billy.'

Jethro returned to the car, and Austin led Cole to the rear of the lodge where a barbecue was smoking gently; the cooking aromas stirred his hunger pangs. The duo entered by the back door, Cole taking in the kitchen layout and the comfortable sofas and chairs dotted around the lounge. 'Very nice, Billy, I'm duly impressed.'

Austin pointed back over his shoulder. 'The dining area is back there off the kitchen, and through here are two double ensuite bedrooms; though I don't expect you're likely to have company this trip.'

'Sadly not, maybe another time if you'll have me back.'

'Jethro is my heart and soul, Jos, we both owe you big-time.'

'You owe me nothing, I did no more than my duty.'

Austin smiled and shrugged, 'Have it your way. I look forward to hearing about your business later.'

Cole nodded. 'We're in the same line of work but my mission is red-flagged, need-to-know. I'll tell you all I can, maybe more than I should, but I may have to leave out some of the detail.'

Austin put his hand on Cole's shoulder and gave it a squeeze. 'I've been there, Jos, I understand. I really do. I promise not to poke my nose in too far. Jethro and I will help all we can.... swear to God. OK, this is your room, we're across the corridor. Anything you need, just ask. See you at the barbie when you're ready.'

Cole took his time showering; lathering and rubbing away the stickiness of the flight. He changed into new clothing and felt re-energised when he joined his friends at the BBQ. Austin was doing the cooking and beckoned Cole to join him. 'Place your order, Jos.'

'Oh dear, I'm a strict vegetarian.'

Billy's jaw dropped. 'Oh no, I didn't know, I suppose I can rustle up some bread and corn on the cob.'

Cole pulled a face, 'Sorry Billy, I should have said.' He smiled and reached forward for a plate, 'Only kidding, ignore me. It looks delicious; fill up my plate with a bit of everything, please.'

Minutes later the three men were seated round a table, each with a plate piled with steak fillets, scampi and crab meat. Cole filled his glass and proposed a toast. 'This is fantastic, raise a glass to the chef.'

The meal continued for the next forty-five minutes; munching interspersed with chat and ribaldry in equal measure.

'Wow that was something special,' said Cole rubbing his belly, 'I reckon if I lived near you guys, I'd have a weight problem come my next medical.'

Appetites satisfied and glasses refilled, Jethro stood and started gathering up the plates. Cole made to help but Austin restrained him. 'Let's you and me get to know each other a bit better, Jos. Jethro has briefed me within the boundaries you've set, but I need to know a bit more if I am to be of assistance.'

Cole nodded, the moment had arrived, he had to open up, but how far should he go was the question. 'I'd want to know who the local drug lords are for a start.'

'That's an easy one, the Romero family, Mexican origin; and the Shkodra lot, Albanian origin.'

'Any aggro between them?'

'Not nowadays, used to be a while back then suddenly it all quietened down. They still bad-mouth each other but that's as far as it goes.'

Cole sighed inwardly. *The Hydra* 'Sounds like someone is pulling their strings.'

'Meaning what exactly, Jos?'

'This is where I can't say too much, Billy, but say there was a layer of organised crime above them, and maybe another layer above that, both exercising control at appropriate levels over the local gangs. Added to that, high level connections with law enforcement. What then?'

Austin looked at Cole, expression clearly sceptical. 'Sounds like a superhero story - unrealistic; everybody is out for themselves in the criminal world.'

'I know where you're coming from, Billy, but just leave the door open to the idea.'

'Have it your way. What else can I tell you?'

'I want to know where the big chiefs hang out, I want to know how I can stop a major drugs' run? In short, I want to rattle the Romeros and the Shkodra set-ups.'

'How are you two getting on.' Jethro joined them, directing his question at Cole.

'Just fine, Jethro. I'm hoping Billy can tell me what I need to know.'

'Except I'm finding it hard to accept Jos's concept of a super drugs cartel. I haven't even heard a whisper about such a set-up.'

Jethro shook his head. 'I think it's feasible, Billy, think about it. Over the last few years all we've been catching are the minnows or big guys long past their sell-by dates. And we've picked up a number of unexplained underworld executions. Come to think of it, over the years there have been a number of notable accidental deaths. Maybe they weren't accidental. It all chimes with major forces at play. Given what Jos has told us, I'm pretty convinced something big is going down.'

Austin looked from Watkins to Cole, several times, then shrugged. 'OK, I'll go along with you guys for now. So where do we go from here, Jos?'

'The pressure is on and I've got to act quickly. I need those addresses I asked for. And, this is the toughie, is there any way I can tap into the movements of your government ministers and top-level military people over the next couple of days?'

Billy sagged back in his chair, 'You're fucking kidding me, right?'

Jethro intervened, his voice strained, 'I don't think so, Billy.'

Cole said nothing. If Billy couldn't, or wouldn't help he'd have to rely on the Embassy to find out what he needed to know, and that risked news leaking out.

'I hope you know what you're doing, Jos. You two have got me thinking about a job I took part in six months back. I was part of a team set up to bust a Romero drug run. Intel was good and the operation went like clockwork, except when we boarded the boat involved there wasn't a sniff of cocaine to be found. Three months after that we got insider intel again and wanted to run the same operation but weren't given the go-ahead by the higher-ups. It fits in with your scenario of people in high places calling the shots.'

'Fits the scenario perfectly.' Cole raised an eyebrow and smiled; Billy was on the hook. Jethro made to fill, the glasses again but Cole declined. 'I need a clear head for what lies ahead. So how much info can you get your hands on, Billy?'

'I **can** get you the movements of our top Officials; just have to do it in a way it can't be traced. I'll work on that tonight. And I can pinpoint a static target for you, one we've not been able to access; we just can't persuade the top brass to authorise a search warrant. We believe there is a drug lab and get this, a big computer installation on a site owned by a big nob front man for the Shkodra cartel.'

Inwardly, Cole was over the moon, three out of four targets were taking shape. That just left the Romero's boat operation to be sorted. 'I'm in dreamland, Billy. Can you get me a map of the site and those names? I'll figure out how to deal with that boat you referred to. I don't think I'll have need of a search warrant.'

Austin laughed. 'By the time you wake up tomorrow morning, I'll have the names you want and I can drive you to the site; it's not far away.'

Jethro frowned and intervened. 'No way Billy Bobs, you're not getting involved. If Jos needs help it will come from yours truly – no argument.'

Austin bristled. 'I'm not some fucking amateur, Jethro. I know the risk and this is as good a cause as I know.'

Cole butted in. 'Why don't you make a start on those names, Billy? They are my official targets and it would be great if you've got a good map. I'll scout out the place if Jethro can run me over. Added to that I'll need to visit the British Embassy in Canberra; they have some stuff I need, including a car. Sorry, but you're going to be my cab driver Jethro.'

Billy raised his hand. You do realise Jos that destroying the Romero boat won't inflict lasting damage? They've got others anchored around the coast.

'I agree, but they favour this one for a reason; I bet it's equipped with all sorts of built-in hiding places for drugs and it's probably got a souped-up engine. I don't suppose you could find out the next run for me?

Billy nodded, 'As a matter of fact I can. You're in luck, I'm due to meet my contact tomorrow for a routine briefing; she'll likely know when it's due.'

'Great, my expedition is getting easier by the minute. How about you get me that map and I'll see if I can persuade Jethro to run me over to Canberra today.' He glanced at Watkins, winking when he got the anticipated nod.

Austin rose and went indoors, returning minutes later with an ordnance survey map which he proceeded to spread out on the table. 'You'll like this, Jos, the site is readily accessed. It's located on the edge of Lake George, this side of Canberra. I'm sure Jethro knows where it is.'

'Sure do, been there, though it was a time back.'

Cole gave a thumbs up. 'OK guys, we have a plan, high fives all round.'

CHAPTER SIX

Later: Canberra

'You're really pushing on with this mission of yours, Jos, I would have thought your first priority was a good night's sleep?' Cole and Watkins were well on their way to Canberra, the sun blazing down, not a cloud in the sky, Cole deep in thought.

'I'm too fired up to sleep, Jethro, and I want to make sure all my stuff has been delivered to the Embassy.'

'I guess so. Just what are you collecting?'

'The main thing is a good quality sniper rifle.'

Watkins snorted. 'I could have provided a rifle, all bored out and untraceable; you should have said.'

'Sure, but I'm also collecting some high-grade explosive devices and a small rocket launcher; I doubt if even you can help me with those. Now, thinking about it, how about I take your advice and grab some shuteye? Wake me up at Lake George, please.' Cole drifted off in minutes but it seemed to him that he'd barely closed his eyes when a firm nudge woke him.

'We're here, Jos.'

Cole looked around, taking his surroundings. 'No cameras in these parts, I hope.'

'Nope, this is one of the quieter areas, and mid-week there won't be too many locals around either.'

Both men got out of the car and Watkins led the way along a well-trodden path to the edge of the lake. 'We get a lot of visitors here at weekends; swimming, fishing, boating, you name it, it's not normally this quiet.' He pointed across the lake to the other side. 'The two nearest buildings you can see in the distance are the two Billy told you about.' He handed a pair of binoculars to Cole. 'Take a look.'

Cole focussed on the buildings for a few minutes, smiling when he saw what he'd hoped for. 'Thanks, Jethro, let's get moving, I don't want to spend too long here in case we arouse suspicion.'

'Very unlikely, lots of visitors have binoculars, especially the birdwatching community.'

'I appreciate that, but I'm being super-cautious. I'd like to hit this place tonight.'

Watkins gasped. 'You're fucking kidding me, man!'

Cole shook his head. 'No, I'm not. Now, I saw an overhead electricity cable running into the site. Can you get me anywhere near where it joins the site.'

Watkins took a look through the binoculars. 'That shouldn't be too difficult, but they'll have a back-up generator, and most likely only lose power for a few minutes.'

'A few minutes is all I need, lead the way.'

The two men returned to the car, each with their own thoughts; one busy planning, one thinking the other was mad. Watkins drove for about fifteen minutes then pulled up at the side of the road and pointed to a wooden pylon about 100 metres away. 'That's your baby, Jos.'

'Won't take much to take that out of the game. Thanks, Jethro, I'm indebted to you. We can head for the embassy now, if that's OK with you?'

Watkins bowed. 'On my way master Jos.'

Twenty minutes later they pulled up half a kilometre or so short of the British High Commission on Commonwealth Avenue in Canberra.

'Thanks, Jethro, I'll see you back at the ranch. I won't hang around here for any longer than I need to.'

Watkins tipped a salute. 'Stay safe man, you know where I am if you need me.'

The Embassy

Cole made his way to the white entrance lodge, apparently idly looking round in tourist fashion. In reality he was checking out the area for any suspicious observers; not that he expected any. He used his mobile to send a text to a number given to him by Gerry Moore to cut through the admission formalities. He waited a few minutes for instructions to filter down to the Lodge-like reception building, then made his way in. He was greeted by a small formally dressed woman in her mid-forties, smiling broadly at the casually attired man before her. 'How can I help?'

Cole returned the smile. 'Jos Cole, Sir Kenneth is expecting me.'

Alison Swan gulped, she'd received the call, but hadn't anticipated her VIP visitor to be dressed in a tee-shirt and shorts. 'Of course, come through Mr Cole.' She pointed at a door.

Cole moved along and waited a few seconds for the door to open. Swan beckoned him to enter, still looking uncomfortable with the new arrival's scruffy appearance.

'Sir Kenneth will meet you at the war memorial.' She turned to a young man seated behind a desk. 'Alex, I'm taking Mr Cole to meet the High Commissioner, I won't be long.'

The young man's face registered surprise at the attention being afforded to Cole, but he didn't voice his curiosity, confining his response to a hand wave.'

'Follow me, Mr Cole, my name's Alison.'

'Lead on, Alison.'

Cole got in tow, admiring the well cared for garden surroundings as he went. He caught his breath when the main building came into view; to his eyes it was an architectural masterpiece. A few moments later, Swan stopped and pointed ahead. 'That's the war memorial, and that's Sir Kenneth sitting on the bench. I'll leave you now, I'm sure I'm not required.'

'Thank you for your help, Alison.'

To Cole's surprise the High Commissioner remained seated, and appeared to be avoiding eye contact. Then it dawned on him that Sir Kenneth was pretending not to know him, so he spent a few minutes admiring the memorial obelisk before strolling over to the bench and sitting down.

'Thank you for giving up your time, Sir Kenneth, I'm sure you've got better things to do.'

Sir Kenneth Rawlins, tall, bronzed and slim, wearing a white single-breasted linen suit, smiled. 'Well now, I'm not so sure about that. Gerry Moore didn't tell me much but I know you're not in Australia on holiday. I also know that I'm not to ask any questions and been told you'll be tried for treason if you reveal anything of your mission.' A smiled played about his lips as he spoke, his expression one of bemusement.

Cole grinned. 'I'll answer any questions you have to the best of my ability, Sir Kenneth. I have to trust someone and who better than yourself.' Cole was being pleasant; he had no intention of saying more than he needed to.

'Thank you, but I think the least I know the better.'

'It's highly likely my business will make the headlines, Sir Kenneth, so be prepared for a shock or two.'

'Enough said, Mr Cole, my imagination is already working overtime. Best if I take you to the real reason for your visit to the High Commission.'

Cole followed Rawlins along a tree lined path to a white painted double garage.

'It's pretty quiet in this area, you shouldn't be disturbed. Leave the garage door open when you depart. You'll find your car inside along with a number of sealed packing cases; lord knows what MI6 has put in them.' The Commissioner extended his hand. 'Good luck, get home safe; I can't wait to read all about your adventure, Mr Cole. The rear exit gate is at the end of the drive opposite the garage. You are expected and won't be stopped and questioned when you leave.'

Cole wasted no time and made his way into the garage, disappointed when he saw the car he'd been allocated. He'd hoped for something like a Porche, but in front of him stood a rather scruffy-looking orange Mini Clubman. *Christ, I hope I don't end up in a car chase. Your dream is over mate, now get cracking and unpack those crates. Make sure you have everything you need.*

Cole cut the binding on the three packing crates stacked at the rear of the garage, meticulously checking that everything he needed had been provided, His eyes lit up when he saw the weaponry and explosives. *Gosh, there's enough here to start a small war, thank you, Gerry.* The smallest crate contained wearing apparel, a selection of combat gear and everyday clothing.

Cole turned his attention to the Clubman and breathed a sigh of relief when he saw a brown envelope on the front seat. The printed sheet gave instructions on how to access the Mini's secure storage compartments. His disappointment surfaced again when he found there were no mention of the Mini having any special features. *I'll bet it's not armour-clad or fitted with bullet-proof glass. You'll just have to be extra careful and not get caught in any crossfire.*

He spent the next hour packing the gear away in the Mini, making sure that the equipment and clothing he needed for his planned excursion that evening were readily accessible. Job done, he pressed the garage's up-and-over door switch and made himself comfortable behind the wheel. *Here goes.* He pushed in the clutch and pressed the ignition button, pleased when he heard the throaty roar of the engine as he accelerated away. *You sound better than you look.*

The pair of tall iron exit gates swung open as he approached and within seconds, he was back on Commonwealth Avenue and on his way to Jethro's beach hut. Long stretches of straight road afforded the opportunity to familiarise himself with the Mini's performance, and by the time he arrived at the Jethro's hut, his confidence had grown.

Bateman's Bay

Cole glanced at his watch as he pulled up alongside the beach hut, 5.55pm; three hours or so rest, necessary preparations and he'd be setting out again.

Jethro and Billy must have heard the Mini arrive and were soon present, offering to lend a hand with any unpacking. Cole turned on the satnav and punched in the code to gain access to the hidden compartment below the front seating pad. Jethro emptied the compartment which contained combat and day-to-day clothes. 'That it?'

Cole nodded, 'That's it.'

Billy interjected. 'Mind showing us the rest of your gear? Strikes me you'll need more than fancy clothing to carry out tonight's mission.'

Cole punched two codes into the satnav, then did the necessary to reveal the arsenal hidden under the rear seat pad. Austin let out an involuntary whistle of amazement. 'Jesus, you could wipe out a small regiment with that lot.'

Cole nodded, 'I guess there is a bit of overkill. To be fair though, the team back home didn't have a lot of detail to work with; this business is so hush hush. You never know what the moment will bring and I'm pretty sure I'll need most of the explosives. Now, if it's OK with you guys, I'd welcome a bite to eat and a couple of hours kip. I suggest we assemble at nine to put the finishing touches to tonight's plans.'

CHAPTER SEVEN

Jos, Jethro and Billy sat around the dining table, each with their own thoughts. A goodly number of sandwiches had been consumed; modest drinking was in progress. Plans and photos covered the table. The discussion had been short; Cole knew what he had to do and, more importantly, how to do it.

'Top you up, Jos?' Jethro reached across, a bottle of Glenfiddich in his hand.

Cole shook his head, 'Would love to but must keep a clear head. I wouldn't want to be stopped by a Highway Patrol looking like this and smelling of whisky. He was dressed in a tight-fitting black outfit that included a Teflon armoured vest.

Jethro chuckled. 'Just tell him you're going to a fancy-dress party, boy.'

Cole laughed. 'Oh yeah, where exactly?'

'Here of course.'

Billy joined in, 'Once you get out of Batemans Bay environs you won't come across any patrols. That area seems to be a no-go zone for police patrols since a few years back; due to a low crime rate, so say the top brass. I must say, Jos, you really look the part. I see you've got two handguns. You must be expecting trouble, not that I want to know anything about that in my professional capacity. Tell me all about it after the event. By the way, I've been going over old photos of the site layout and I picked up an anomaly you might be interested in.' He pushed across three high level drone photos. 'Look at these.'

Cole placed them side by side, studying them closely, then looked up puzzled. 'They look pretty much the same.'

Austin pushed a fourth photo across. 'Now look at this one.'

'Identical except for the faint vapour trail, a boiler perhaps?' Jos looked at Billy quizzingly. 'So, what am I missing?'

'Well, as far as we know the site is served by electric heating, so why the vapour trail? And why doesn't it show up on any of the other three photos?'

Cole's interest sharpened. 'You've obviously figured it out so you tell me.'

'I reckon this building houses the diesel generator providing the emergency electricity supply for the site.'

Cole snapped his fingers. 'Of course! So, it only fires up when they run a test or there's a power cut. Thank you, Billy, I reckon I've got to change my plan of attack just a mite. Show me on the site plan exactly where this building is located.'

'Can't miss it, it's on the extreme right-hand side looking from the lake.'

'Thanks, Billy.' Cole stood and stretched. 'It's getting dark out there, time Jethro and I were heading off.'

Austin nodded. 'Wish I was going with you two guys. Good luck, Jos; you too Jethro.' He stepped forward and gave his partner a hug. 'Mind you come back in one piece big fella.'

'You bet I will, I'll be back home before you know it'

Cole and Watkins made their way outside to their cars, shaking hands and wishing each other good hunting.

'Are you sure about this, Jethro? I appreciate the back-up, but you've got so much to lose if this goes pear-shaped.'

'Shush buddy, let's get this show on the road; I'll lead the way. When I pull over, you pull over and I'll point out your route. I reckon it's about an hour and a half drive.'

Watkins pulled away, closely followed by Cole. Their journey was uneventful. Both drove just below the speed limit, both rehearsing in their head what lay ahead. Forty minutes passed and Watkins signalled he was pulling over. Cole pulled up behind him and took the opportunity to apply some blackening to his face.

Watkins grinned at him. 'Looking good man, you're nearly as black as me. I'll be going straight on; you're taking that right fork just ahead. Check we got the same time, 22.41 for me.'

Cole pulled his sleeve up and checked his watch. 'Spot on.'

Jethro nodded. 'We'd better push on; my aim is for the lights to go out at 23.00 precisely. Hit them hard, Bro.' With that he made his way back to his car and drove away.

Cole didn't linger, the talking was over, the action was about to begin. Ten minutes along the lane, he pulled off the road onto a farm track and bumped along it for around a quarter of a mile. He had switched off the headlights and was grateful for the bright moon and a clear sky. Up ahead he caught sight of the lake. *Nearly there, Jos. Let the fun begin.* But first he had to turn the car round, ready for a quick getaway if one was needed.

The electrified fence loomed on his right, and he could see the site lights around the buildings about six hundred metres away. The terrain was flat as a pancake. There were no trees to provide cover; darkness was his friend, the moon an unwelcome intruder. He checked his watch, his gut tightening when he saw there was only two minutes to go, if Jethro was running to time. Ten seconds left and he began counting down in his head, *three, two, one, zero.* Nothing but an anti-climax. He forced himself to relax, a minute or two either way was of no consequence. *Fuck it, I hope you're OK Jethro; heaven forbid you've had an accident. Maybe the explosive charge has failed. Fuck it, how long do I give him?*

Ten miles away, Jethro, was getting out of his car; he had miscalculated the journey time and was cursing as he strapped the explosive in place to the pylon. *Shit, Jos will be getting worried; you've fucked up Jethro.* He ran the hundred metres or so back to his car and pressed the detonator button. The explosion seemed massive; the pylon instantly collapsed like a matchstick. An eerie silence replaced the noise. *Job done. Over to you, Jos.*

Cole smiled broadly when the site lights went out; the fence no longer electrified. He wasted no time getting the cutters into action, relieved by the ease with which they severed the fence wiring. It took him less than two minutes to make a good-sized access. He could hear shouts issuing forth from the buildings and see torch beams jiggling about as the locals dealt with the blackout. A few dim emergency lights had come on inside most of the buildings. He pulled down his infra-red goggles and saw three figures running towards the generator building presumably to fire up the engine and restore the electrical supply.

He unslung the rocket launcher and took aim. *Sorry guys, wrong place, wrong time.* He pulled the trigger and watched the trail of the missile for the few seconds of its flight. The building disintegrated before his eyes as missile made contact. Debris flew in all directions; three broken bodies were further evidence of the destruction. There was no time to linger and admire his handiwork; the noise of the explosion brought staff running from the line of buildings. Some were armed, others not. Most gathered in the immediate area of the carnage, some bent over their fallen colleagues. Cole started to run towards them; there was no time to waste.

Someone must have heard him or caught sight of his outline in the moonlight and the group turned to look in his direction; a few raised their weapons. Cole was prepared for this eventually and drew the gun from his left-hand holster and fired. There was no need to aim, it wasn't that kind of weapon. He pulled the trigger and the scene before him was filled with a blindingly brilliant light. Shouts of despair could be heard. It would be hours before they could see properly again, some might have lost their sight completely.

When its affects had been described to him, Cole had felt a degree of unease; surely such a weapon wouldn't be allowed under the terms of the Geneva Convention. The lab chief had laughed out loud and told him bluntly. *'Only use it if you need to, and stay away from Geneva.'*

This wasn't the occasion for moralising, there was a job to be done. He holstered the flash gun and ran toward the nearest building and went inside. There was a bank of computers around ten metres long and three metres high, red warning lights were flashing as the equipment gasped for its life-blood…electricity. Cole swung his shoulder bag round across his chest and ran to the far end where he fastened a magnetic explosive charge and pressed its activation button. He now had three minutes to get clear of the building. He ran forward and repeated the process twice more as he made his way along the computer bank to the exit. Two armed men suddenly appeared in the doorway; Cole drew his Walther immediately and shot them both before they could respond. The men fell to the ground clutching their chests, their bodies blocking the doorway. Cole jumped over the sprawled corpses and raced away, throwing himself to the ground some thirty metres clear of the building.

Three massive explosions followed in quick succession and he felt bits of tiny debris hit his body. There was no time for admiring his work, there was more to do; he pushed himself to his feet, immediately conscious of the eerie silence that follows a blast of that magnitude. He raced towards the next hut, Walther in hand, ready to kill. Another bank of computer towers stood unattended and he repeated the procedure, this time setting the timers to two minutes. He made a quick exit and was safely grounded when the charges went off.

Cole hurried across to the three remaining buildings and entered the nearest without caution. The last bank of computer towers was accompanied by six work stations, two of them attended by one man, one woman. Both raised their hands in surrender when they saw his gun. His finger tightened on the trigger but relaxed when he saw the terror on their faces. It was time to add a bit of confusion. 'Get out.' He barked in Russian, pointing at the door behind him, 'Quickly, quickly.' Both dashed forward and disappeared through the door without further urging.

Cole fastened three more charges, again setting them to two minutes and raced outside. A man and two women stood nearby, gaping at the neighbouring building ruins. Their colleagues milled around wailing, their sight stolen by the earlier flares. Cole shouted at them in Russian again. 'Get clear, get clear.' Whether they understood or not he didn't care. He raced to safety and threw himself to the ground to await the blasts. The explosions sent tremors through the ground, and as before debris covered him in dust and grit. He pushed himself to his feet, and looked for the man and woman; they were still on the ground, moving and emitting low groans.

There was no time to worry about casualties, especially those involved in drug trafficking. He had the two remaining buildings to deal with. He raced to the nearest and went in through the open doorway, taking in the deserted scene before him. It was a laboratory, no doubt used for testing and processing drugs. Analysers, scales, mixers and equipment he'd never seen before sat on top of benches alongside packaging material.

But the real prize was stacked along the furthest wall; boxes of drug compounds stacked six high with a street value of millions of dollars. What he was about to do would hurt the cartel badly; they would be out of action for months by the time he'd finished.

An open door led off the lab and he crossed over to check it out, slamming it backwards on its hinges to ensure no-one was hiding behind it. He heard a gasp from the left-hand corner and his infra-reds picked out a figure crouched down at the side of one of the stacks of boxes. Cole strode over gun in hand and grabbed hold of an arm. Its owner squealed in fear; it was a

70

woman. He pulled her to her feet and pulled her across to the door and into the lab.

'Get out, go, go, run.' Cole used Russian again, still seeking to confuse. The woman didn't linger and was out of sight in seconds. Cole set three timers to two minutes, threw one into the store room followed by two into the lab and dashed for the outdoors. Time was passing and he was desperate to complete his mission. He ran to the next building without seeking cover from the explosions.

The door was wide open and he stepped inside, his eyes taking in what lay before him; chairs, tables, sofas, a TV, a small bar - a recreation area. There were three doors at the far end, one had a toilet sign, another was open and he moved across to it cautiously; it was a kitchen. Stealthily he sidled along to the third door and eased it open. Crouching low, he peered into the darkness, his ears straining for sound. It seemed empty and he was about to stand when he heard a movement. He pulled down his infra-red goggles and scanned the room, smiling when he saw a dog tethered in a corner. A shot rang out, and a bullet thudded into the wall inches from his face. The infra-reds picked up the flash; Cole wheeled half-right and fired three shots. His attacker dropped poleaxed to the floor. The dog seemed unphased by the events and just licked at dead guy's face. Cole took a second to untether the dog and was about to usher it out when the explosives went off. The whole building shook but the wall and roof absorbed the blasts. *You got lucky Jos.*

Time to get out of here. He sprinted over to the door and was about to exit when a jeep screeched to a stop about twenty metres away. Four heavily-armed men leapt from their seats and formed a square, military fashion. *Fuck it, the cavalry's arrived.* Cole took aim, he could drop one, maybe two, but four meant the odds weren't on his side.

Suddenly a shot rang out, quickly followed by another; two men fell, almost certainly dead. The other two dropped to crouch position with their backs to Cole, weapons extended, pointed in the direction of the shots. Cole took aim and fired; the man on the right toppled over, dead or dying. The remaining man threw down his weapon and raised his hands. Another shot rang out and the man dropped like a stone.

For the first time, Cole caught sight of a car about a hundred metres away. His rescuer was clearly a friend and could only be one person, the redoubtable Jethro. *Finish the job, Jos.* He set the last two explosives to one minute and sprinted away grinning widely as his suspicions were confirmed. 'What the hell are you doing here, Jethro? You said you wouldn't get involved in a gunfight?'

'Saving your fucking arse, that's what I'm doing. Now cut the chat and get in the car. Let's get the hell outta here before more reinforcements arrive. We'll collect your Mini on the way.'

CHAPTER EIGHT

Later

Watkins got back before Cole and he and Austin were standing outside the beach shack when he arrived. They saluted and started clapping when he got out of the Mini. Cole was on a high, the whole operation had taken just over four and a half hours including the three hours travel. With luck he'd get a good night's sleep.

'Sorry we ain't playing Hail to the Chief for you, that sure was a sweet operation. Let's get you inside and changed, then I'll get us all a drink. Wash that black stuff of your face; I want you outta my territory soon as.' Jethro chortled.

Cole didn't need any further encouragement he desperately wanted to freshen up.

He showered quickly and changed into a tee and cargo pants; a quick glance in a mirror showed no sign of the tiredness he felt. His two friends stood as he joined them, Austin had a bottle of champagne in hand and popped the cork, then poured three glasses and reached one to Cole. 'Well done, Jos.'

'I second that.' Jethro clicked his glass.

Cole shook his head. 'It was a joint operation and you probably saved my hide back there, Jethro; I was out-gunned four to one.'

'My pleasure, Jos, though I'll bet you would have downed them without my help.'

Austin raised a finger, seeking silence, pointing to an earbud. 'Breaking news.' He walked over to the television and switched it on, the screen filled immediately with a scene of carnage. The huts were still belching out flames and smoke; six fire engines were on the scene and firemen were still trying to quell the flames. Two ambulances and four police vehicles were also in attendance.

A reporter on site was addressing the camera. 'Very little is known about the buildings behind me or the purpose to which they are put. The Responders answered an 'anonymous alarm call and found a number of dead bodies lying on the ground outside the building when they arrived. A number of staff have been taken to hospital with gunshot wounds along with others who seem to have been blinded. Some staff have been traumatised by the attack; others unharmed, but for reasons unknown at this time are unwilling to be interviewed. The Police are trying to contact the owners of the site and will make a formal statement later. I'll now return you to the studio.'

Austin switched the TV off, smiling broadly. 'You've achieved more in a few hours, Jos, than we've done in years. This will hit the Romeros hard; Australia owes you big time.'

Cole was beginning to feel embarrassed at the praise being heaped upon him, Gerry Moore didn't do praise and he didn't expect it. 'Guys, I'm going to be unsociable and hit the hay. I'm knackered and I need some time out to study those papers you gave me, Billy. My mission is only half done. By the way, back there I spoke in Russian in the hope it will stir things up between the Romero gang and the Shkodra. I don't speak Albanian but Russian should be near enough for the uninformed.'

Austin shook his head, mouth open. 'That's brilliant, Jos, fucking brilliant. I can't wait to see how the Romero retaliate. Have another glass of bubbly before you go.'

Cole shook his head. 'I'll decline thank you, I have work to do, sorry.'

Austin made to protest but Jethro put a hand on his shoulder. 'Jos is right, Billy. Let's all say goodnight.'.

Cole nodded, 'Sleep well, guys, see you in the morning, if I'm still around when you get up. I have no idea what these papers will lead me to. Real sorry it's got to be this way, but I promise we'll meet up in the months ahead and paint the town red.'

Jethro watched as his friend left the room, a mixture of sadness and disappointment on his face; he felt sure Cole wouldn't be joining them for breakfast. He put his arm round Austin's shoulders. 'Bed time, buddy, I need some shuteye.'

In the privacy of his bedroom, Cole scanned the lists given to him by Billy, very quickly picking out his next target, Edward 'Ted' Harris, Minister for Home Affairs. He smiled when he saw that Harris would be in Canberra for the rest of the week. A quick internet search on his burner phone duly provided details of the minister's residence.

Moore had provided him with the addresses he needed when she briefed him on his mission but a double check never went amiss. And besides, it was useful to know what the place looked like. Next, he searched for Patrick 'Paddy' O'Connor, Australia's highest ranking police officer who, it turned out, would be meeting the State Governor in Canberra the following day. Another internet search confirmed what Moore had told him. *All systems go, Jos.*

Cole packed his bag, glancing at his watch in the process, 2.10am. He had time to run through his plans - time to clear his head – time for a lie down. He would aim to leave around 4am, hoping Jethro and Billy would be in a deep sleep and he could sneak away unheard. He felt guilty at the thought of running out on his hosts, but he'd make it up to them another day.

Canberra. Early next morning.

Police Chief, Paddy O'Connor had been in his office since shortly after 5am. His phone had been red-hot since the news broke of the attack on the Romero set up. He had put the entire force on full alert and charged his sub-lieutenants with finding out who had been responsible. The Minister, Ted Harris, had been on his back demanding to know who had committed the outrage. The pressure didn't end there; the Hydra's Leader had contacted both of them demanding answers they couldn't provide. They both knew they would have to identify who was responsible or face the consequences.

As Head of Hydra zone 5, Harris had contacted Pablo Romero to see what he knew of the attack on his empire. Romero had provided such detail as he could; the entire drug factory set-up was a write off. He recounted that the assailant had spoken in what sounded like Russian, and he suspected that the Shkodra were mounting a takeover bid. He would be taking his revenge.

Harris could see where this was heading and sought to take control of the situation. 'No Pablo, there are to be no reprisals until I have carried out a full investigation. I will ensure that the instigators are dealt with severely. I promise that your factory will be rebuilt to the highest standard. You will take no further action, do you understand?'

'Yes, of course. I hear what you say Number 5.'

Romero slammed the phone down. 'Fuck you, Number 5, this is a matter of honour, I will deal with this outrage my way. He reached for another mobile and sent a WhatsApp to his two lieutenants. *Assemble at the warehouse in twenty minutes, bring ten of our best with you, we have business to attend to.*

The Romero Warehouse

They were all there; Enrico Murrato, Pablo's number two, Marco Bonneti next-in-line, and ten toughies. They were all eager for action and revenge, no matter what it involved.

Romero addressed his team. 'Our factory has been destroyed by the Shkodra cartel; it's probably still burning as I speak. Our entire drugs stock has gone up in flames; we won't generate a single dollar anytime soon. We will all suffer because of those bastards. This cannot go unanswered. Agreed?'

There were growls and utterances of anger all around the group.

Romero shook his fist in the air. 'Death to the Shkodra. Grab your weapons and grenades and get moving. You're are going to hit them now and hit them hard. Enrico and Marco take five men and a van each, show them what happens when they mess with the Romeros. We lost eight good comrades and another ten are blinded; get out there and even the score, no holds barred, man or women. Don't come back till the job is done. Leave no-one alive.'

The Shkodra estate.

Forty minutes later the two Romero vans drew up near the gated entrance to the Shkodra estate. Enrico and Marco got out of their vehicles and discussed their next move before returning to brief their men. Marco reversed back twenty metres, then accelerated forward to crash the car into the gate. The gate collapsed and Marco drove on; he knew the site layout from times gone by when the two cartels were on better terms. Enrico's van followed close behind, both racing along a narrow tarmac road towards the Shkodra drug factory. They were there in minutes.

Their presence had been caught on the gate's CCTV and the alarm sounded. Men and women were gathering outside the huts, waiting for directions from their supervisor. They saw the vans coming towards them, but it was curiosity that filled their thoughts, not concern or fear. How wrong they were.'

Inside the vans the windows had been rolled down and the occupants sat with automatic weapons at the ready. Marco slowed the van to a fast-walking pace and his men opened fire relentlessly. Enrico's van followed, its men firing indiscriminately at the dead and the injured, male or female it made no difference. At the end of the line of huts the vans turned and drove back, stopping at each of the four huts in turn. One van covering the other whilst a team entered to continue the slaughter. There were sounds of explosions as grenades and makeshift Molotov cocktails were ignited and thrown.

The operation lasted barely fifteen minutes. Every hut was in flames, their contents destroyed and not a single Shkodra operative left alive. The annihilation complete, Enrico gave the order to depart and for each van to take a different route back to the warehouse. Both vehicles got back to their base in under twenty minutes; if there were any responders on their way to the carnage, they didn't see them. No-one had been left alive and it was not until the following day, when the dayworkers reported for duty, that the alarm was raised.

Next morning

Newspapers reported that over thirty drug factory workers, unarmed men and women, had been slaughtered during an attack by unknown parties. Officials were tight-lipped, but the most likely reason for the attack was inter-gang warfare. The police were investigating the possibility of a link between this attack and the one on the Romero set-up the previous evening.

CHAPTER NINE

Day Three

Cole slid out of bed, and headed straight for the bathroom to freshen up and shave, his head buzzing with the options he was considering for the day ahead. It was 4am and his couple of hours' sleep had been sufficient to rejuvenate him. Back in his bedroom he dressed and shoved the last few items into his backpack He was being as quiet as possible, seeking not to disturb his friends. He crossed the lounge and was reaching for the front handle when he heard a whisper.

'Going somewhere, boy?' Jethro was sitting in an armchair in pyjama shorts. 'You leaving without saying goodbye?'

'I guess I am, Jethro. I didn't want to trouble you and Billy any more than I had to; you've done more than enough already.'

'And what if I want to help?'

Cole shook his head. 'What lies ahead is nowhere near as difficult as last night; I'm happy I can handle my next assignment singlehanded. That, and the fact that there's too much at stake for Billy; his whole career would be in ruins if it became known he'd been in any way involved. Think about it, if you got tagged the trail would lead back to Billy by association. I knew you would want to help, so I was trying to sneak away and avoid a situation like this. I'm grateful, Jethro, I really am, but it's best I go on my own this time.'

The big man sighed. 'I guess so, but dammit I want to get involved. I haven't had so much fun since I retired from the SAS.'

Cole smiled. 'I know, Jethro, but believe me, what I'm doing is just the beginning, big things lie ahead and my guess is you'll be up to your eyeballs in action; this is only the beginning. You mark my words.'

Jethro's face clouded with disappointment. 'I know you're right and Billy must come first.' He rose and strode over to Cole and gave him a massive hug. 'You be careful man, very careful. I hate fucking funerals, good friends especially.' He pulled opened the door. 'Off you go and don't look back, I won't be waving you goodbye.'

Cole dumped his backpack on the passenger seat, pressed the ignition button and gently eased the Mini forward until he was well clear of the hut. It was still dark as he raced along the highway toward the outskirts of Canberra, getting ever closer to the home of Edward 'Ted' Harris, Zone leader 5 in the Hydra organisation.

He was on the lookout for a church close to a small crossroads; Harris lived not far from there. It came into view much earlier than he anticipated and he had to brake heavily to pull into a bus stop lane. It was dark and silent, perfect for what he had to do. Only an occasional owl shriek broke the silence as he strode forward hugging the hedge. There were only a handful of houses in the area, all of mansion proportions. They all had entrance drives and large steel gates, none of which were closed. Cole raised an eyebrow and pursed his lips. *Trusting sods, maybe tomorrow's headlines will change that attitude.*

The first house was called Valhalla, the next Serendipity, the third was the Harris residence, Paradise. Cole smiled when he saw the name. *Not for long, Ted. Let the party begin.* He made his way up the curving red gravel drive, keeping close to the rhododendrons that lined the edge.

Paradise came into view; an attached double garage stood on its right. There were no cars parked outside so he ran over to the garage, cursing when a security light came on. He quickly moved to the side of the garage out of sight of the house. The light would remain on, but if someone did happen to be up and about and looked out, they would see nothing of concern and conclude the sensor had been activated by a flypast owl or a fox.

Cole continued along the side of the garage, nearly tripping over a pile of watering cans in the process. The resulting noise didn't bother him; noise was an element of his plan. He pulled up his mask, leaving only his eyes to be seen, and sidled along the rear of the garage. Half-way along the wall he found the door he was hoping for and tried turning the handle. He gave himself a mental thumbs up when he found the door was unlocked; not many people lock doors to outhouses when they're in residence and the Harris family was no different.

He entered and felt around for a light switch, giving up almost instantly and resorting to his torch. There were two cars, Ted Harris's black convertible Rolls Royce, the Minister did himself proud, and alongside it a cherry-red Citroen, presumably his wife's. He swung the torch round and found what he'd hoped for, a connecting door from the garage to the house. He moved to the Rolls and gave it a heavy shoulder nudge, instantly triggering the car alarm; in the confines of the garage the noise was deafening. He turned his attention to the Citroen and repeated the process and was rewarded by a piercing alarm.

Upstairs in the main bedroom, Peggy Harris nudged her sleeping husband. 'The car alarms have gone off, Ted. Can you hear them?'

Harris raised his head from the pillow and stopped himself cursing. His wife was right. 'Dammit, I was in a deep sleep. I'll need to go down and reset the buggers.'

'Sorry, honey, I can't think why that would happen.'

Harris drew a sharp breath, 'Christ, maybe it's an intruder.'

Peggy Harris shuddered. 'We should call the police; I'll get my phone.'

'No, dear, it'll take them too long to get here. I'll deal with it.'

Peggy Harris bit her lip. 'Be careful, honey, there's some bad people around nowadays.'

'I'll take my gun.'

Harris pulled open his bedside cabinet drawer and took out a revolver; he was licensed and competent, having practised on the police department's indoor firing range. He made his way out of the bedroom and down the stairs to the lounge and from there to the utility room, switching on lights as he went. The alarms were sounding ever-louder as he approached. He started to relax; an intruder would be gone by now.

Harris took both sets of car keys from their hooks and walked over to the door to the garage. It was locked and bolted and it took a few seconds to open the door. He stepped into the garage and reached across with his left hand to switch on the lights. The garage flooded with light and made him blink. He barely had time to process his first sight of the man standing on the far side of the garage before a shot rang out. The bullet struck the centre of his forehead and he fell backwards into the house. Cole moved round the cars and fired another shot into Harris's heart. A waste of a bullet, but better to be certain.

Both sets of cars keys had were lying near the dead man's feet; Cole retrieved them and pressed both keypads in turn. The Rolls alarm ceased but the Citroen carried on; he needed to be closer to the car. He walked towards it pressing the fob repeatedly, breathing a sigh of relief when the alarm stopped.

So far everything had gone to plan but he wasn't finished yet. He moved back to Harris and unceremoniously dragged him by his feet to the rear of the Rolls where he opened the boot and bundled him in. *Welcome to Paradise, Mr Harris.* Cole slammed the boot lid down and made his way over to the utility room and from there followed the light trail to the staircase. He sneaked a look round to see that it was clear.

Peggy Harris had heard the shots and was trembling with fear and apprehension. *It was an intruder and Ted was shooting at them. Christ, what do I do? Phone the police? No Ted wouldn't like that. He'd want to show how brave he was and impress the public.* She waited a few minutes then shouted, 'Ted, are you OK?' There was no reply, maybe he couldn't hear her over the noise of the alarms. Suddenly there was silence; Ted had sorted the problem. *I must have imagined I heard shots. No, I'm sure I heard shots.'*

She gasped when she saw the masked man, gun in hand, and instinctively raised her hands. 'Please don't shoot, I'll do whatever you want.' Then she remembered Ted. 'Where's my husband? Where's my husband? What have you done to him?

The man said something she didn't understand. He was a foreigner, what was he saying? The man repeated his instructions; he sounded European - German - .no - Eastern European. She shrank in fear as he stepped towards her, sinking to her knees. He was beside her now, looking down at her. She felt small and insignificant when she looked up at his masked face. The eyes were staring, pitiless, almost evil. 'Please don't hurt me; I'll do whatever you want.'

He grabbed her pyjama jacket collar and hauled her to her feet. He was shouting at her again. *Fuck it, why don't you speak English. Tell me what you want*

Cole pushed her towards the door and out onto the landing. She offered no resistance. *Shit, he's speaking in that lingo again, what in hell's name does he want?*

Cole motioned her to go down the stairs, following a few steps behind her. *Maybe when she got to the bottom of the stairs, she could make a break for it. Don't be mad, you can't outrun a bullet.*

She reached the bottom of the stairs and turned to look at him. He spoke again, more words she couldn't understand. Cole pushed her towards and into the lounge, nudging her along whenever she hesitated. Finally, she understood what his intentions were. *He wants me to go to the utility room, the garage. Ted, oh my God, I hope he's OK. He wants to tie us up together, they always do that on TV. Ted must be OK. He could have killed me upstairs. It's going to be alright. I'll do whatever he wants.*

She reached the door to the garage and looked in. *Where are you, Ted?* There was no sign of her husband. *What now?* She stopped and looked round at him. He mouthed more instructions in that language of his and pointed left; more words only one of which she recognised - Citroen. Fear filled her again, he was going to kidnap her, hold her to ransom. Cole pushed her along to the rear of her car. *Where are you, Ted? What has he done to you, my darling?*'

Her assailant was speaking again, waving the gun.

'What do you want me to do? Speak English for fuck's sake.' Peggy Harris was near breaking point and yelled the words at her captor.

Cole opened the boot and pushed her head downwards. She resisted and straightened up but gave way when he raised the gun threateningly. *Do what he says Peggy.* She climbed into the boot and crouched herself into as small a presence as possible. The gunman was reaching up to the boot lid and she put her hand protectively over her head; it came down and she was in darkness but at least she was unharmed. She heard the boot lock operate then silence. Peggy Harris breathed a huge sigh of relief; she was alive, but for how long and where was Ted?

Cole was pleased with the scenario; his alternative plan had been to plant a magnetic car bomb under the Rolls. The resultant explosion when the car pulled away would undoubtedly have killed the driver, but he had no way of guaranteeing who would be driving or if they would be accompanied. As it was, no innocent party had been injured and one of the Hydra's leading lights was dead.

With luck it would be a few hours before the alarm was raised by which time he would be well clear of Paradise. He closed the connecting door to the house, switched off the garage light, shut the side door and ran back to the Mini.

A mile or so along the way he threw his victims' car keys into a ditch. *Mission accomplished, Jos, give yourself a pat on the back.*

CHAPTER TEN

Canberra

Cole felt relaxed as he drove towards Australia's capital, the toughest elements of his mission had been accomplished; the final phase would be a piece of cake, or should be if the unexpected didn't come along to spoil the party. He was driving as fast as the speed limit allowed, following the curve of the road, not cutting corners, making sure he wouldn't be hauled over by a police patrol; not that he had seen any.

Cole was heading for the small block of apartments where Commissioner O'Connor resided; better known as Paddy O'Connor – the undercover deputy who secretly reported direct to the Hydra's leader – who secretly kept tabs on the late departed Ted Harris. O'Connor was the Head of Australia's police service, feared by both his staff and the criminal fraternity.

Cole glanced at his watch - it was nearly 6am, later than he wished; Canberra would be in the process of wakening up.

O'Connor had chosen the location of his part-time residence to be near the centre of power. Parliament House was less than a mile away, so Cole was in familiar territory, having visited the British Embassy a couple of days previously

A short distance ahead he saw a small public car park and pulled in, pleased to find that he was its sole user. He got out of the Mini, then climbed into the rear seat and opened a tan leather briefcase; it held what he needed to carry out the final stage of his mission. A few minutes later he returned to the front seat and took a final look in the rear-view mirror before setting off. *'Not bad, Jos, some women might prefer your new look in this age of facial hair.'* He had donned a fulsome head of blonde hair combed back in a quiff. The wig was accompanied by a blonde horseshoe moustache. Happy with what he saw, he started up the Mini and began the short journey to O'Connor's Senate Apartments, a block of twenty small but luxurious dwellings. The police chief's main residence was in Sydney, where he lived with his third wife Carole.

Cole had studied online estate agent photos of Senate House and readily spotted the yellow brick-built building as he approached. He turned right off the main highway, took the first left and parked up. It was early and he knew he might be observed, but that was a chance he had to take; his disguise would offer some protection. He left the Mini, and briefcase in hand, walked back along the way he had come, arriving at Senate House in under ten minutes. Without hesitating, he walked up the entrance drive and followed it round to the rear of the building and the entrance to the car park which effectively formed the ground floor.

All he had to do now, was find O'Connor's car. Fortunately, the guy was a publicity seeker and there were numerous online photos of him in the red Morgan he used in his leisure time. Cole very quickly found it parked opposite the entrance, facing outwards, ready to go. He strolled casually across to the car; to an onlooker it would appear he was admiring the iconic British motor.

He knew there would be security cameras recording his presence but wasn't concerned. By the time the forces of law and order started their manhunt he wouldn't be wearing his disguise. He ducked down behind the boot, slid a slim, saucer-like magnetic explosive device from his briefcase and placed it in position on the petrol tank. That done he moved round to the driver's door and fastened another to the underside of the car. The devices were now active, any attempt to remove the devices, or car movement over ten kilometres per hour would result in massive explosions.

Cole left the parking area immediately and walked calmly back to the Mini. His job was done; fate and time were in control now. His next destination would be the British High Commission, but he had time to kill, and he was hungry. He took the main road out of town, cruised through the suburban layer, and drove aimlessly for an hour, eventually parking up on the outskirts of Queanbeyan.

It was time to revert back to normality; he removed his wig and moustache and stowed them in one of the Mini's concealed compartments. He took a look round to ensure no-one was anyone in the vicinity and finding the coast clear, removed the false magnetic number plates. Back in the car he snapped the number plates in two and put the four pieces into a red 'destruction' bag. It would be retrieved by authorised Embassy staff and destroyed without opening.

Hunger pangs were beginning to gnaw at him and he followed the signs to the riverside where he hoped to find a decent café for breakfast. There were a few to choose from and working on the 'locals know best' belief, he chose one with a well-filled carpark. Most of the vehicles were commercial and professional drivers really did know where best to dine out.

Cole made his way in and was greeted immediately by a cheerful middle-aged woman who led him to a small table with a view of the river. She introduced herself as Gladys and handed him a menu. 'What can I get you to drink, darling?'

'A large pot of strong tea please.'

She raised her eyebrows. 'A Brit eh, what brings you to these parts?'

'Business in Canberra with a bit of pleasure thrown in.'

She nodded and moved away, returning a few minutes later with the tea. 'Ready to order?'

'I'll have your Big Breakfast without the tomatoes, please.'

'Be with ya shortly, darling.'

The café was busy with most of its tables occupied by a one or more customers. The sound of conversation was hushed and not intrusive; no-one was showing him any interest. Behind the service counter a television, at a very low volume, was showing the morning news. Cole could make out scenes of the Romero and Shkodra factories in the background; a solitary Fire Engine was still in attendance on each site. In both places the police presence amounted to three or four vehicles. A high-ranking police officer was being interviewed and Cole wished he could hear what was being said. He seemed to be the only one interested; perhaps those present had had their fill of the news the previous night.

Suddenly the scene changed, an announcement was being made from the studio; a banner headline read - Large Explosion Outside Canberra Apartment Block.

His waitress returned with a heaped plate. 'There ya go fella, enjoy.'

'What's that about?' Cole nodded in the direction of the TV.'

She shrugged. 'First I've heard of it, you know as much as me. An explosion of some kind, I bet it's a gas main.'

Cole started devouring his food, only occasionally glancing at the TV; his basic needs had taken over, a typical fry-up English breakfast had his full attention.

Someone turned up the TV volume and Cole, along with others, gave it his attention; fighting off a smile when the announcer informed viewers that Australia's Commissioner of Police and been killed in a car explosion.

The cause was believed to have been an explosive device. One witness in the area claimed she heard two explosions in quick succession and was describing what had followed. The scene switched to the Senate Apartments block where two Fire engines and four police vehicles were on site. The area was cordoned off and traffic was being diverted.

Job done, Jos, enjoy your breakfast.

BATEMANS BAY

Miles away, Jethro Watkins sat watching the morning news, eyes wide, his head shaking slowly from side to side in amazement. *Fuck me Jos, I sure am glad I'm not on your kill list.*

AUSTRALIAN SECRET INTELLIGENCE AGENCY

Edgar Tomlinson, Head of ASIS, hurried into the main office. 'Attention everybody. The Police Commissioner has been assassinated right here in Canberra on our fucking doorstep. 'Everybody, and I do mean everybody, get onto this outrage right away; check every communication source you have access to. I want answers, and I want them fast. 'Billy will lead on this. Steve, Tim and Billy, my office, now.'

Billy Austin's heart missed a beat, it had to be Jos.

PARLIAMENT HOUSE.

Prime Minister Malcolm Henderson was reading over papers in preparation for business later that day, when his Personal Assistant entered his office, her face strained.

'What is it, Val?'

'The Commissioner of Police has been murdered, Prime Minister; right here in Canberra, less than a mile along the road.'

The colour drained from Henderson's face, his head shaking slowly from side to side in disbelief. 'Murdered? Murdered? When? How?'

'A car bomb, less than fifteen minutes ago.'

'I can't believe I'm hearing this. Why hasn't Ted Harris been in touch, this is his area of responsibility? Get him on the phone, right this minute.'

'I knew you would ask, Prime Minister, and I've tried but he's not answering his secure phone - his house phone - or his mobile.'

'What? That's ridiculous! Get onto his PA and get him to find out what's going on. Tell him I said it's top priority. Something big is going on, the Romero incident, the Shkodra attack, Paddy O'Connor assassinated. This feels bad to me. Report back when you know anything and let me have Paddy's wife's mobile number; I'll have to phone her.'

Val Clarke went back to her desk and phoned, Olaf Reid, Ted Harris's top assistant. 'Olaf, it's Val Clarke here.'

Reid cut her short. 'I can guess why you're calling; the PM wants to talk to Ted. Join the club. He's not answering his phones and he's overdue for a meeting.'

'Maybe you should get the Police to check this out.'

'No way, we'd have eggs all over our faces if he's just overslept or forgotten the meeting or whatever. I was just leaving to drive out to his place when you phoned. I'll phone in when I get there.'

'The PM's worried, Olaf, very worried.'

'We all are, Val, believe me. I'm going now.'

The Harris residence, Paradise

Olaf Reid pulled into the driveway, parked and scrutinised the front elevation windows. Everything looked normal except for one pair of upstairs window curtains that hadn't been drawn. He walked quickly over to the front door and rang the bell repeatedly, then used the large door knocker, slamming it full force for at least twenty seconds before giving up. He was beginning to feel uneasy.

Reid made his way round to the rear of the house and scanned the garden and the rear elevation; there was nothing out of the ordinary. Somehow, he had to get inside the house, that's where the answer must lie. He'd visited many times and knew there was an interconnecting door between the garage and the house. Once inside the garage he switched on the lights. Ted's Rolls and a Citroen were parked, gleaming, no sign of damage. Turning back to the interconnecting door he hammered on it with his fist, shouting, 'Ted, Ted, are you in there?' He continued hammering. 'Ted, Ted where are you?' Then he heard it - a strained female voice from behind him, one he recognised. 'I'm here, help me.'

He wheeled round, puzzled, there was no-one in sight. 'Is that you Peggy. It's me Olaf Reid, where are you?'

'I'm locked in the Citroen boot.'

Reid ran over and tried the boot and found it locked. 'I can't open it; I'll have to ring a garage for assistance.'

'There's a spare set of keys for both cars in a flower pot on the top shelf on the wall behind you.'

Reid turned and reached up for the pot and fished out the keys, immediately pressing the Citroen fob and raising the boot lid. A dishevelled and blinking Peggy Harris sat up and reached out her arms. Reid helped her out of the boot and steadied her as she tried to stand.

'Bless you, Olaf, thank God you came. I might have died in there.'

'Do you know where Ted is, Peggy?'

She shook her head and explained what had happened. 'Please excuse me, I must change; I've been in there all night. I need to get to the toilet and clean myself.'

'The door to the house is locked.'

She took the flower pot and removed a key and hurried over to the door. 'I'll get back as soon as I've freshened up; then we can search for Ted.' Without waiting for a reply, she opened the door and scurried away upstairs.

Olaf Reid's stomach was churning, he was certain he knew where Ted Harris was. He pressed unlock on the Rolls key and, nerves on edge, opened the boot, turning away gasping in horror when he saw the staring eyes and bloody face of his former boss. He slammed down the boot lid; he had three calls to make - the police - the Prime Minister and Ted Harris's personal assistant. They could all be dealt with quite formally, but how was he going to tell Peggy Harris her beloved husband was dead.

He felt sick, vomit reaching for his mouth; he fought back the nausea and used his mobile. The Deputy Commissioner answered immediately and Reid explained the situation, stressing the need for specialist support for Peggy Harris. He also remembered to make a plea that the media were not informed at this early stage. The other calls followed - the Prime Minister promised to get there as soon as he could - Harris's secretary burst into tears. The poor woman was fraught and he wasn't sure if she took on board his instructions regarding a media blackout.

His tasks done Reid sat down on a garden bench. The Romeros, the Shkodra, Paddy O'Connor and now Ted Harris, his head was swimming. *What the fuck is going on? This just can't be a series of co-incidences.* A siren-wailing police car swept into the drive and parked at the front of the house. *So much for a news blackout.* But he parked his anger for the moment; it was not the time for remonstration.

'You phoned the police?' Peggy Harris had returned dressed in casual clothes, clearly anxious but trying to control her emotions.

'I thought it best, Peggy. They are trained to deal with situations like this.'

'He's never gone missing before, but he deals with very strange people from time to time; maybe he's been kidnapped. It wouldn't surprise me.'

Reid just stared at her; he didn't have the heart to tell her that husband has been murdered. Before he could rustle up some words of comfort, a Police Superintendent accompanied by two Sergeants arrived at the rear garden. One of the Sergeants, a woman, walked immediately over to Peggy Harris and took her by the arm. 'Could you and I go indoors, Mrs Harris? I'd like you to take me through the situation from start to finish.'

Peggy Harris shook her head, 'I've already...'

The Sergeant gently guided her away. 'I know but this is for the records. Please.'

When they'd gone, Reid addressed the Superintendent. 'Ted Harris is in the boot of the Rolls Royce, he's been shot. His wife doesn't know yet; I didn't have the guts to tell her. Would it be alright if I left now, I'd rather not be around when she finds out?'

'Not a problem, Olaf, though we'll need a formal statement from you in due course.'

Queanbeyan Café

Cole settled his bill and made his way out to the Mini; it was time to wrap up the mission. He took out a burner phone and texted the High Commissioner. 'Deception. Be with you in an hour or so.'

British High Commission, Canberra

The drive was uneventful and the rear gates to the High Commission were opened by the Security Guard as soon as Mini came into sight. The High Commissioner was waiting for him in the grounds when Cole parked, got out of the Mini. The two men shook hands wondering how to begin their conversation.

Sir Edward looked troubled. 'If you have anything to do with recent events in Canberra, Mr Cole, you've been very busy?'

'No comment.'

A frown crossed the politician's face and Cole raised both hands apologetically. 'It's best you don't know, Sir, believe me. It'll all come out in due course, though hopefully not my name. Now, if you don't mind, I'd like to change and get on my way.

It may not seem like it, but I greatly appreciate all the help you and your staff have provided. Gerry Moore might tell you more about what's going on, but I'm limited in what I'm authorised to say, sorry. I will say though that everything that has happened is fully justified, you have my word. By the way, there is some red bag stuff in the car for secure disposal; it would be very bad news if it fell into the wrong hands.'

'That's not a problem, leave it with me.'

Cole nodded his thanks. 'One final request, I'd be grateful if you could arrange a taxi for me; tell the driver to pick me up at the rear gate.'

Sir Edward was starting to relax. 'Count it as done. You're right of course, it is best I know as little as possible.' He smiled, 'I think I'm going to redact you from my memory, Mr Cole.' He turned to leave, then turned back. 'Jos.'

Cole held the High Commissioner's gaze, wondering what was about to be said.

'I just want to wish you good luck.'

Cole smiled and nodded. 'Much appreciated, Sir Edward.'

CHAPTER ELEVEN

Day Three

Cole climbed into the taxi and settled in the back seat, dressed casually in dark blue shorts and a light blue tee.

'Where to, boss?'

'Canberra Railway Station.'

'Going far?'

'Sydney.'

The driver looked at his dashboard clock. 'Next train is in twenty-five minutes; I'll get you there in plenty of time. I like Sydney, a lot more goes on there than Canberra; unless of course politics is your business.' He looked at Cole in his rear-view mirror, seeking a response.

'I'm sure you're right.' Cole replied blandly not wanting to get drawn into conversation.

The driver took the hint and drove on in silence, pulling up outside Canberra Railway Station around 12 minutes later.

'That'll be sixteen dollars, please.'

Cole passed him a twenty. 'Keep the change.'

A smile broke out on the driver's face and he saluted. 'Thank you, mate.'

Cole made his way into the station ticket office, noting that the train would depart to schedule. He purchased a first class single then made his way across the concourse to the platform where the train stood ready to leave. There weren't many fellow passengers to be seen and he had a first-class compartment to himself. *Your lucky day, Jos.* He had barely made himself comfortable when the train gave a small jolt and his four hours plus journey to Sydney began.

The events of the last few days had drained him, mentally and physically, and within minutes he had fallen into a deep sleep. Nearly three hours passed before he woke up; his nerves had settled and he felt refreshed. Travel wasn't his favourite pastime but at least it was restful. His thoughts inevitably drifted to planning the days ahead. The chaos he'd created in Canberra had been a massive success and he was surprised that Gerry Moore hadn't been in touch. She must have received reports of what had taken place and put two and two together to work out he had been responsible. Maybe she had a dilemma? She would be pleased about Harris and O'Connor, but on the other hand he had worked outside the agreed plan and could have jeopardised the main operation. She could hardly pat him on the head for disobeying orders. *Bollocks, it's history.*

His intention was to get to Sydney's main railway station and from there take the shuttle to Kingsford Smith International Airport, known as Mascot Airport by the locals and Sydney International by everybody else! If all went well, he would book a flight to Mumbai, preferably the 4.10pm with Sri Lanka Airways. Otherwise, it would mean spending another six hours waiting for one of the late-night departures. He would take the best class of travel on offer, Business or First; he wasn't picking up the tab.

Sydney International Aiport

When officials looked at his passport, they would find that he was Richard McIntosh, a British National. The purpose of his visit, if asked, was sales. It was up to him to come up with a storyline as to what he was selling, and he had settled on computer software for analysing marketing trends.

He knew who his prime targets were but was still undecided as to whether to go rogue and make a direct attempt on a couple of the big crime syndicates. The two main syndicates, one simply known as The Company, and the other the Mumbai Mafia, were notorious. Their leaders seemed to be immune from prosecution, but that was the very nature of the Hydra. He had the basis of an idea, but would need the help of an old friend who lived in Mumbai and might be able to help him.

Cole, as Richard McIntosh, passed through Passport Control without barely a glance and made his way to a lounge to wait for the boarding call for the flight to Mumbai, whose airport had a name so long he couldn't remember half of it. He'd managed to purchase Business Class, but resolved not to overdo the free drinks.

Despite the luxury travel, the fourteen-hour flight, with a forty-five minutes stop in Colombia, proved to be purgatory; eating, sleeping, and drinking despite his resolve, did little to relieve the boredom. The only highlight proved to be a film, Wicked Little Letters, which had him laughing out loud. But all things, good and bad, come to an end and the Airbus landed a little ahead of schedule, shortly before 6am.

Mumbai

Along with other Business Class passengers he was one of the first to get off the plane, and with no hold luggage, first in line for Border Control. The usual formalities were carried out without a hitch and he moved on to Customs. The Officers on duty waved him through and he was quickly on his way to the hotel he'd found on the internet. Rydges had two advantages - it was immediately adjacent to the terminal building, and it had a gymnasium; he felt in need of a good workout. The Receptionist gave him a broad smile and welcomed him to India; he booked himself in for three nights and was allocated a room on the fourth floor.

He'd had a breakfast of sorts on the plane and felt sluggish rather than tired, so his first destination was the Gym where he spent thirty minutes on a treadmill, and another thirty toning his muscles. His exercising complete Cole returned to his room for a cold shower. It was now 8.30am local time and he decided to relax for another 30 minutes before phoning his contact, Anika

Chopri, a woman he'd met at university some years ago. She now worked for the Ministry of Law and Justice, and with luck, would provide the information he needed.

At 9.00am he phoned her mobile, relieved when it rang out and was answered after a few seconds.

'Hello.'

'Anika, it's Jos Cole, I'm in Mumbai. I'd like to meet up for lunch today if you're free?'

'Jos! My goodness, that is a surprise. What brings you to Mumbai?'

'I'll tell you when I see you. It's to do with my work and it's confidential.'

'Hmm, sounds like a fairy story to me, Jos. I'm working, so my time will be limited, but of course I'll meet you. I have to tell you that I'm engaged to be married and our yesterdays are history.'

Cole knew she was alluding to the affair they had had at Uni. 'He's a lucky guy whoever he is, and I'm jealous, but I assure you, this trip is strictly business. I need some information that you might be able to help me with. It would be great if you could bring your laptop in case you have to look something up. I'm pressing my luck, but it would be ideal if we could meet somewhere near the British High Commission.

'I'm intrigued, Jos. I'll meet you in the coffee lounge at the Grand Hyatt Hotel at 12.00. Don't be late.'

Cole had another call to make, and dialled a mobile number supplied by Gerry Moore. His call was answered on the third ring. 'Deception.'

'Eureka. There's no need for introductions, I know the backstory.' The Deputy High Commissioner, Diane Fitzwilliam, verged on being brusque. 'I've been fully briefed and I'm of the view that it's best if you don't show up at the Commission; it could result in questions I don't want to deal with.'

'Thanks for the warm welcome, Commissioner.' Cole responded sarcastically. 'I have my job to do and I won't take up any more of your time than I need to. Where's my car?'

Fitzwilliam wasted no time in giving Cole the details for collection and return of the car. 'Is there anything else I can help you with?' She sounded irritated, her voice unwelcoming.

'Nothing I can think of, but I have your number if anything crops up.'

'I'll ring off then, good luck.'

Cole sighed. *Maybe I'd be the same in her position.*

He left the hotel and wandered through the Arrivals concourse to the taxi rank. Cabs were plentiful and he was soon comfortably settled in the overly-cooled rear seat of his air-conditioned transport. 'Maharashtra Nature Park, please. I'm meeting a friend at the car park.'

The journey in heavy traffic took all of forty-five minutes, but Cole had time to kill and wasn't bothered. As advised, he found his car, a slightly worse for wear white Fiat Panda, in parking bay 56 of the underground car park. He retrieved the magnetic box fixed to the exhaust and used the enclosed key fob to open the boot where he found a small suitcase. It should contain what was needed for his mission. *Check it out, Jos.* He climbed in behind the wheel and slid the seat back into a comfortable driving position. Making sure there was no-one in the vicinity he opened the case, his eyes lighting up when he saw the two Walther PPKs and a silencer. *Bingo*

Cole set out for the Hyatt and somehow, despite Mumbai's traffic congestion and his limited knowledge of the area, he arrived at the hotel with five minutes to spare. He quickly parked and made his way into the restaurant. He looked around and found a quiet table in the furthest corner of the dining area. A waitress appeared at his table almost as soon as he sat down but moved away when he explained he was waiting for a friend.

Minutes later he caught sight of Anika; drop-dead gorgeous, dressed in the smartest business suit he'd ever seen, its pale green colour contrasting beautifully with her pale brown skin and dark hair.

He rose to greet her; memories of times past flooding in. Dressed as he was in tee-shirt and shorts, he somehow felt at a disadvantage. If she shared his misgivings, she hid any sign of disapproval, smiling and reaching out both arms to greet him, though offering only a light kiss on his cheek and kept me at arm's length.

'You look more beautiful than ever, Anika. My wardrobe is minimal so I couldn't dress up for the occasion.'

'Liar, you never were a snappy dresser, but you're still a handsome bugger.' Before they could continue their conversation, the waitress returned and enquired what they would like.

Anika replied instantly. 'A skinny latte and a dark chocolate croissant, please.'

Cole nodded. 'I'll have two of the croissants and a large black Americano. The waitress smiled, made a note and headed off to the bar.

'So, when's the big day, Anika?'

'We hope to get married later this year.'

'I must give you my address for the invite.' Cole raised an eyebrow and grinned cheekily.

Anita laughed. 'Don't hold your breath, Jos, nice as it would be to have you there. Now, let's cut to the chase, why am I here?'

Cole shot her a warning look as the waitress returned with the coffees and croissants. He smiled his thanks and grabbed a croissant. 'Hmm, these are good, I'm hungry.'

Anita smiled. 'Ditch the padding, Jos, let's have your story and what you want from me. Last time we were in touch you were in the SAS.'

'I'm with MI6 now.'

She burst out laughing. 'Stop it, Jos, be serious.'

'I've never been more serious, Anika, you have my word. I'm afraid I can't tell you much about why I'm here, I'm sworn to secrecy.'

Anika was genuinely stunned. She studied his expression for a few seconds; there wasn't a trace of mischief, in fact his whole demeanour was serious, almost tense. 'Go on, tell me why you're in Mumbai.'

'You've heard of The Company and the Mumbai Mafia.'

Her eyes widened. 'Shsss, keep your voice down, they're notorious. They run the criminal underworld over here and have spies everywhere. They seem to be able to survive whatever the law throws at them.' She paused for a second, her expression thoughtful. 'But hold on, we're thousands of miles from the UK, they're not your problem.'

'That's where you're wrong, Anika. I'm part of a worldwide operation, set up to inflict damage on both organisations.' He was revealing more about his mission than he should, much more, but he had no option but to trust her.

She went silent. 'I can't believe what you're telling me, and I don't think I want to hear anymore. I work for the Minister of Justice and Law and if I wasn't hearing it from you, I'd be reporting this conversation to him.'

'I strongly advise keeping your mouth firmly shut, darling; there are corrupt politicians and officials all around you. I've already said more than I should, much more, but I need help and you're the only one I know who can provide it. I'll get to the point, can you tell me who handles the money-laundering for these people; in other words, their accountants? Please tell me if you know, it's important - very important.'

She tilted her head, puzzled. 'Eliminating their accountants would hurt them, but it wouldn't have a long-lasting effect.'

'You're right, it wouldn't, but that's just part of the package; a much bigger package I can't un-rap for you. So, will you help me or not?'

Anika nodded and took a small notebook out of her handbag and began writing, tearing out a page when she'd finished and handing it to Cole. Everything he needed was there; two names and surprisingly, their addresses. 'How come you can rattle off the addresses of these guys?'

'It's my turn to play dumb. Let's just say that we've been trying to pin something on them for as long as I've been with the Department. We've tried all sorts of surveillance but they've been ahead of us every step of the way, slippery as hell. They both work from home, and take on limited private work to cover their main activities. You can track them down on-line, I won't look them up on my laptop, it would be traceable. I presume you're not here to wish them happy holidays?'

Cole nodded his understanding. 'From what you've said, it sounds to me that they are being tipped off by someone on the inside. I can't tell you what my plans are but the outcome will make media headlines. When you leave here it will be best you forget you ever knew me. Rest assured, Anika, whatever the headlines say, the people involved are fully deserving of their fate.'

Anika stiffened and fear flitted across her eyes. 'You're scaring me Jos, scaring me big time. 'Suddenly she reached forward and squeezed his hand. 'I'm going now, this is all way above my pay grade; please be careful, I wouldn't want to lose you.' She stood and kissed him on the cheek, then whispered in his ear. 'I still fancy you.' With those parting words she hurried away.

Cole's eyes followed her all the way out of the building, wishful for what might have been.

CHAPTER TWELVE

Cole now had the names of two accountants; Krish Argawal who worked for The Company and Ajay Babu who worked for the Mumbai Mafia. Cole searched the internet on his burner phone and quickly confirmed their addresses. Both lived within walking distance but CCTV cameras were everywhere and it would be best to go by car. The plates were false and ultimately, if it came to it, the High Commission should be able to deal with any enquiries. *No time like the present, Jos, let's get this show on the road.*

Argawal's residence

First up was Krish Argawal, 42, born and educated locally. Cole got in the car and followed the route offered by his burner phone satnav; the car was fitted with satnav but it was another potential source of evidence. The journey took ten minutes and led him to a leafy street, populated by colonial style bungalows well concealed by shrub-filled gardens. He drove slowly along the avenue and turned into the house named Svarga, noting the CCTV as he walked towards the door.

By chance, Argawal, a small thin man, was on his way out and heading towards a covered parking area when Cole pulled up. He stopped and turned back, speaking in Hindi. 'How can I help you?' He squinted at Cole, 'I don't think we've met?'

'Are you Mr Argawal?'

'I am. Who are you and why are you here?' Argawal's English was perfect.

'We haven't met but I've heard a lot about you and your work for The Company.'

The accountant's face hardened. 'I haven't the faintest idea what you're talking about and I'm asking you to leave.'

Cole reached into his briefcase. 'If you don't mind, would you please take a look at this.'

Argawal shook his head. 'Not interested, now please go before I call the police.'

'The police will be here soon enough, I assure you.' Cole pulled a Walther, silencer in place, out of his briefcase and fired two shots, twin holes appeared instantly, one in Argawal's forehead the other in his heart. Cole removed the silencer and screwed it into place on the second Walther before returning it to the briefcase.

Now what shall we do with you, Mr Argawal, we don't want you cluttering up this well-tended garden? I know, car boots are in fashion of late, let's give you a hand.

Cole retrieved Argawal's car keys and dragged him over to a yellow Tata Nexon where he opened the boot and unceremoniously bundled in the body. That done he slammed down the boot lid and made his way to the house. Cole knocked loudly on the door and waited for a few seconds before selecting a key from Argawal's keyring and opening the door. 'Hello. Hello. Is there anybody there?'

His wishes were answered, the house was empty. He began the search for the CCTV recorder, eventually finding it in a room set up as an office. In seconds he'd removed the recording disk and was on his way back to the car. *Sweet as a nut, Jos. Now for Mr Babu.*

Babu's residence

His next target's dwelling was located to the north of the High Commission and Cole had to retrace his journey; taking just over thirty minutes to find another leafy street of colonial style bungalows. He drove along the street, passing Sukha, barely able to see the house because of the lush blossomed hedgerow. The street turned out to be a dead end and he had to execute a quick three-point turn and drive back to the bungalow. This time he drove straight in, noting there was a car parked in front of house. *Oh dear, looks like you have a visitor, Ajay.*

He reversed back and set the Fiat ready for a quick getaway. The second of the two Walthers in hand, Cole headed to the house. If there was a CCTV camera fitted, he didn't spot it as he moved to the building and sidled along the front wall. The two front rooms had large bow windows and Cole edged carefully to the first, sneaking a quick glance – a large comfortably furnished lounge hung with paintings and abounding with ornaments, including a stuffed full sized Bengal tiger, but no people. The next room was an equally large dining room, housing an eight-place cherrywood table, chairs and two cabinets, one of which was laden with decanters and bottles; this room too was empty.

There were no side windows as he made his way round to the rear of the property, where he paused briefly to admire the large garden set out with flower beds in full blossom. As he drew near to a window, he could hear groans and the sound of pleasure. Cole stole a quick glance in, drawing back immediately he caught sight of the couple having sex on the bed - Ajay standing - his partner lying face down arms wide. *Damn, there's two of them.* Cole quickly shook off his concerns; he wasn't short of bullets.

He ducked down below window level. and still bent over, hurried along to a rear glazed door where he tried the handle; the door swung open and he stepped inside onto a colourful mosaic-tiled passageway. The door to the bedroom was open and ecstatic noises were still issuing forth; Cole pondered on giving them time to finish their pleasures but quickly dismissed the thought and stepped inside gun in hand. He knocked loudly on the open door to get attention.

'Sorry to interrupt, Ajay, game over.'

Babu looked over his shoulder, passion draining away in an instant when he saw the gun in Cole's hand.

'Who the hell are you?' he barked in Hindi.

'Introductions aren't necessary, Ajay. I'm here on business.'

Cole was taken by surprised when Babu's partner, a twenty-something handsome young man, stood and turned to face him, terror on his face. He garbled something in Hindi to Babu that Cole didn't understand. Babu replied but whatever he said didn't calm the young man down; his agitation continued to be expressed in fear-filled words and quick glances between Cole and his partner.

Babu sought to calm him down with words but to no effect and in desperation he eventually slapped his partner viciously across the face, causing him to sink to the floor in tears.

'That wasn't nice, Ajay, smacking a sweet young chap like that.'

'Cut the crap, Englishman, what the fuck do you want? There's no money in the house.'

Cole smiled. 'That's a surprise I would have thought the Mumbai Mafia's accountant would be rolling in it.'

'I've got nothing to do with the Mafia.'

'Don't play games Ajay or I'll have to get nasty.'

'You don't know who you're messing with Englishman. I suggest you leave now and get out of Mumbai. In fact, get out of India as soon as you can; you're a dead man if you hang around these parts. The Mafia's got a long reach.'

Cole smiled. 'Big talk, Ajay. Thing is, I'm holding the gun. Now, I'm in a bit of a hurry and I want you to take me to your safe and open it.'

Babu sneered. 'Fuck off, Englishman.'

Cole shook his head, slowly a couple of times. 'You sure about that? I really hoped you would co-operate.' Cole was grudgingly impressed when the Indian stood his ground, smirking, showing no signs of fear. Cole sighed, and pulled the trigger twice; the young man's head shattered and he fell backwards to the floor. 'Now look what you've made me do to that sweet young man.'

Babu momentarily gaped in amazement, then turned to swing a punch at Cole who swivelled away and slammed the butt of the Walther into the accountant's face shattering his cheekbone. He joined his partner on the floor, kneeling, cradling his face, blood trickling through his fingers.

'On your feet idiot, or I'll put a bullet in that thick skull of yours.'

Babu, still naked, pushed himself to his feet. 'Can I put on my dressing gown?' He nodded across to a wardrobe.

Cole smiled. 'Nope, I like you just as you are. Now lead me to your office.'

This time there was no resistance. Babu led the way out of the room and along the passage to his office. He hesitated in the doorway and Cole pushed him violently, causing him to stumble into is desk. Behind it, built into the wall, was a large safe.'

Cole nodded. 'Open it.'

Babu shook his head. 'I can't; it's more than my life's worth.'

Cole pointed the Walther at his victim's groin and raised an eyebrow. 'Well?'

'OK, OK, I'll open it, don't shoot.' Without further delay, Babu moved quickly to the safe and dealt with the two dials, then swung the door open, revealing six shelves of legers and papers.

'Answer me a question, Babu. How come none of the police raids have ever found these accounts?'

After a brief hesitation, Babu muttered. 'We get to hear about the raids and clear the stuff away.'

'Thank you, Ajay. I have to admit you're well organised. Tell me, do you ever think about all those unfortunates you help supply with drugs?'

Babu screwed up his face. 'Course not, they're a load of shit.'

Cole nodded. 'A load of shit, just like you, Ajay.' Two shots followed and Babu fell to the floor, his dead eyes staring at the ceiling.

Cole went over to the safe and pulled out a number of ledgers and papers, scattering them on the floor. He also found several bundles of 500-rupee banknotes which he stuffed into his pockets.

'Thank you, Ajay, it's been a pleasure.'

Cole strolled back to the Fiat, smiling every step of the way. *Not a bad day's work, Jos.'* There was more to do but that would wait until later that evening. He programmed the burner satnav and just under an hour later, was sipping a cup of coffee in his airport hotel bedroom.

CHAPTER THIRTEEN

Rydges Hotel

By the time it reached 11pm, Cole was well fed and rested. He had eaten in the hotel and made a bit of a play about feeling tired and having an early night; he gave a generous cash tip courtesy of the late Ajay Babu's stash. Back in his room, he ordered a bottle of Bollinger and invited the wine waiter to have a glass; the offer was politely declined. A generous tip was effusively accepted. Cole wanted to be remembered and was confident he would be.

Next on his death list were, Vishna Arya, Minister of Law and Justice, the Hydra's top man in Asia and his undercover deputy, Kana Bedi, Chief of Defence. Gerry Moore's contacts were well informed; both men were attending a conference in Mumbai and both were staying in the Trident Hotel in Bandra. Yet again Moore had come up trumps; this time via a hotel insider as Cole was about to find out.

Moore had arranged for her contact to phone Cole and his burner mobile buzzed at 00.18; Cole swiped the phone and waited a few seconds. 'Deception.' the voice had virtually no accent, neither Indian or British.

'Eureka.'

'Arya room 612, Bedi room 583. They have both retired for the evening.' The call ended immediately.

Cole ignored the elevator and went down the stairs to the ground floor, then along a short corridor to a door used for deliveries. It could only be opened from the inside and he planned to use it later when he returned. He pulled the door closed and used a small folded paper wedge to hold it in place; a crude solution and it might get found, but that was a chance he had to take.

Trident Hotel

Traffic was light on his way to the hotel and barely twenty minutes had elapsed as he drove past slowly looking for a parking place. Less than two hundred metres ahead he pulled into a vacant space behind a line of cars. He rolled the window down for some fresh air and could hear music belting out from a night club up ahead. There was a group of young people drinking outside and if they chanced to see him it would suit his plans.

It was time for an image change and he resorted to his blonde moustache and wig again, cursing when it proved difficult sticking them in place in the limited light afforded by a nearby street lamp. *Best you can do, Jos, let's get moving.* He reached for his phone and hit the last number redial button, relieved when it was answered immediately.

'Trident Hotel, how can I help?'

It was the same voice he'd heard earlier. 'Deception, I'm outside.'

'Eureka.' The call ended.

Cole swung his small backpack round his shoulders and slammed the car door closed. The intended loud thud caused some of the night club party to look round, but their attention ended as quickly as it began when they saw Cole turn towards the hotel. Hopefully at least one of them would remember the blonde-haired guy when the police made enquiries.

At the entrance to the hotel, he drew a calming breath, then elbowed his way in via the revolving door to a large carpeted entry hall being careful to leave no fingerprints. The reception desk was on the far side of the hall apparently unattended, but as he approached, a tall lightly tanned man of European appearance came out of a door behind the reception desk.

'Good evening, sir, how can I help?

'Deception.'

'Eureka. I've dealt with the security cameras. Please be as quick as you can. I can't leave it too long before I call the maintenance people. Here's your master door entry card, take it with you when you leave and get rid of it.'

Cole nodded. 'Thank you. I won't say goodbye when I leave. If that's OK?'

A brief smile crossed the guy's lips. 'That won't be necessary.'

The lift stood waiting, doors open; Cole moved across quickly and entered. He pulled on latex gloves, then pressed the button for the sixth floor. *Game on.* He checked his watch, it was 1.03am. The lift rose silently and speedily before slowing and stopping smoothly. The doors slid open silently and Cole stepped out into a deserted corridor. A wall sign opposite pointed right to rooms 600 to 650 and he strode quickly along the carpeted corridor to room 612. One of the Walthers, equipped with a silencer, was readily accessible in his now open backpack. Cole scanned the door entry pad with his master pass and pushed the door open, the Walther at the ready.

The room was in darkness. A gentle snore confirmed that the room had an occupant but he had to be certain it was Vishna Arya, Minister of Law and Justice. He felt around the wall next to the door, found a couple of light switches and pressed both down. The room flooded with light and Cole strode forward to the bed, recognising his victim immediately. Arya stirred and was in the process of waking up. 'What the…' were his last words. Cole pulled the trigger and a neat hole appeared in Minister's forehead. Cole stepped forward and fired again, this time at Arya's heart.

He pulled the sheet up to cover the corpse, then uncoupled the silencer and swapped Walthers in preparation for Bedi. The gun change would hopefully add to the confusion; two guns would suggest two killers A stray thought crossing his mind. *Sorry Vishna, I don't think that counts as dying peacefully in your sleep.*

The silencer installed on the second Walther, Cole opened the door and looked out. Unsurprisingly, at that time in the morning, the corridor was still deserted. The lift stood waiting, but Cole avoided using it and took the stairs down to Floor Five where the door sign sent him left to Room 583. Cole swiped the entry pad and pushed the door open, surprised when he found all the lights were on. Walther in hand he walked swiftly forward and found himself in a small lounge. Papers were scattered on a table, a brandy decanter and crystal glass keeping them company.

He looked around the room and crossed to two adjacent doors, a glance revealed light coming from under the one on the left. Cole listened but there was only silence. He reached for the handle. *Please don't be having a crap.* The need for caution was gone; he pushed the door fully open and found himself face to face with Kana Bedi, Chief of Defence, wearing a white dressing gown.

Bedi saw the Walther, but hardened soldier that he was showed no sign of fear. He spoke in Hindi and calmly enquired. 'Who are you and why are you here?'

Cole smiled and although he had no idea what Bedi had said, replied. 'I'm from the MI6 and I'm here to kill you' Two shots, two holes and the white dressing gown instantly stained with blood. Bedi crashed down onto the ceramic tile floor. Cole cringed at the thud. *Ouch.* He quickly removed the silencer and returned it with the Walther to his backpack. He glanced at his watch, 1.13. *Well done, Jos, it's been very productive ten minutes.*

The corridor was still empty and Cole hurried back to the lift and pressed the call button; in seconds the cabin arrived and the doors opened. Cole entered and hit the ground floor button, softly humming 'Time to say goodbye.' as the lift descended. The Receptionist saluted his guest and reached for a phone, nodding and smiling as and Cole responded with a thumbs up.

'Hello, it's the Trident Hotel; we have a problem with our CCTV system, none of the cameras are working.'

'Sorry about that, be with you in fifteen minutes.'

Cole returned to the Fiat and settled in behind the wheel. The street was deserted, although the nightclub was still operating at full blast. He punched in the code for one of the concealed compartments and watched as a drawer slid out from below the rear seat. He removed his wig, moustache and latex gloves and dropped them into the drawer along with the Walthers and silencer. Another code entered and the drawer slid closed at 01.21. *Mission accomplished, Jos, give yourself a medal.*

There was still the car to be dealt with and he sent a text to deputy High Commissioner Diane Fitzwilliam telling her he was finished with the car and it could be collected from Rydges hotel car park in the morning.

Rydges Hotel

It was 01.41 as Cole made his way to the Deliveries door at the rear of the hotel, relieved when he saw the paper door wedge still in place; the Fates had been kind to him. Unsurprisingly, given the early hours, the stairs and corridor of the hotel were still deserted and he was soon within the safety of his room.

He felt knackered, mental tension taking its toll rather than any physical effort. Sleep was calling, so other than teeth cleaning, ablutions would have to wait until the morning. Before he sought the sanctuary of his bed, he booked an alarm call for 7.30am. This would serve to prove that he was in his room in the early hours, should any enquiries be made in the aftermath of his day's activities. His final action was to switch off the TV he'd left on when he set out on his killing spree; if either of the rooms adjacent were in use their occupants have heard it; another small deception.

His flight to London was scheduled for 9.30am; he would have plenty of time to catch up with his sleep on the plane.

CHAPTER FOURTEEN

Mumbai Airport

Cole, or Richard McIntosh if you believed his passport identity, walked confidently towards a Border Control booth and presented his passport. The official glanced at him and scanned the passport, his eyes flickering when he saw the diplomatic status.

'Please follow me, sir.' The official left his booth and guided Cole across to a colleague and explained the situation.

Cole was then asked to place his small suitcase on the scanner conveyor and ushered through without a body scan.

The luggage scan complete Cole collected his suitcase and wandered through to airside; he had chosen to arrive latish to reduce the idling around time often spent reading uninteresting literature, or browsing in shops with no intention of buying. Spending time in one of the luxury passenger lounges didn't appeal; he would be swanning around on a plane for the next ten or so hours. In the event he didn't have to hang around too long, the flight was on schedule and he was pleased to board the British Airways Airbus A350-100 when the call came for Business Class passengers to board.

A young steward asked for his boarding card as he stepped off the bridge into the cabin. 'Welcome aboard Mr McIntosh, your seat is second on the right.'

Cole smiled and made a mental note to remember his new name. He passed two other passengers on the way to his seat; both women, both slightly familiar. *Celebrities?* He allowed himself a smile. *How long would it be before celebrities outnumbered ordinary folk?*

Time passed, the plane filled with passengers, the safety instructions were duly delivered and the plane began its journey along the runway before lifting effortlessly into the air on its way to Heathrow non-stop. The pilot welcomed all those on board, and advised that the estimated arrival time was 07.10 GMT. *Must remember to reset my watch to GMT*

Cole lowered his seat to reclining position and waited for the opportunity to speak to one of the cabin staff.

'Can I offer you a drink Mr McIntosh?' A young smiling dark-haired stewardess stood looking down at him.

'No thanks.'

'We'll be serving food shortly. Do you have any allergies?'

Cole returned her smile. 'Nothing to eat or drink thank you. I'm going to get some shut-eye, it's been a hectic week. What time do you serve breakfast?'

'Breakfast is served at 5am, but if you get hungry in the meantime, or want a drink, just press the call button.'

'Perfect timing, please forget me until breakfast time.'

The privacy shells provided in Business Class were impressive and Cole genuinely felt he was in his own little world when he put his head on the pillow seeking sleep.

Cole slept soundly until around half past four, when his waking process began. He gave himself a few minutes to fully shake off sleep mode, then made his way to the toilet cubicles to partake of all the usual refreshing morning activities. By chance, he met the stewardess he had spoken to earlier and requested two pots of porridge and an orange juice for breakfast; a full English breakfast could wait until he landed at Heathrow.

He was half way through his second pot of porridge when his phone vibrated with a text from Moore to say he would be met at the airport and brought to Thames House for a briefing. *Damn, there goes my full English. How the hell did she know what plane he was flying back on?* He snapped his fingers and smiled. *She is head of MI6, Jos; she probably arranged to be tipped off when you went through passport control.*

The pilot's ETA proved to be accurate and the Airbus touched down at 07.06, five minutes early. Business and First-Class passengers were favoured as always and Cole was on his way to Border Control within minutes of the plane being connected to a bridge. He presented his passport; the official checked his likeness and nodded to a small tubby man Cole had never seen before. The man smiled, and walked forward eagerly, right hand extended. 'Mr McIntosh, sir? I'm Bert from Thames House, pleased to meet you.'

'Likewise, Bert. You're new, aren't you?'

'Yessir, Mr McIntosh, just started this week.'

'I hope that you're enjoying your time with us.'

'Oh yes, most definitely, Mr McIntosh.'

'That's good, Bert, lead the way.'

The journey to Thames House was slow, the morning traffic relentless, but it gave Cole time to think; think about what he'd say to Moore. He had exceeded his brief and wasn't sure how she'd take it, but what's done is done he told himself; if he got a rap over the knuckles he'd survive.

Thames House

Eventually they were at Thames House and parked up. *Not long now until the Moore postmortem.* Cole gave his thanks for the lift and was on the point of getting out of the car when a thought struck him. 'Bert, you do know my name isn't Richard McIntosh, don't you?'

'Of course I do, Mr Cole. I was just playing the game as instructed.'

Cole smiled. 'Next time we meet, the name's Jos.'

Bert Hagen smiled. 'Thank you, Mr Cole.'

As he made his way to Moore's office, Cole primed his brain with answers for whatever she threw at him. Sal Galt was on station in the outer office and came round her desk to give him a hug and a kiss on the cheek.

Cole beamed. 'Thank you, Sal. Best welcome back I've ever had.'

'I've been worried about you, Jos, I know just how dangerous it's been for you. You're looking great so whatever you got up to didn't do you any harm.'

'Put it down to a good night's sleep, I slept for almost all of the flight.'

Gerry Moore's voice cut in from the desk intercom. 'When you're ready Sal, please show Cole in; I don't have all day.'

Both Cole and Gault stifled a laugh, both pulled a face.

'Best go through, Jos.'

Moore sat behind her desk and studied Cole as he entered. Cole for his part took two strides forward, stood to attention, clicked his heels together and saluted. 'Commander Cole reporting for duty, Ma'am.'

Moore leaned forward on an elbow. 'Cut the antics, Jos. Grab a seat; we've got some work to do, serious work. Firstly, well done for completing your missions successfully; they made headlines all over the world. I trust you got full co-operation from our local people?'

'Can't fault them; they did everything asked of them.'

'Good. I've received comprehensive reports, official and unofficial, so there's no need for you to go into any detail at this time. Hopefully, you didn't incur any injuries?'

'Not even a scratch.'

Moore sat back in her chair, framing her next question carefully. 'Other deeds hit the headlines whilst you were away; notable killings in Canberra and Mumbai for instance. They weren't resultant from your actions, or were they? I mean, I've gone over your brief, and tried to recall any verbal instructions I gave you but there's no mention of gangland executions. There's been four in total, two each in Canberra and Mumbai. I have to assume they have something to do with you. You appreciate that, sooner or later, questions will be asked and I have to give the right answers?'

Moore swivelled her monitor screen round and brought up displays of local Australian and Indian newspaper headlines. Speculative links had been made between the killing of the officials and the gangland bosses. Rumours were rife. There was even a leak about the same Walthers being used to commit the killings in Mumbai and a mention of the killer's Russian accent in the Canberra gang attacks. Somehow, one Mumbai reporter had got a hold of a photograph of Bedi and his partner and headlined the gay relationship. So, what can you have to say, Jos?'

Coe shrugged. 'I guess I could deny any knowledge of the killings you're referring to, or I could perhaps say I simply used my initiative to help fulfil the overall objectives of the missions you put in place.'

Moore raised an eyebrow and cradled her chin in her left hand. 'Meaning what exactly?'

'Your ultimate aim is to destroy the Hydra and you've chosen to execute the top brass; we've made a start on that. But important as it is, it does little to deter the gangs. Sure, a bit of co-ordination gets chopped but they are free to follow their usual routines unchecked. I was on the spot and I had local intelligence to act on so I used it to put the main factions in conflict with each other. I'll bet they're at each other's throats even as we sit here chatting. I did what you're always preaching to your agents, *'You're on the spot, use your initiative, do what's best.'*

Moore smiled, tapping her lips with her forefinger. 'I thought you would say that. I want you to write up a report for me and fill in the detail.'

Cole was surprised by the request. 'Are you sure you want it on record? I won't reveal any of my sources, no matter what.'

'Yes, I do want it on record, but no, I don't want your sources named. As for stirring up gangland, I personally like the idea, though I'm not sure everyone will share my view.'

Cole's curiosity was aroused. 'Meaning?'

'Well, the Australian and Indian governments for starters. Big names taken out of the picture at the same time as top drug dealers; that's too much of a co-incidence to ignore. And it's potentially embarrassing for both governments, don't you think? But let's leave that subject for now and get down to some real business.'

'I'm afraid I've had to add to your European mission.' Moore handed over a brown folder. Cole opened it and began to leaf through the pages; there didn't seem to be anything new. Moore was watching closely and knew Cole was in for a shock. Sure enough, his eyes opened wide when he reached section three. He glanced at Moore, taking in her apprehension. What he was reading just couldn't be true, though the facts as presented were convincing.

Cole's heart was racing as his eyes left the dossier, mixed emotions were taking hold; anger, sadness, apprehension. He shook his head. 'I just can't believe what I've just read; somebody must have got it wrong, seriously wrong.'

Moore sympathised with Cole; she had suffered the same emotions. 'The facts are convincing, Jos. We just can't ignore them. I've checked them out best I can and sadly can't fault them. Everything I've learned points to him being an undercover Hydra second-in -command.'

Cole shook his head, and waved his hand. 'I can't take him out, he's one of us. I've been under his command, served with him; he's an inspirational leader.'

Moore had anticipated Cole's reaction, and had her response ready; it was time for persuasion not instruction. 'I know it's close to home but we can't just deal with foreign bad guys; we have to take care of our own when the need arises'

Cole hesitated; in principle, Moore was right. 'Yes, but in the other instances it was straightforward. The top guys and the Big Man's spy deputies; why suddenly is there another name in the frame? Why is the Hydra suddenly adding in an extra undercover deputy?'

Moore shrugged. 'I can't answer that, but the British Isles, Europe, the Balkans and Russia is a massive, highly populated, multi-cultural land mass; I reckon I could justify having an extra undercover lieutenant to look after my interests.'

Cole didn't want to be convinced. 'This man has put his life on the line for this country of ours and he's always gone the extra mile for his men. I've met him a number of times, I just can't believe he's a bad guy.'

Moore continued to maintain a persuasive tone. 'I'm sure you would agree that the most successful criminals are all very believable. They know how to play the double game, that's why most of them are never brought to justice.'

Cole nodded, sadness and reality starting to take hold. 'What's the source of your information?'

'Field intelligence, I might check it out with Mitch Rosetti when I get the chance. I'll continue to carry out enquiries but I'm convinced our man has joined the Hydra. And another point worth mentioning, our man has a reputation for wanting to give criminals a second chance. He's recruited some questionable thugs into the Special Forces.'

Cole was on the back foot. 'I guess so but as far as I know they've all reformed and given good service to the country.'

'They would wouldn't they, if the rewards were high enough, that's the nature of criminals.'

An awkward silence followed, finally broken by Moore. 'So that's it, Jos. You know what you have to do and if it makes it any easier for your conscience, remember that you are just obeying orders, doing what you're paid to do.'

Cole nodded reluctantly. 'I guess so. I wonder if Rosetti will confirm our intelligence. And I still wonder how he has been able to find out so much about the Hydra when we've barely scratched the surface?'

'He claims to have a high-level informant inside the Hydra. Most organisations have a leak if the price is right. It's a question I've asked myself, but I trust him and he's never let me down.'

Cole rubbed his forehead, finding it hard to argue with what Moore had said. 'How's Rosetti getting on with his side of the business?'

Moore shrugged. 'Don't know, I'll be meeting him later this week and I'll get the full picture then.'

Cole sighed deeply and shook his head. It was time to go. 'I think I've heard all I need to. If it's OK with you I'll head home and give some thought to the days ahead?'

Moore nodded. 'Good luck, Jos. The sooner this mission is put to bed the better. I'll call a car for you.'

'No thanks I'll walk home, I need to clear my thoughts and come to terms with what I have to do.'

Just as he reached the door, Moore called out to him. 'Jos, I meant to ask how are your old mates Jethro Watkins and Anika Chopri doing these days?'

Cole wheeled round. *Christ am I under surveillance? No, not possible, she's fishing.* A smile replaced his anger. 'Didn't get a chance to catch up with them. I had other things on my agenda.'

'That's a shame.' Moore smiled knowingly, her eyes following Cole as he turned and left the room. *'Don't let me down, Jos, there's too much at stake.'*

Sal Galt was in the process of retrieving some files when Cole entered her office. A glance was enough to tell her that he was deeply troubled. 'Alright, Jos?'.

'I guess so, Sal. Though I can't say I'm looking forward to the immediate future.'

Galt knew better than to question him; instead, she stepped forward and gave him a long hug. 'You be careful, Jos, I'm looking forward to that dinner date you offered me. Come back to me with a date when you've done whatever you have to do.'

Cole smiled for the first time that day. 'I'll hold you to that.'

CHAPTER FIFTEEN

London

Cole was in no hurry walking back to his apartment, he had a lot of thinking to do; killing General 'Tiger' Wilson, someone he admired, a brother-in-arms, was completely against the ethos of the SAS. But what could he do? Orders were orders and had to be obeyed or he would have no recourse but to tender his resignation. He needed to investigate further, find out more about Wilson. *You've happily acted on the information provided to assassinate European officials, Jos, so why should Wilson be exempt? Because he's a Brit? Because you served under him? Because he's SAS like you? Bollocks, Jos, he could be as bad or worse than any of the others. And yet - dammit. Park it, Jos. You're not getting anywhere; focus on the other elements of your assignment.*

Back in his flat, Cole settled down on the sofa a whisky by his side, and re-read his briefing papers twice over. The first decision he had to make was Italy or Poland, or more precisely, Rome or Warsaw? He decided on Rome before the temperatures started to rise.

His target was Guido Bassanini, twin brother of Mario Bassanini, the Minister of the Interior. Both were known to be close associates of high-ranking Army General Staff and board members of the Banca d'Italia. Mario's office was in the Chigi Palace, an architectural wonder whose construction started way back in 1562 and had been the home of Italian government since 1961.

Both brothers lived in the Parione district, which was, according to the internet, *a maze of tree-lined streets and avenues, and elegant palaces and parks with lush gardens extending along the banks of the Tiber.* Not for the first time Cole wondered if he was living on the right side of the line; the bad guys always seemed to do very well for themselves, or at least the top brass did. *And why just take out Guido? It seemed more than likely that the pair were in partnership; maybe Guido was calling the shots?* Cole took two decisions; Rome would be his first stop and, if the opportunity presented, he would eliminate both Guido and Mario.

He was about to move over to his desktop to check travel and accommodation options when his burner phone buzzed. *Must be Moore.* He opened the line but said nothing, waiting for Moore to bark out his name.

'Hello, is anybody there? The voice was female, husky, American, but not heavily accented; a New Englander Cole guessed.

'I think you have the wrong number, darling.' responded Cole amiably.

'Deception, **darling**.' the last word emphasised.

Cole tensed, this contact was definitely not in the script, but she had the codeword.

'Eureka. Now who are you and how did you get this number?'

Ms Husky let out a giggle. 'I'm in the same business as you although my travels confine me to North America, South America and Africa. My hobby is Greek mythology.'

Cole was intrigued. The voice knew the operational zones and her reference to Greek mythology clearly alluded to the Hydra and she had his telephone number? 'This is against the rules, **darling**, my brief says we are to operate entirely independently. I think I should terminate this call now.'

'But you haven't rung off, have you, **darling**? I bet you're as curious as I am about your opposite number. I admit I'm breaking the rules, but I would like to know more about you, and how you're getting on with your mission. Be honest, aren't you curious about me and how I'm getting on?'

Cole's brain cells were working at breakneck speed. He **was** curious, very curious, and that husky voice had its attractions. 'You're way out of line here, Miss Whoever-you-are, but you are right; I am curious, so what do you suggest?'

'My mission is on hold for a week or so, maybe we could meet and chat face to face.'

'Before we explore that, fill me in on how you got this number, or the call really does end now.'

'You know how I got it; same way as you got mine. My boss and yours agreed that we were both to remain anonymous but exchanged our numbers for use in an emergency.'

Cole still wasn't happy; curiosity was hardly an emergency. 'And your boss's initials are MR.'

'Mitch Rosetti, you got it right first time. This is getting boring, let's cut to the chase. Are we meeting up or not? I'm sure we both have something to gain, and I've got time on my hands.'

'I can't see that this is an emergency, but being honest, yeah, I would like to meet my opposite number. Problem is, unlike you, I don't have time on my hands. I'm heading off to Rome tomorrow or next day.'

'Sounds good to me. Tell you what. How about you delay your flight until the day after tomorrow and I'll head for Rome on the first flight I can get? I'll even book us a couple of rooms in my favourite hotel.'

Cole took a deep breath; this was way out of line. 'OK, I'll go for that, though Gerry Moore will lynch me if she finds out.'

'I promise I won't say a word to her.' She giggled. 'I'm going now. I'll phone you back with my flight and hotel details. We can exchange our travel aliases then.'

'Sounds good, I'll await your call.' Cole terminated the call and sat back to think. Ten minutes later he picked up his burner phone and rang Gerry Moore who picked up immediately.

'Deception.'

'Eureka. To what do I owe the pleasure Jos, assuming it is a pleasure?'

Cole went through the nature of the call from Ms Husky, ending with a question. 'You definitely didn't give Mitch Rosetti my name?'

'Certainly not. We both agreed to exchange minimum information. We both agreed that both our set-ups might have a leak'

'I thought that was the situation. She didn't use my name by the way, just referred to me as darling. It's what we do now is the big question?'

Moore snorted. 'Come off it, Jos, **darling**, knowing you, you've already decided. So pray tell me what you're going to do?'

'My instinct tells me to go along with her for now, meet up in Rome and see what I can find out. I wondered if you could sound out Mitch Rosetti without mentioning this call. Maybe even find out who his agent is? It's not unreasonable for either of you to check out progress. In any case he'll have read the newspapers and know what's happened so far. Come to think off it, has there been anything in the American newspapers?'

144

'Not that I'm aware of, and that's been a concern of mine, more so given this call. Regardless though, I want you to go ahead with your mission as planned; there could be a simple explanation for all this. Be careful, Jos, very careful. I'll get back to you when I've spoken to Mitch.'

Later

'Hi Mitch, how are you?' Gerry Moore despite her concerns did her best to sound upbeat.'

'I'm good thanks, Gerry. To what do I owe this honour.'

'Flattery will get you everywhere, Mitch. Despite what I said when we met last, I thought we should touch base regards our current projects'

'Really! That's a bit of a switch, Gerry? You were the one who insisted on secrecy! But OK with me, up to a point. I've kept an eye on the Australian and India media, your operative certainly left his mark. A much bigger mark than I expected, I have to say.'

'Me too, but an opportunity presented and all our agents are licenced to exercise their initiative dependent on circumstances. I wouldn't want it any other way. I haven't picked up anything in the newspapers from your side of the Pond. Are matters proceeding?'

'Gerry, I can assure you that both North and South America have been dealt with according to plan. To the south there were no members of officialdom involved, but you have my assurances that the targets are no longer functional. Gangland killings are ten for a cent in the southern continent which is why they don't make headlines. Up north, my girl got smart and made her first hit look like natural causes. The other has been attributed to an accidental electric shock. Pretty clever, don't you think?'

'I am impressed, Mitch. I don't have any female agents on my staff at this time; you must let me have details of your recruitment and training programme.'

'I've slipped up, Gerry, said more than I should have. And what about your near neighbours. When does that campaign get launched? And I know it's a guy, because you just told me you don't have any female agents.'

'Touche, Mitch. My guy will be setting forth this week. And what about your other targets?'

'There's been an unexpected delay, due to unplanned high-level politicos visiting, courtesy of the President. I gotta go, Gerry, I've said all I want to at this time. I wish your boy luck. Speak soon.' Rosetti rang off leaving a very pensive Gery Moore with the phone still held to her ear.'

Later

'Deception.'

'Eureka. Jos it's me. I didn't get too far with Mitch, but his agent is definitely a woman, so that fits. North and South

America have been put to bed. The Far East is on hold due to Presidential business taking place there in the very near future.'

'Do you believe him?'

'I've no reason not to, Jos.'

'Do you trust him.'

'In our line of work, it pays not to trust anybody; watch your back when you crawl into bed with Ms Whosoever. I mean it Jos, be careful, super-careful.'

'Don't know about **crawling into bed,** but I will be on my guard every step of the way. Is everything set up for me in Rome?'

'Yes, everything is as laid out in your briefing notes. Good luck, Jos.' Moore ended the call.

A very reflective Cole reached for his briefing notes. Even as he began to read through them, a new plan was forming in his head. He would be travelling as Peter Crossways, without diplomatic credentials on this occasion. He fired up his laptop and searched for flights to Rome, one-way only; his timetable had to be flexible. His new passport and credit cards were clipped to the file, the essentials were in place. Within minutes he had booked a one-way afternoon flight out of London Gatwick later that day. A day earlier than suggested by Ms Husky but it suited his plan. The flight was scheduled to get him into Rome around 5.30pm.

It was just gone noon by the time he'd packed and had a relaxing shower; all that was left was to do was book a taxi.

Come on Ms Husky it would be nice to hear from you before I set off. Cole booked his taxi for 2pm, allowing an hour to get to Gatwick gave him plenty of time to go through the departure processes.

The clock was ticking and he was getting restless when his phone finally buzzed at 1.38pm. He and Ms Husky exchanged passwords and Cole wasted no time in getting to the essentials.

'We'll have to be brief; I've got to leave shortly for a meeting, sorry. I'll be travelling under the name Peter Crossways.'

'I'm travelling as Jessica Andretti; I'll reduce that to Jess. I've taken a couple of rooms at the Rome Cavalieri; it's on the Via Alberto Cadiolo.'

'Your pronunciation is excellent, Jess, you sound like a local, almost as if you had Italian blood in your origins'

'Thank you, Peter. I do my best. I fly in on Monday; I presume you'll join me then? If I'm not around, just use my name when you turn up at the hotel and they'll make you welcome. We're on the top floor; the views are amazing. I've taken adjacent rooms to make things easier.'

'Sounds good to me, Jess, I'll keep you posted. You haven't told me your real name.'

'No, I haven't, have I.' Ms Husky giggled and rang off.

CHAPTER SIXTEEN

Rome: Day One

Cole's Easyjet flight touched down in Rome at 5.37pm - a noisy flight, full of kids and alcohol-fuelled travellers. The privileges of First and Business class, alas not available on this short haul journey. He took his turn in the aisle queue and a slow ten minutes elapsed before his feet hit the tarmac. Cole stepped up his pace and wove his way through the throng to get into the terminal building of Rome's Ciampino airport.

He was looking forward to this mission. Unlike those to date, this one was being handed to him on a plate; with the proviso that his targets maintained their normal weekend habits. The brothers Bassanini routinely joined each other most Sundays for a family gathering. Usually a few friends were invited, in Cole's opinion, Hydra accomplices.

Cole/Peter Crossways joined the queue of travellers waiting for a taxi, pleased that it was short. 'Parco Egerio please.'

The taxi driver obviously enjoyed his pasta, a goodly portion of his stomach folded over the steering wheel. 'Si Signor, but Parco is big.' He spread his hands to convey his meaning.

Cole nodded his understanding. He had expected the question and had his answer ready. 'Piazzale Metronio per favore.'

The driver smiled and tipped his forehead. 'Si, signor.'

Cole then buried his head in a guide book and the driver seemed happy to let the conversation end at that point. As they drove along, Cole soaked up the passing edifices and architecture It seemed to him, that if it wasn't for the modern traffic, much of Rome looked like it had been lifted from its glorious past and transplanted to the present. He suspected that inhabitants of days gone by would still be able to find their way around this glorious city.

Around forty minutes later a park appeared on his left and he caught sight of a road sign which told him he was on the Via Della Navicella; his journey was nearly over. A few minutes later, the driver pulled over into the Piazzale Metronio and pointed to his meter. Cole swiped his credit card and got out of the taxi, pleased to find that the temperature was comfortable.

He tugged out the handle of his wheeled suitcase and made his way down the Vialle Metronio, then turned left along the Via Tracia. Cole was on the lookout for a battered, dusty, black Fiat 500. The intention was to stay clear of the embassy and only seek its assistance if absolutely necessary. He breathed a sigh of relief when he saw his new chariot ahead, a 100metres or so short of the Via Gallia. *Game on, Jos*

The street was deserted and Cole immediately removed the magnetic box from its hiding place under the driver's side wheelarch and retrieved the ignition key. Having loaded his case into the boot, he got behind the steering wheel and entered a street code into the satnav. Out of habit he glanced around again to ensure he wasn't being watched. The coast was clear and he set off on his way to his overnight stay; a small embassy safe house.

The journey took a nervy fifteen minutes; adjusting to driving on the right and coping with Rome's traffic, was a test for any driver. Cole was pleasantly surprised to find that his accommodation was a small villa which looked like it had been around since the middle-ages. He pulled onto the drive and parked near the front door, disappointed that there was no garage to hide away the Panda.

Cole looked around, taking in the neighbourhood; it was quiet but the villa had very little frontage and was in the line of sight of houses opposite and along the road. *Hmm, no cover, not ideal.* He proceeded to unload his suitcase and use the code he had been given to open the key box. *So far, so good.*

Despite its outward appearance, inwardly the villa was a gem with all mod cons and very comfortably furnished. Everything he required for his short stay was laid out on the kitchen worktop - artisan bread, eggs, croissants, milk, coffee, tea, spread and marmalade. The sight of the food made him feel peckish and he resolved to have a croissant and coffee before retiring for the evening.

There were two double and one single bedroom; he chose a double at the rear of the building away from traffic noise, although all the windows were double-glazed. Before he settled there was one vital matter that required his attention. Cole returned to the kitchen and manhandled the tall refrigerator out of its alcove and removed the cardboard box behind it.

His eyes lit up when saw its contents; a SakoTRG M10 sniper's rifle complete with silencer, one of the best. There was also a good quality telescopic sight. His hunger pangs momentarily left him and he set about adjusting the rifle's length of pull and cheek height. *Perfect.* Provided the line of sight was clear, tomorrow's operation would be a piece of cake. He screwed the silencer into place and hefted the rifle to try it out for ease and balance. *Perfect.* Completing the preliminaries he adjusted the telescopic sight to his vision and took a few imaginary shots. *Bring it on.*

There was nothing else to be done, he could relax; it was time for that croissant and a cuppa before retiring for the night. He didn't set a wake-up alarm on his phone; he would no doubt wake around his usual time and on this occasion an early start wasn't necessary. There would be plenty of time to kill before setting out on his mission.

CHAPTER SEVENTEEN

Rome: Day Two. Embassy safe house.

Cole rose around 8am, cleaned his teeth then promptly doused them with a cup of strong black coffee. He had slept soundly and felt rested and refreshed. He looked forward to the day ahead., but had time on his hands and hated hanging around doing nothing. *What to do? Get exercising, Jos.* He pulled on a pair of shorts and embarked on a round of exercises, starting off with a hundred push ups, followed by a hundred squats. The exercises were over fairly quickly and he repeated them before ending with a series of stretches.

His stomach decided it needed to join in the exercise regime and he made himself a couple of slices of toast accompanied by another coffee. All that done, and it was still only a few minutes after 9am. The hands of the clock barely seemed to be moving. Next on the agenda was a shower and shave, on this occasion they were activities he took the opportunity to dwell over. The endless rush of water flowing over his body was both soothing and stimulating. He reflected that it might just be the longest time he had ever spent in a shower, at least without company.

The outside temperature was already approaching the low seventies and best suited to a tee shirt and shorts. Last up, Cole put on another of his blonde wigs and looked at himself in a mirror, pleased with what he saw, a typical tourist.

There was still time to kill and he tried finding BBC World News on television, but without success. He continued surfing the channels for another ten minutes. *What a load of crap.* Cole's boredom was reaching new depths and he sought another pre-occupation. He scanned the well-stocked bookshelves and settled on one of Lee Child's Jack Reacher novels, Die Trying. *He always fancied himself as a book hero. Hope the title doesn't prove prophetic, Jos.* He glanced at his watch, 9.45am; there was still had an hour and a quarter to kill if his briefing notes were accurate.

Villa Romulus

Some miles away the Bassanini households had gathered and were getting ready for a busy afternoon. Mario, Minister of the Interior, lives in Villa Romulus with his wife Emilia and their two sons, Enzo age 12 and Nicolo aged 10. Emilia has blond hair, cut short, urchin style and has a countenance reminiscent of Audrey Hepburn.

Mario has invited Gianni Rizzo, a very senior civil servant to join them for a family barbecue. Rizzo is employed by the government and deals with the tax returns of mega-rich Italians.

He is happily married but his wife of many years hasn't been invited. Emilia has met Rizzo in the past and doesn't like him and neither does Mario, but he is acting on a request made by his brother Guido.

Guido lives next door in Villa Remus; he is unmarried and intends to stay that way. He will be accompanied by his current partner, Lucia, a dark haired, well-endowed Italian beauty. Guido has also invited Gabriella, who is perfectly proportioned with waist length jet-black wavy hair. She will be available for Gianni's entertainment, not that the civil servant is aware of this arrangement. Gabriella, she has never shortened her name, will be well rewarded for her presence and whatever services she provides.

It is nearing noon, and the boys, Nicolo and Enzo, are getting restive, but Emilia has insisted they await Signor Rizzo's arrival before going outside to play. Tables have been set up for lunch near the massive outdoor swimming pool. Emilia and Gabriella have completed the food preparation and Mario has a large leg of lamb, slowly roasting in the barbeque; he too is getting restive. Several bottles of champagne are chilling; all that is missing is Signor Rizzo. Mario smiles when he hears the doorbell and the boys rush away to greet the guest of honour.

'Welcome Signor Rizzo, I'm Enzo, I'm twelve years old.' He holds the door open with a bow.

'And I'm Nicolo, I'm ten years old, please come in.' He too bows and stands back inviting Rizzo to pass into the hallway. Rizzo is average height and build, handsome in a rugged sort of way and has a broad smile. 'Please, you must call me Gianni, pleased to meet you both.'

'Have you brought your swimming trunks? We have a super swimming pool.' Nicolo is keen to show off his swimming ability. 'I'm the youngest but I can swim faster than my brother.'

Enzo protests. 'Oh no you can't. Let's get in the pool and I'll prove it.'

Rizzo looks on bemused, not sure what to say. 'I'm sure you are both very good swimmers. I'm afraid I'm hopeless at swimming; in fact, I never really learned to swim.'

The boys looked at each other, pulled a face and shrugged.

At that point Mario joined them, and ushered the boys away. 'Off you go, boys; help mama put the food on the tables. Come, Gianni, follow me.'

'Yes, Minister, thank you for inviting me.'

'Forget that Minister nonsense, this is a friends' occasion; keep the formalities for work. Let's pop a bottle of champagne.'

Gianni Rizzo smiled dutifully. 'Thank you, Mario, that's very gracious of you.'

Rizzo didn't really believe the Minister considered him to be a friend, and experience had taught him not to trust politicians. Bassanini wanted something and Rizzo was curious to find out what it was. 'A glass of champagne would be lovely but I mustn't drink too much, I'm driving.'

Mario waved his hand dismissively. 'No, no, of course not; although I can always get a taxi for you if needs be. Let's go outside to the pool, my brother will be joining us shortly. He lives next door and we share the pool.'

Embassy safe house

Not far away, Cole finished a chapter and checked the time, 11.45, it was time to move. He returned the book to its place on the shelf, then set about checking all of the rooms he'd used, making sure he had gathered up all his belongings and left everything tidy. That done, he grabbed his suitcase and tucked the Sako M10 wrapped in a small carpet under his arm, then made his way outside.

This time the street wasn't deserted; no-one was in the immediate vicinity but couples and individuals could be seen out for a stroll or attending to their cars. Cole would never know whether they afforded him their attention or not. He quickly put his suitcase in the boot and deposited the rifle on the back seat, then got behind the steering wheel. His destination wasn't far and he had committed his route to memory to avoid keying the Bassanini postcode into the satnav.

Villas Romulus and Remus came into view on his left, an impressive identical duo on a tree-lined avenue, their frontage and sides protected by a high ornate iron boundary fence. Each

157

villa had its own majestic tall iron gate, topped with gold-painted finials, set back a couple of car lengths from the road. Without doubt they were electronically controlled.

Cole drove past the villas and took the first turning on the left, then left again into a quiet street of old terraced houses, relieved when he immediately found a roadside parking space in front of the house the Embassy had rented for a month. The house has been chosen because it looked directly onto the rear of the Bassinini villas. Cole took a quick look around before getting out of the Fiat; it was lunchtime and the street was empty. *Looks like the neighbours are getting ready to tuck into their vino and pasta.*

Still wrapped in the carpet, Cole carried the Sako M10 under his arm he approached the door, the key provided for him ready in his right hand. Within seconds he was indoors, wrinkling his nose at the musty smell. The staircase lay immediately ahead to the right and he made his way up to the first floor. The door to a bathroom was partially open on the first-floor landing and provided the sole source of lighting. In the semi-gloom, Cole needed to peer carefully to spot the very narrow set of stairs leading to the small attic bedroom.

He made his way up the stairs and pushed open the door, blinking when he found himself bathed in full sunshine. He quickly crossed to the small oriel bay widow and looked out at the scene beyond. The garden was around 15 metres long, mostly paved and bordered with flower beds. A small fountain, looking somewhat forlorn, stood near the boarded perimeter fence, its water spout barely a trickle.

In the distance, maybe a hundred metres away, across their rear gardens, he could see the Villas Romulus and Remus. Their residents were either splashing in the pool or engaged in conversation. Cole scanned the scenes left and right, smiling when he caught sight of a young couple sunbathing in the nude; themselves their sole source of interest. Further along, an elderly couple, newspapers on laps looked like they were dozing on a garden bench.

Cole pulled on a pair of polythene gloves; he had been careful not to touch anything since his arrival, as always keen not to leave any fingerprints. Embassy staff would probably clean up when Cole gave the all-clear, but why take a risk? The window had been well oiled and opened quietly and easily. *Thank you, Embassy staff.*

Cole knelt down on the floor, resting the end of the barrel on the window ledge and put his eye to the telescopic sight. Three men were engaged in conversation, the Bassanini brothers and another he didn't recognise. *Get out of the way. Be patient, Jos, there's no urgency.*

To the left of the three men, Emilia, Lucia and Gabriella were engaged in conversation, bursts of giggling issuing forth and occasionally reaching Cole's ears. *Hmmm a gorgeous trio by any standard. I'd be delighted to spend time with any of you. Keep your mind on the job, Jos.*

One of the ladies broke off and moved away, shouting at the two kids in the pool. Guido Bassanini shouted across to the women and one of them moved over to join the three men. Cole cursed. *Fuck it, four heads in the mix now, I'll never get a clear shot. Patience, Jos.* The four heads appeared to be at arms-length in the eye-piece of the telescopic sight. Momentarily, Cole wished he could lipread, not that he was clear what benefit it would bring.

Guido nodded imperceptibly at his brother; it was time to advance their plan a little further. 'Gianni, I've just remembered something I need to discuss with Mario and I think I should do it now before the champagne takes over.

'I know the feeling, no problem, Guido. I'll take a stroll round the garden with Gabriella if she'll accompany me' He smiled at her and put his hand round her waist.

This was the opportunity she had been waiting for. 'Yes, I'd like that. But before we tour the garden how would you like a guided tour of Guido's villa? It's beautiful. Is that OK with you, Guido?'

'Of course, off you go.'

Gabriella took hold of Gianni's hand. 'Come with me.'

Gianni smiled and put his hand round her waist. 'Lead the way, Gabriella.'

Lucia excused herself. 'I'll go and give Emilia a hand with the food, I can't see those two rushing back.' She winked and licked her lips.

Guido waved her away.' You've got a one-track mind.'

'He's typical man, just like you.'

Inside the villa, Gabriella walked straight to the stairs. 'Let's start upstairs with my bedroom, it's lovely.'

Rizzo's pulse quickened; his visit was proving to be more rewarding than he had expected.

'In here, Gianni.'

The centrepiece was a four-poster bed, made up with a gold silk coverlet. She turned to Gianni and kissed him. 'I've never made love in a four-poster bed before; I think it would be very romantic. What do you think?'

'I would love the experience, lead the way.'

Outside

Meanwhile Guido and Mario poured themselves a champagne and made their way over to a wooden bench where they sat down, smiling at each other.

Guido laughed. 'Wouldn't surprise me if they weren't at it already; she won't waste any time, if I know her.'

'Are you bedding her?' Mario enquired of his brother.

'Of course, wouldn't you? I can arrange for you and she to get to know each other?' He raised an eyebrow.

Mario shook his head. 'No thanks, Guido, I'm happy with Emilia.

Guido shrugged, 'If things change, let me know. In the meantime, let's toast to the future.'

That was the moment when Cole pulled the trigger; Mario barely had time to gasp when Cole took his second shot. The two brothers fell into each other and that was how they were found when Gabriella and Gianni returned to the swimming pool fifteen minutes later.

Cole wasted no time wrapping up the rifle and making his way back down the stairs. The street was still deserted and he was in the Fiat and on his way within seconds. The satnav was already set for Stazione Roma Centralle, the railway terminal. He arrived twenty minutes later and began searching for a parking place. After a few circuits of the area, he turned down the Via Castro Pretorio and squeezed the Fiat 500 into a vacant space. *Small cars do have their advantages.*

He used his mobile to dial the number he had been given. It was answered in after six rings. 'Yes?'

'Deception.'

'Eureka. Where are you?'

'Via Castro Pretoria about half-way down. You have the car details?'

'Of course, and I have an ignition key. Just lock up the car and dispose of your key. I'll leave here when I end this call; it'll take about half an hour for me to get there.'

'I'll be gone by then.'

'Sure, good luck.'

Cole recovered his bag from the boot, locked up and headed back towards the railway station to get a taxi. His ultimate destination was the Waldorf Astoria, otherwise known as the Rome Cavalieri. But before that, he had some serious shopping to do. As he walked along, he suddenly realised he was still wearing his blonde wig. *Fuck it.* He looked around and with no-one nearby he snatched from his head and stuffed it into his bag. *Tut, tut, Jos, a black mark.*

Cole made straight for the station taxi rank, pleased to see there was no queue and a string of drivers waiting for custom. The driver at the head of the queue sat behind the wheel reading a newspaper which he immediately folded away when Cole appeared at his side.

'Signor?'

'Via del Tritone per favore, il Rinacente.' Cole made the effort, but knew his pronunciation wasn't great.

'You are on holiday, sir?'

'More business than holiday, I only have a few days. I wish I had longer, there is so much to see in Rome.'

The driver shrugged. 'Rome is the eternal city; we will be here if you can come back again.'

The Waldorf Astoria would be posh and Cole had travelled light with fairly basic apparel. Truth to tell he was more Marks & Spencer than Calvin Klein. He needed to make some serious purchases. *You really are out to impress Ms Husky, Jos.*

Ten minutes later the taxi pulled up in front of the five-floor edifice that was the Rinacente department store. He had a mental list of his requirements. That was the easy bit; it was making choices he would struggle with. Cole collected a small trolley and checked the store guide to locate the luggage section; the first item on his list was a decent suitcase. He chose a red hardshell wheeled case, one that would be easily spotted if he had to resort to hold luggage on his next flight.

That done, he wheeled his way to the lift and ascended to the third floor. The lift slid to a gentle stop, Cole stepped out and began his marathon shopping spree - a pack of boxers - a decent summer suit - a white linen tailored fit jacket - a casual zip jacket - a belt – three colourful shirts – a pair of shorts – six pairs of socks – two pairs of loafers. Every piece a designer brand. *Well done, Jos, let's go and settle up. I hope Ms Husky approves of my new wardrobe.*

The woman on the till nodded her head in appreciation and said something in Italian he didn't understand. He patted his chest. 'Inglese.' She smiled but said nothing. *Doesn't speak English.*

Cole put the case up on the counter and gesticulated in a manner designed to ask the woman if she could fold his purchases into it. The woman smiled and nodded her understanding then happily did as he had requested. Packing complete, he settled up with MI6's Gold American Express credit card. Moore would throw a tantrum but he'd plead expediency and offer to refund the department. It wouldn't be a problem; he'd banked the rupees he'd stolen in Mumbai and his bank account was bulging. He thanked the woman and gave her a ten euro note. Transaction complete he left the store and hailed the first taxi that came along. 'Waldorf Astoria per favore.'

CHAPTER EIGHTEEN

Rome: Day two. Cavalieri Hotel

An immaculately-uniformed doorman stood waiting outside the Waldorf when Cole's cab drew up and immediately moved forward to take his luggage. Cole, Peter Crossways as he now was, handed over his newly purchased suitcase, but held onto his working bag containing the Walthers. Cole walked through the impressive foyer to Reception and presented his passport. The Receptionist, a young man, scrutinised Cole's passport and extracted the necessary details, then looked through his bookings register. 'Room…' He hesitated and checked again, Crossways wasn't dressed like he belonged in such a luxurious suite, but it seemed to be the case.

'Room 502, Signor Crossways. Your friend, Signorina Andretti, has Room 501, although I believe she out at the moment. I'll call a porter to take you to your room.' He pressed a button and a porter literally appeared out of nowhere.

'Luigi, take Signor Crossways to room 502.'

Was it his imagination or was the porter taking a sniff and giving him the once over; the sooner he had a wash and changed the better. *Have yourself a long relaxing bath, Jos, make the best of the situation. Lord knows what Ms Husky would think of me if she could see me in this gear.*

The lift rose rapidly to the fifth floor and the porter led Cole to his room, scanned the entry card and ushered him in. He put Cole's baggage on a luggage rack and stepped back. 'Do you require anything else, Signor?' He handed Cole his entry card. 'You can take it with you when you go out or deposit it in Reception; the choice is yours.

Cole nodded and handed over a 10 euro note for which the guy tipped his forehead.

The Waldorf-owned Cavalieri hotel sits on Rome's highest hilltop and offers spectacular views, so Cole wasn't disappointed when he went out onto the balcony. Everything about the hotel, its art, its décor, its service, its three-star Michelin restaurant could be summed up in a single word - luxury.

Suites 501 and 502 had a connecting door and it was time to meet Ms Husky if she was around, albeit Reception had said she was out. He knocked on the door and waited a few seconds before knocking again. There was no rely and he reached forward and turned the handle but the door was locked. Cole sighed and spoke to himself. *Probably for the best, Jos, gives you the opportunity to have a bath and draw the razor over your face.*

Twenty minutes had passed, Cole had shaved and was lying in the bath soaking in scented foaming water when he heard a knock on the bathroom door.

'Who is it?'

'It's me, can I come in?' The unmistakeable voice of Ms Husky.

'I'm in the bath, you're more than welcome to join me.'

The door opened slowly and his visitor stepped in, Cole made sure he was well covered with bubbles and smiled broadly. *Gosh, she's absolutely stunning.*

'Welcome Ms Husky, and thanks for booking me in to such a classy suite. I didn't think our first meeting would be like this, not that I'm complaining. But before we go any further, I'd like to be formally introduced please.'

Ms Husky giggled; it was becoming her trade mark. 'That'll have to wait until we pop a bottle of champagne. I have one on ice in my room; come and join me when you've dressed.'

She made to leave but Cole stopped her. 'Wait.' She turned back and looked at him expectedly.

Cole struggled for words; he felt like a schoolboy on his first date. *Why was this happening.* 'I'm not given to flowery words but I just want to say, I think you're absolutely stunning.'

'Thank you, kind sir, join me when you're ready. And Peter, don't be too long.' Her expression and her voice seemed seductive. *Wishful thinking, Jos*

After she'd gone, Cole slapped the water in frustration. *What the fuck are you thinking of? Get a grip. She's a hired killer, just like you; nothing less, nothing more.* But his self-reprimand didn't match his feelings. She **was** beautiful - her smile was dazzling - her hazel eyes were round and wide set - her cupid lips invited a kiss. *Shut up, Jos, you sound like a judge at a beauty contest.*

She had certainly made an impact - she dazzled - she was confident - yet something about her projected a certain vulnerability. *Knock it off, Jos, your imagination has gone haywire, you'll be writing fairy stories next.* An image of her close-cropped hair, blonde with pink tones and highlights, filled his mind's eye. She was stunning

Cole climbed out of the bath and quickly dried himself, leaving his hair damp and tousled. He dressed quickly in his newly acquired attire then knocked on the interconnecting door, entering when he heard her call. 'Welcome to room 501, Peter'. She extended her hand to greet him, her grip lingering and gentle. He could sense her appraising him.

'And before you ask, my name is Toni Denard, Italian-French origins but mainly Irish-American ancestry. The Italian and French sides go a long way back. Grab a seat and I'll pour you a glass of fizz.'

She walked across to a coffee table, Cole's eyes following her; curvy but modestly so, his ideal woman. *Cut out this beauty judge act, Jos, it's wearing thin. Just enjoy her company.*

Toni returned with a crystal champagne flute in each hand. She was making her own appraisal and liked what she saw; lean and well-muscled, but not overly so. Around six foot tall, a handsome but not a pretty-boy countenance - wide-spaced light blue eyes and a dazzling smile, when he used it. *Just remember he's an assassin, Toni. Don't let your guard down.*

'I've introduced myself, your turn now, **Peter**.' A smile played about on her lips.

Cole took a sip of the Champagne, licking his lips in appreciation. 'I'm no expert but this is good stuff, Toni.'

She waved her hand. 'It's a Bollinger, but I just buy what I fancy at the time. Truth to tell, I like most champagnes. Now, your name please, your real name.'

Cole smiled, 'Jos Cole. We're way out of line, exchanging names and being together like this. I'm sworn to secrecy and I'm sure you are. We both know what we do for a living and both know we shouldn't talk about it. So where do we go from here?'

'I get it Jos, and added to that, I know we have no reason to trust each other. But we're here now so, let's just take time to get to know each other, in the old-fashioned way. I don't know for sure how long I have before being recalled to continue my mission. In the meantime, I got bored and curious about my opposite number. And do you know what?'

Cole raised his eyebrows. 'I've a feeling you're going to tell me.'

She nodded. 'Probably shouldn't say it, but I like what I see. Now let's deal with the champagne, talk about Rome and how we spend the next few days together.'

Twenty minutes later, the champagne gone, Denard glanced at her watch. 'It's time we went down to dinner.'

'Lead the way, we'll avoid using names just in case we are overheard.'

The Head Waiter led them to a table for two, situated in a window alcove in the far corner of the room. He and gave both of them a copy of the evening's menu and moved away.

'I've already ordered the six-course taster menu for both of us, I'm sure it will be good. I hope that's OK?'

Cole nodded. 'Sounds good to me; you really are pushing out the boat.'

Denard shrugged. 'I don't get to do it very often, and every time might be my last.' Sadness crossed her face momentarily.

At that moment the Wine Waiter arrived and before he could say anything, Denard ordered another bottle of Bollinger.

'I hope you don't mind. We get a small glass of something or other with each course, but champagne is my preference and I'm determined to spoil myself this trip. You too if I get the chance.'

Cole smiled and reached across the table to take her hand. 'Count me as spoiled.' With some reluctance, his eyes locked on hers. *There was something there he didn't understand.* He eased his hand away. *What the hell are you playing at Jos?*

The meal lived up to expectations, albeit a bit decorative for Cole's tastes, but he wasn't going to complain.

They filled in on their life history and explained the pathways to their current employment. The more they talked, the greater his admiration grew; she could be serious, she could be funny. All through the dialogue though, he couldn't help but wonder if she had a hidden agenda and was telling the truth. Not that she said anything to arouse concern; he was just suspicious by nature.

Coffee arrived and Denard invited him to have a liqueur.

'I don't think I should, I've already over-indulged'

She waved over a waiter, 'Two Drambuies, please.'

'You're a very determined woman, aren't you?'

She nodded. 'Wouldn't be where I am today if I wasn't.'

'I guess not.'

'So, what will we do tomorrow?'

Cole shrugged. 'Well, we're in the Eternal City so let's go see what it has to offer.'

'I was hoping you would say that. I think we're done here; the bill will be charged to Uncle Sam. I'm ready for a good night's sleep.'

Cole noted that she stumbled slightly as they rose to leave. *Methinks you've had a glass or two too many, Toni.* He put his arm round her waist as they walked across the restaurant and kept it there on the way to the lift; it was still there when they reached her room. Denard fiddled in her purse for her room pass, letting out an expletive when she let it fall. She leaned against the doorframe as Cole retrieved it and opened the door.

Again, there was a slight wobble and Cole gave her a supporting arm as he led her across to her bedroom. On reaching the bed she flopped down on it, watching as Cole put on the bedside light and switched off the main. Her eyes didn't leave him as he went to the bottom of the bed and removed her shoes.

'Thank you, Jos.'

'My privilege, Toni. Thank you for a lovely meal and one of the most enjoyable evenings I've ever had. I'll bid you goodnight. Breakfast will be in my room, 8.30.'

Was it his imagination or did she frown briefly? *Wishful thinking, Jos; she just thinks 8.30 is too early a start.*

Without looking back, deep in thought he made his way to his suite.

CHAPTER NINETEEN

Rome: Day Three

Cole got up around 7.30, had a shower and reflected on how he was going to deal with Salvatore Armati, the Boss of Rome's Mafia, the Mafia Capitale. Moore had suggested a method, but had agreed that ultimately circumstances on the day would dictate. Cole checked his phone for messages, not in the least disappointed to find he hadn't received any. It was 8.20, breakfast was due in ten minutes.

He went across to the interconnecting door and knocked loudly, Toni Denard answered immediately, 'Be with you in a sec, Jos.'

The door opened and she stood there in a white towelling dressing gown that barely reached her knees.

'And how are we this morning, Toni?' Cole was smiling his thoughts already going in one direction.

'I'm fine thank you, though my memory of last night is a little hazy. I feel good though.'

'Sleep well?'

'Like the proverbial English log, thank you.'

A knock on his door interrupted their conversation. A voice called out, 'Room service.'

Cole moved across to open the door and invited the petite dark-haired waitress to enter. She smiled dutifully and wheeled her trolley across to the small dining table where she set out their breakfast then left. If she was surprised at Denard's state of dress it didn't register on her face.

'What have you ordered for us Jos? I pray it's not one of your traditional English breakfasts.'

'Thought about it, but knew better You have a choice of cereals, fruit, toast and tea or coffee.

'Coffee for me please and I'll help myself to whatever.' Her dressing gown opened slightly as she stood and she was quick to cover up, her cheeks reddening slightly.

'Jos.' Her tone, almost apologetic, secured Cole's full attention. 'I'm sorry I had too much to drink last night.'

'Didn't notice.'

'Liar! I just want to thank you for being a gentleman.'
Cole raised his eyebrows seeking an explanation. 'Meaning what exactly?'

'For not taking advantage of my, er, condition. Me drunk, lying on a bed., most men would have shagged me the night long.'
Cole smiled. 'Maybe I don't fancy you.'
Disappointment crossed her face. 'Oh. OK, understood.'

Cole stepped towards her and took her in his arms, kissed her passionately, then stood back. 'There was nothing I fancied more last night than climbing into your bed and shagging you the night long, as you put it. But I'll only do that when I know that you want me as much as I want you.'

Toni smiled. 'Thank you, Jos. I think I'll have a slice of toast.'

Cole laughed out loud. 'Thank you for that gentle brush off.'

'No, I didn't mean it to sound like that. I was …'

Cole kissed her again, gently this time. 'Shsss. Let's focus on the next few days and just let things happen.'

Their chat lasted around an hour, with Cole explaining that he wanted to complete his mission, then fly onto his next destination on Saturday.

Denard nodded. 'That gives us four days before you fly off, one of which will be taken up with Salvatore Armati.' She sighed and looked unhappy. 'Oh well, it is what it is. I wish we had more time. I'm going to have a quick shower and leave you to plan the days ahead.'

Cole nodded. 'I wish we had more time too; let's see what the comes along. For now, meet back here 10.30 and we'll set off on our tour of Rome.'

Toni Denard returned on the dot of 10.30, dressed in a tight-fitting pale green top and a pair of cropped equally tight-fitting white shorts.

'Wow, you look like a million dollars.'

176

'Thanks, Jos, I'm a sucker for flattery. Keep it coming.'

'It's not eye-wash, Toni, I really mean it.'

They held each other's eyes for a few seconds. Both knew what it meant, both afraid to reveal their innermost feelings. Denard put her arm around Cole's waist and motioned him towards the door. 'Let's get out of here; we've got to get into tourist mode.'

Cole smiled and nodded, 'You're right, first stop the Vatican, though I don't have a religious bone in my body.'

'Me neither, but I've wanted to see the Sistine Chapel for as long as I can remember.'

Cole guided them over to the taxi rank. 'We're going to be doing a lot of walking, so we'll take the quickest means of getting to the Vatican.'

Unusually, the queue to get into the Chapel was short, and it wasn't long before they found themselves gazing agog at Michaelangelo's iconic ceiling and art work. 'You don't have to believe in God to be blown away by this place.' observed Cole.

'That's true, but, just like us, he was hired to do a job. He didn't do it out of love for Christianity. Nowadays it's a good money-earner; at twenty-five bucks a head, it generates a nice income for the Holy Father. I bet Michaelangelo wishes he was on a percentage of the take.'

Their tour continued; they admired the San Pietro but skipped the Muesi del Vatican both agreeing they wanted to walk in the sunshine, their destination the Ancient Centre.

Cole had committed the route to memory and led them through the Piazza San Pietro on the way to the Ponte San Angelo where they stopped to gaze at the boats on the river River Tevere.

'This is idyllic, Jos, I could stay here forever.'

'I guess I could be persuaded if you were part of the deal; though there are other places I want to see.'

She gave him that look again, posing questions he didn't want to answer. 'Right, enough of the river-gazing let's head onto the so-called Ancient Centre.'

They spent the next two hours wandering aimlessly, admiring Rome's never-ending landscape of ancient architecture, both marvelling at the skills of the designers and their builders.

'I wonder how many piazzas, palazzos, towers and churches there are in Rome, Jos?'

'Too many to see in one day, that's for sure. I don't know about you but I fancy a coffee, and lo and behold I spy a café on the edge of that piazza across the road.'

'I fancy a bite to eat if that's OK.'

'Sure, but eat small. I'm taking us out tonight and, I warn you now, it will be traditional Italian, not at all like that super deluxe dinner you treated us to last night.'

'Suits me, let's go.'

Toni took control of the ordering; a pot of coffee and a sharing plate, a spuntino as the locals referred to them, were quickly on the table. The eats didn't last long but they dragged their coffees out, both happy to relax and rest their feet. Jos sneaked a look at his watch. 'Time we were moving on; I want to see the Pantheon and a bit more of this district before we head back.'

'Lead the way, master, your humble slave will do thy bidding.'

Another couple of hours went by, both in awe of Rome's grandeurs, most notably the Pantheon, the last resting place of many Italian monarchs.

'Jos, I've loved everything I've seen, but I think I'd like to go back to the hotel, have a shower and rest up before we go out tonight.'

'Good idea, look out for a taxi.'

Twenty minutes later they were back in their rooms, arranging to meet in Toni's room at 7pm.

'Thanks for today, Jos, it was all I hoped for. Just one thing left me puzzled.'

'And what would that be, might I ask?'

An impish smile played round her lips. 'The statues of Italian male gods and warriors.'

'Yeah, what about them?' Cole asked warily

'Well…you guys always seem proud of your manhood, and keep it tucked away for the most part. Whereas those guys have it all on display and there isn't too much to admire. I just wondered where you stood on the subject?' With that she let out one of her inimitable giggles and skipped away to her room.

Left to himself Cole checked his phone, mildly surprised to see that he had missed a call from Gerry Moore, which he duly returned immediately.

'Deception'.

'Eureka.'

'Hello Jos, where have you been? You missed my call.'

'Apologies, I was doing the tourist bit, playing the part. There lots of signal dead spots in Rome.'

'Hmm. Anyway, purpose of the call.; your friend is going away for the weekend, off to his country residence. He'll be there as of Friday afternoon.'

Cole frowned. *Shit.* 'No problem, I'll deal with it.'

'And there's been another development.'

'What kind of development?' Coles steeled himself for what was to follow. A development in Moore's vocabulary only meant one thing.

'You'll have to take a trip to Budapest; the Ambassador needs your advice.'

'But.'

'No buts, just get the job done.'

Moore rang off. *Fuck, fuck, fuck.*

Cole stripped off and headed for the shower, his temper slowly abating as the stream of refreshing water poured down on him. He was towelling himself down when there was a knock on the bathroom door.

'Jos, I need your help.'

It didn't sound urgent so he quickly finished his drying and pulled the towel around him and opened the door. Toni stood just ahead of him, in her dressing gown, looking radiant as ever. Cole looked left and right around the room and over her shoulder through the open door to her suite. 'What's wrong?'

'Nothing's wrong, Jos. I need you, that's all.'

She stepped towards him, her gown falling open, but he had only a split second to catch a glimpse of her nakedness before her arms were around his neck and she was kissing him with unbridled passion. Next, she was pulling at his towel and throwing it onto the floor. Her arms round his neck, he lifted her and strode to his bed, laying her down gently. There were no preliminaries, their lovemaking was over almost as quickly as it began and they lay side by side hearts thumping in heaving chests.

'I'm sorry, I couldn't hold back.' Cole felt embarrassed., it felt like their lovemaking had only lasted for seconds. Toni put a finger to his lips. I'm not sorry. I got what I what I needed. Next time will be different.'

Next time was only a few minutes later, each exploring the other, each savouring the other's sounds and movements. In that final climactic moment, Cole gazed up at her and knew that lust was giving way to love. Afterwards, they lay beside each other, saying nothing. Flirting with sleep, hoping the moment would last forever.

Cole broke the silence, 'It's time we made a move, darling. I think I'll have another shower.'

'We could shower together.'

Cole shook his head. 'Not this time, I don't trust myself. I'm saving that experience for another time.'

She pouted. 'Spoil sport, I was just getting to know you.'

Cole watched her pull on her dressing gown, smiling as she made an exhibition of tightening the belt around it. She blew a kiss before she turned away. As she reached her bedroom, she stopped and looked over her shoulder. 'Thank you for a wonderful day, Jos, and by the way, you've got a lot more to offer than those statues.'

Thirty minutes later they were strolling, arm in arm in the warm evening air looking for a traditional trattoria. They found Villa Guissepe on a small side street, led there by the sound of romantic Italian music.

'I like this kind of Italian dining much more enjoyable than the formality of the hotel restaurant, Jos.'

'I was hoping you would, because I plan for us to do the same tomorrow.'

Later

Back in their rooms at the hotel, Toni hugged Cole. 'Thank you again for today, and for this evening; I feel happier than I have for a long time. I hope you don't think I do this with every man I chance to meet. It's been a long time, a very long time, since I felt like this.'

'I know what you mean, truly I do. In fact, I've **never** felt like this.'

Her grip around him tightened, her head rested on his shoulder. 'This is going to sound strange, but I don't think we should share a bed tonight. I want to reflect on today and what it means to me. Is that OK with you?'

Cole smiled, 'You won't believe me, but I feel exactly the same. I'll order breakfast; my room, 8.30 again.'

CHAPTER TWENTY

Rome: Day Four

'Cereals, fruit and toast, same as yesterday.' Cole poured coffee for both of them. 'Missed your company last night.'

'Missed yours. In fact, ….' Denard glanced behind at Cole's bed, her tongue tracing her lips.

Cole forced himself to shake his head. 'Uh, uh, it's tempting but we have a busy day ahead; let's save ourselves for when we get back. I've booked a car and driver for the day; we've got a lot of sightseeing to do.'

'Where have you got in mind?'

'Well, I thought we'd start with the Catacombs; they are twenty-five kilometres from here on the Via Appia Antica. When we've done those, there's the Colosseum, the Palatine, Santa Maria Maggiore and, last on my list, Trajan's Forum and Markets. I'll brief the driver and he can decide on the order of visits.'

'Gosh! Why are you cramming so much in? We've got another full day before you fly back to London. I've got some news too, my target is hanging around doing trade deals, so I can fly back to London with you. I'll stay at your place, and you can show me round London. I've been before but not done it justice. Besides, I'd have other things on my agenda and I don't mean work.'

Cole sighed. 'I wish it was that easy but there's been a change to my schedule.'

'What kind of change?'

Cole hesitated. This was yet another breach of security; Moore would be furious if she knew. 'Salvatore is on the move; he's heading off today to his country retreat for the weekend. I'll have to deal with him there tomorrow.'

Toni shrugged. 'That's no big deal, we'll deal with him there and have the rest of the day to ourselves. Get to his place before he's due and a single shot will see the job done.'

'That won't work. First, I'm not sure of the timing – second, I don't have a rifle – third, I don't have a car and he lives miles away to the south of Rome, a place by the name of Latina.'

Denard looked puzzled. 'Surely you've got access to all the gear you need?'

'I can get a car, but I'd have to arrange it through the Embassy with all the usual protocols and I'd like to avoid that if I could. And by the way, this isn't a sniper take-out.'

'How are you going to do it?'

Cole smiled. I'll tell you later when I've fixed up a car and found out a bit more about Signor Armati.'

'I've got an idea. Why don't I hire a car and drive us to Latina? Who knows, if a distraction or cover is needed when we're there, I might be able to help.'

Cole shook his head. 'You take enough risks carrying out your own missions without taking chances for me,'

'Balls! I'm coming with you, end of story. When we've had breakfast, I'll book a car for tomorrow while you do your research on Armati. Get that lot out of the way and we can go on that amazing tour of yours.'

'Thank you, Toni, I'm so damn lucky to have you on board.'

'You'll have to make it up to me one way and another over the course of the day. **And**, you're sleeping with me tonight. I won't take no for an answer.'

Cole leaned forward and kissed her gently. 'I think I've just got the bargain of a lifetime. Now, let's get tucked into this breakfast.'

The Tour

Their driver turned out to be a middle-aged overweight guy called Rocco who was clearly bowled over by Toni, and never missed an opportunity to give her the eye in his rea-view mirror. But he proved to be a gold mine of information and knew the road network, literally like the back of his hand. Added to that he had a wealth of knowledge about Rome's buildings, architecture and folklore. It turned out that he'd been a university lecturer in times gone by and had retired to write a book about Roman mythology. 'It didn't sell well,' he said ruefully, a smile returning when he added., 'though it did earn me a good review and an interview on television. I might write another someday.'

The catacombs of San Callisto were vast and cut out of a soft porous volcanic rock. After an hour or so of looking at graves cut into the rock Toni expressed her wonderment. 'This is mind-boggling; why the hell didn't they just dig ordinary graves?'

Cole shrugged.'Lord knows. They were a superstitious lot in those days. I've had enough, let's go get us a coffee.'

Seated outside in an a nearby café, sipping coffee and chewing on a croissant, Cole decided on taking his companion further into his confidence. 'Toni.'

'Oh, oh, that sounds ominous, out with it.'

'I'm not going back to London when I'm finished here. Sorry, darling, but I've been lumbered with another engagement.'

She looked at him sharply. 'Are you trying to ditch me? Give it to me straight if you are.'

Cole gripped her shoulders, his expression earnest. 'Not at all, honest darling; Moore sprung it on me last night.'

She relaxed a little. 'Where are you headed?'

'Budapest.'

'Who's the unfortunate this time?'

'I don't know who. I don't know why. I don't know how. I'm pissed off to tell you the truth.'

She reached across and took his hand. 'I'll come with you, I've never been to Budapest, it'll be fine. Nil carborundum illigitimas.'

Cole squinted at her. 'What the hell does that mean?'

'Don't let the bastards grind you down.' She let out a giggle then got serious again. 'So how do you find out what's expected of you in Budapest?'

'I have to report to the Embassy and take it from there. I really am fed up with this business.'

'Why don't you chuck it all in. I'll do the same and we'll set up some kind of security business. We'd be in control of our own lives. What do you think?'

Cole was literally gobsmacked. 'You never cease to amaze me, Toni! At this moment in time, I can't think of anything I'd rather do more.'

'Is that a yes, or a no?

'It's definitely not a no, it's just…' Cole struggled to find the right words, 'it's just that I love my country and don't want to let the service down. I want to complete this mission. I need to see it through to the end.'

'I understand that, Jos, I really do. Like you, I have unfinished business to attend to, but more than anything, I want us to be together. And I ask you, what's more important at the end of the day, work or life?'

Before Cole could reply, Rocco appeared at their table, 'Signora, Signor, apologies for interrupting but we have much to see. If you want to do everything on your list we must get on our way.'

Cole apologised. 'Of course, sorry. I'll settle up and we'll join you shortly.' The bill settled, Cole returned and they strolled back to the taxi. 'I feel like I'm reliving that old film, Roman Holiday; I'm your Gregory Peck and you're my Audrey Hepburn.'

'She was gorgeous.'

'And so are you. I never thought I could ever feel this way. I think it's the first time I've ever been truly in love.' She squeezed his hand but said nothing. *I wonder if you've ever been in love, Toni?*

They climbed into the taxi and had barely time to fasten their safety belts before Rocco accelerated away.

'Rocco, we do want to see those places I mentioned earlier but have to be back in the hotel by six; I'll rely on you to keep us on course. OK?

'OK, but don't blame me when I hurry you along. Let's see it's 11.30, allow an hour for each place plus travel-time and lunch.'

Cole interrupted, 'We'll skip lunch, maybe eat a sandwich on our way round.'

Rocco pursed his lips, 'I reckon 6.30 is the earliest I can get you back to the hotel if you want to do the sites justice.'

'Agreed, now put your foot down, Rocco.'

The Colosseum was breathtaking and took more time than allowed, so it was 6.45 when Rocco pulled up outside the hotel. Cole added a fifty-euro tip to his bill and they both thanked Rocco profusely for his services.

'My pleasure, enjoy the rest of your evening. He kissed Toni's hand, and turned to Cole. 'You are a very lucky man, Signor.'

'Very lucky. Arrivederci, Rocco.'

Back in Toni's room, they only had one thing on their mind, both tearing at the other's clothes like first-time teenagers. Afterwards as they lay back in recovery mode, she was first to speak. 'I needed that. Sightseeing is great but…'

Cole put a finger to her lips. 'I know, but we have a long night ahead of us. We need to get moving if we don't want to eat too late. I'm headed to the shower.'

'I'm coming with you.'

Cole smiled. 'Great, but no funny business.'

Her impish smile returned as she glanced down. 'OK, but you had better put that away it's distracting me.'

Later

Somehow, they survived the shower and set out into a balmy evening to find another old-style trattoria, heading this time in the opposite direction to the previous night. They walked arm in arm, listening out for the strains of music. Everything seemed perfect until four youths appeared from a side street ahead of them. They stopped when they saw Cole and Denard; two leaning against a wall, the other two mid pavement right in front of them.

Cole sensed trouble but said nothing. The tallest of the quartet blocked their path, cupping his non-existent breasts and leering at Denard.

'Fucking asshole: She swung her right leg karate-style and caught him mid-crotch. He dropped to the ground crying in pain and she smashed her left foot into his face. The three remaining youths gaped briefly, then gathered their courage; one pushed off the wall to join in. Denard's right foot repeated its attack and he doubled over. Her left knee flattened his nose. The third youth bunched his fists and stepped forward.

It was time for Cole to get involved; he swung a left, connected, and blood splattered from the guy's nose Another punch to his guts brought him to his knees, his hands in front of his face defending himself. The fourth youth drew a knife which Cole kicked out of his hand. Toni finished the youth off with another crotch-targeted kick. The guy dropped like a stone to the pavement shrieking in agony. She grabbed his hair and dragged him to his feet. 'Next time I'll cut your fucking balls off.' She ended her warning by pulling his head down and kneeing him in the face.

The first guy she'd downed started to recover and pushed himself up on one arm, pointing at her. 'Fucking bitch, I am

Mafia, you'll pay for this. Toni stepped towards him and grabbed his hair. 'And I am Armati's cousin, so watch your filthy mouth or you'll end up in the Tevere.' Her warning given, she pushed him down and kicked him in the ribs, sending him into shrieks of pain.

Cole looked at her with a mixture of amazement and admiration. How could such a loving, caring woman be so violent, so cruel? *Don't forget she's a killer, Jos.* For a moment it looked like she was considering doing further damage to the youths. He put his arm round her waist and gently led her away.

'Top marks, Toni. I'm not going to upset you anytime soon. Are you really related to Armati?'

'Nope, but that punk doesn't know that. And you weren't exactly gentle yourself, Jos. Oh dear your knuckles are bleeding.' She pulled a hanky from a pocket. 'Let me wrap them.'

Cole grimaced. 'And what about your lovely feet? Those were mighty kicks you delivered and you're just wearing loafers.'

Denard grinned. 'Specially made for me; they have hidden steel caps, back and front. Look, there's an eatery ahead. Let's go, I'm absolutely ravenous.'

A fulsome meal followed, each gently continuing the exploration of the other's life story; each subconsciously searching for some kind of re-assurance that they really were falling ever-deeper in love.

They were on their guard as they set off for the hotel, but the youths had gone. It was a warm evening and they were totally relaxed as they strolled along under a starry sky. Romance ruled once again. Back in the hotel they quickly retired to bed together; if the street confrontation and a generous meal had tired them, it didn't show.

CHAPTER TWENTY-ONE

Rome: Day Five

In Cole's mind, cereals fruit and toast for breakfast was on the threshold of becoming a tradition, a boring one; Toni was happy with it but he was starting to long for a traditional fry up. Resigned to his fate he acted as mother and poured the coffee. They had had their showers separately and were both dressed ready for the day ahead.

'So, tell me how and when you're going to take this Armati guy out of the equation, Jos? You've been kind of close-mouthed on the matter?' She ladled a goodly helping of marmalade onto her toast, and looked at him expectantly.

He grimaced, 'You won't like it. And to be honest, it's not how I like to do things, but I'm under orders.'

'OK, you've made your excuses and blamed your superiors, so enlighten me, please'

Cole replied in just one word. 'Novichok.'

Denard paused mid-bite. 'Novichok? That's the Commie way of doing things. I thought the West was above all that?'

Cole shrugged. 'Told you! I knew you wouldn't like it. It has its merits though; it's easily concealed in a small perspirant spray container and I can bury it quickly when the job's done. Added to that, if I don't get it right first time, I reckon I've got enough for another ten attempts.'

Denard sat back, her thought processes weighing up what she'd just learned. 'The thing is, Jos...as I understand it... with Novichok you come in contact with the stuff but you don't keel over dead straight away. So how will you know if you've been successful before you fly off to Budapest?'

'That thought had occurred to me, but everybody knows who this guy is and it'll hit the headlines pretty quickly if he dies. If he survives, I guess I have to come back to Rome and do it again. If that does happen though, I'll ignore my orders and give him a couple of bullets.'

'I suppose so, but I still don't get why your Chief wants you to resort to Novichok.'

'To be fair to her, she explained that an element of this whole Hydra business is to generate fear and, equally importantly, confusion. Moore and Rosetti don't want the Hydra to know that it's the CIA and MI6 who are on their tail. You said yourself that Novichok is traditionally a communist state means of assassination, so it's very likely it'll stir up confusion and get them thinking it's down to Russia or one of their eastern European allies.

Denard nodded. 'I guess so. You mind you're careful when you use that stuff, a gust of wind and spray can go anywhere. It's risky, Jos, be ultra-careful. So, what do we know about Armati, other than the fact he has a shack in Latina?'

Cole refilled the cups with coffee. 'We know that he heads up the Rome mafia. We know that he's a leading light in Europe's branch of the Hydra; a major asset in fact. He's a computer whizz kid - a leading light in the field of Artificial Intelligence. He's the brain behind most of the major software hacks that have bedevilled the world in recent times.

Now, I'm not a techie, and don't really know what I'm talking about, but what if he could hack atomic missile control centres or bring the financial world to its knees? We know he has a massive mansion on a hill near Monti Semprevisa. It's a very secure set-up apparently with all the latest security gadgetry; it's a bit of a fortress.'

Denard raised an eyebrow. 'And you're going to breeze in there and spray Novichok on his door handles?'

Cole laughed. 'Not exactly his door handles.'

'So out with it, Jos. What's the plan? I'm your chauffeur, remember?'

Cole kissed her. 'How could I forget. This is what we're going to do...'

When Cole had finished explaining his plan, Denard nodded, somewhat grudgingly. 'It might work, but it's not without risk. I reckon at best it's got a fifty-fifty chance of success; lucky you have a fall-back position. It's time we were on the move; I'll go and collect the car. I'll send you a text when I get back.'

Half an hour passed, then forty minutes, then forty-five. Cole was starting to worry if she had been involved in an accident, when his phone bleeped. *I'm outside.*

Cole put on a light jacket and left his room, but on this occasion didn't make for the lift. He had agreed with Toni to make it look as though they were going out separately, so the forty-five minutes had served them well. He also wanted to avoid being seen getting into her car. That being the plan he opted for a staircase that led to the rear of the hotel.

On reaching the ground floor Cole stepped out onto the terrace, greeted the elderly couple who were seated there reading, then made his way across the lawn to a service yard. Exiting the yard, he turned right, away from the hotel, and walked the hundred metres or so to where Toni had parked up in a white Fiat 500.

'Good morning, driver. First stop Latina, and put your foot down.'

'Yes sir, Mr Cole.'

'I was starting to get worried about you. You've been gone the best part of an hour?'

'I had some shopping to do.'

'Shopping?' Cole echoed, 'Shopping? Want to tell me about it?'

'Later, darling. I presume you've remembered to bring your pepper pot with you?'

'Yes darling, three bags full darling.'

Toni let out one of her giggles. 'Sounds like I've upset you. You'll thank me later on, I promise. Tell you what, just to calm you down, you can put that warm hand of yours on my knee.'

It was Cole's turn to laugh. 'Can't see that calming me down, quite the opposite. You keep your mind on your driving and I'll save the goodies for later.'

An hour later, twenty kilometres short of Latina, Toni pulled of the highway into a shaded layby. Cole looked at her enquiringly.

'Pray tell me why you have pulled into a layby?'

'Now, don't get all uppity with me, but given your plan, I don't think it's the best idea for you to stroll into your destination dressed in a pale blue Armani suit. And if I'm to help, I shouldn't be wearing my best Stella McCartney outfit.'

Cole's heart sank, she was right. He would look totally out of place. 'Stupid me, it would have been daft. Something modest will attract less attention. So, just what have you been up to, darling?'

'I've bought us this lot. I hope I've guessed your sizes correctly.' She reached over to the back seat and pulled forward two large plastic bags. She glanced in one and handed it over. 'These are yours.'

Cole reached in and pulled out a grubby-looking T-shirt, a pair of ragged shorts and a pair of hiking boots. Toni registered the disapproving look on his face. 'Got them in a second-hand shop; now stop gaping and get changed. We're headed for hiking country, just another pair of happy wanderers.' That said she pulled off her top and pulled on a crumpled, creased stained, white tee-shirt. 'Get a move on, Jos, stop ogling. You've seen it all before.'

'Got to hand it to you, darling, good thinking. I should have thought of this scenario. I'm going to lay the blame at your doorstep, you're too much of a distraction.' He slid out of his trousers and struggled into a pair of tight-fitting, ragged denim shorts; that done he put on a black over-sized tee-shirt.

'How do I look?'

'Don't ask. Get those hiking boots on and we're on our way.'

Their change of dress complete and their clothes folded away neatly in the plastic bags, the duo were ready to go. But Cole had one further change to make. 'What about this, sweetheart?

'What about what?'

'Close your eyes, darling, humour me.'

He reached into the inside pocket of his discarded jacket, retrieved his blonde wig and put it on.

'You can look now.'

Her eyes widened when she saw the wig. 'Hey, you look great. I'm not sure which Jos Cole I like best. When we end up together you might have to go blond for me.'

Cole's heart missed a tiny beat. *It was happening, they were being drawn together. What they shared wasn't going away anytime soon – theirs was a future in the making.* 'I don't think there's anything I wouldn't do for you, Toni.'

'On that romantic note, before you get other ideas, I think we'd best get on our way. Have you got Armati's trattoria café address for the satnav?'

'Yip. I'll punch it in.'

'Turn the voice off please, Jos; you can be my navigator.'

Latina

The satnav skirted the town and directed the car towards the hills. Time passed quickly and Cole punched the air when the satnav showed that they were nearly at their destination. 'Slow down, Toni, it's not far ahead. Drive past and look out for somewhere to park. A small church lay ahead and Cole pointed. 'Over there behind those cars.'

They parked up and Cole took a few seconds to retrieve the Novichok and latex gloves. 'All set.'

Cole raised a hand and circled it around slowly in every direction. 'We're in luck, there's not even a breeze.'

'Let's hope it stays that way.'

They both got out and began to stroll slowly back to the Trattoria Palmarola. As most walkers would do, they stopped briefly from time to time to take in the scenery.

Cole tutted, 'His car's not here, we'll go in and order a beer and a sandwich. Being poor hikers, we can't order anything expensive.'

'I hope this gamble pays off, Jos.' She was alluding to Cole's briefing notes regarding Armati driving a Maserati sports car and lunching regularly in the Palmarola. 'There's no guarantee he'll come here today.'

'I'm feeling lucky. I can't see him coming here for the weekend and not visiting his favourite haunt.'

'Let's hope so. My Italian is better that yours, grab an outside table and I'll go in and order.'

'I don't like the thought of you going in by yourself amongst those randy Italians.'

'The place looks quiet, and anyway I can look after myself; I'm wearing my steelcaps.' She winked at him, 'And, I've got this tall muscled bodyguard watching out for me.'

Cole chose a table under a large parasol where he could look into the pub and keep an eye out for a Maserati. The Trattoria wasn't busy and only a few minutes had passed when Denard returned. 'Refreshments are on their way.'

Time was dragging and no sign of Armati. They were on their second beer and Cole was starting to feel awkward. *Maybe*

I've made the wrong call. Denard had guessed where his thoughts would be and kept stum.

Cole broke the awkward silence, 'We'll give it another ten minutes then call it a day. I've got some head scratching to do to find another option.'

But miracles do happen – suddenly a red, open-topped Maserati pulled up in front of the trattoria, its deep-throated engine purring until the driver cut the ignition. A white Fiat Punta pulled up behind it; two swarthy toughies got out and stepped forward to the sports car, one going left, the other right. Each pulled open a door. The driver got out first, closely followed by a large-breasted blonde wearing the highest heels Cole had ever seen. Her lipstick matched the colour of the Maserati, her eyelashes defied gravity. Her white tight-fitting silky outfit left little to the imagination.

Armati looked younger than his thirty years; he was lean, average height, bronzed from head to toe and as handsome as they come. His attire shouted quality, though it was just a simple bright-yellow open-necked shirt and pale blue linen shorts. The blonde clung to him as he walked into the trattoria; the owner appeared and Armati was welcomed profusely. The toughies sat down inside; one on each side of the door, guarding their master.

'Get ready, Jos, let's get this over with. I'll go in I'll settle the bill and do my best to distract them. She made her way into the trattoria drawing admiring glances from both of Armati's bodyguards.

Cole stood and discretely pulled on the latex gloves then wandered over to the Maserati where he stood looking at it admiringly, listening out for whatever Denard had planned as a distraction. He heard a shout and saw that she had made an old-fashioned stumble into one of the guards. All attention was on her as Cole walked round the car spraying the door handles and the steering wheel with Novichok., all the time praying that there wouldn't be a sudden gust of wind.

Meanwhile, Denard was apologising profusely to the guard, who was in no hurry to take his hands off her shoulders. She pointed down at an undone shoe lace and bent down to tie it, giving the guard a close up of her cleavage. The other guard's eyes were taking in the rear end view. Both were oblivious to Cole as he took the opportunity to walk back to the Punta and spray all the door handles. *I'm afraid there's going to be a bit of an outbreak, Signor Armati.*

Denard expressed her thanks for the third or fourth time then walked away to rejoin Cole, leaving the two guards to slump back into their seats and find solace in a glass of wine. Armati and his companion had briefly eyed the commotion then returned their attention to the menu and a bottle of champagne.

'What a performance, darling, you deserve an award.'

'Rest assured Jos, I'll claim my award back at the hotel. By the way, I took the liberty of ordering dinner to be served in our room tonight.'

'Perfect. And believe me, it will be my objective to reward you handsomely.'

On the way back to the hotel they stopped at the roadside to change back into their original clothing. Their discarded gear would have to be dumped in a waste bin on their way to the airport in the morning. Disposal of the Novichok would be dependent on Signor Armati's death.

Back at the hotel, they entered by the same way they left; Cole by the hotel's rear entrance and Denard via the main entrance twenty minutes later. She made a point of stopping at reception to enquire if there were any messages for her, seeking to register that she and Cole hadn't returned to the hotel together.

CHAPTER TWENTY-TWO

Budapest Day Six

Cole and Denard were settled in their seats, travelling First Class in an airplane bound for Budapest; happily sipping their coffees and reflecting on the recent past.

'I really enjoyed Rome, Toni, and hope we can go back one day, free of the background stress. I shall always remember it as the place I first fell in love.' Cole was enjoying his new found romantic outlook, one he never thought he possessed.

She laid her head on his shoulder. 'Me too, darling. I keep thinking we ought to get out of this game; I really do believe life would be better for us on the other side of the fence.'

'I'm coming round to that way of thinking.'

Denard saw the opening and piled on the grief. 'I hope you mean it, Jos. Look at us. You'll be going to the Embassy, some shit will be piled on you, and then what? You'll have to return to the UK and start all over again.'

'You're right, of course you are, Toni. I promise I'm giving serious consideration to standing down when I've completed this mission.'

Denard kissed his cheek. 'And meantime, I'll be left worrying about you every time you're out of my sight.'

'Same goes for me, babe; you're not immortal as far as I know.'

Denard let loose one of her giggles. 'I haven't told you everything. Which reminds me, I can't help out on your latest exploit, sorry. I got a message last night instructing me to report to the US Embassy in Budapest as soon as possible after landing. This is what it's like when we're at someone's beck and call.'

'What's that about?'

'Search me.' She laughed, 'They might want me to take out some troublesome Brit. One good thing though, we'll have free accommodation and hotel expenses courtesy of Uncle Sam again.'

Cole laughed. 'Whatever. We'll do what we have to do, then have a few days enjoying Budapest; it's another one of the many cities I've never visited.'

The next two and a half hours passed in silence for the most part, each contemplating their future and the path ahead. Both were taking the opportunity to relax; they knew it wouldn't last. Cole's new persona according to his passport was Terry White, Denard's was Marcella Gizzi.

The plane landed on time at Ferenc Liszt International, around twenty kilometres south-east of the city. Connecting a bridge to the aircraft was carried out speedily and the duo were amongst the first in the queue for passport checks. Denard was beckoned to a desk, Cole to another; the passport scanner did its job and they were duly welcomed to Budapest. Customs barely gave them a glance and less than ten minutes later they were at the head of a taxi queue.

'Let's see, Cole checked the time, 'it's coming up to midday. What say we meet at the Szchenyi Istvan Terrace at 2pm? It runs alongside the Danube and there's bound to be a cafe in that area.'

'Hell, I can't pronounce that; type it into my phone for me.'

Cole smiled and did the necessary. 'I doubt if I pronounced it right anyway. Don't make any arrangements for a car; I'm pretty sure something will be lined up for me. I'm not sure if the embassy will have lined up accommodation for me but we can deal with that in due course.'

A taxi drew up and with a parting kiss, Denard was on her way. Cole got the next taxi and instructed the driver to head for the British Embassy on V. Szabadsag. *Toni's right, life really would be much simpler if they were free of the reins of government.* He used his burner phone to call the Ambassador on his way to the Embassy and was answered immediately.

'Who shall I say is calling?'

'Terry White, I think you'll find the Ambassador is expecting this call.'

'Hold please and I'll see if she is free to take your call, Mr White.'

'Nicola Watson.' The voice was refined and had a friendly tone.

'Deception.'

'Eureka, Mr White. I've been expecting you. I have an envelope and a sealed briefcase for you, both delivered yesterday by diplomatic courier. You must be important.'

'I'll explain when I see you, Ambassador. I'm in a taxi on my way to the Embassy now.'

Watson chuckled. 'I'd better get the kettle on then, see you shortly.'

The driver was silent the entire trip, maybe he didn't speak English, maybe he didn't like Brits. Cole was indifferent; he had plenty to think about. The driver seemed determined not to show Cole the best of Budapest, or maybe the back streets were the quickest route. He muttered something Cole didn't understand, but whatever his problem was it didn't slow him down and a few minutes later he pulled up outside the embassy.

'How much?

Mr Surly pointed at his meter which showed 12,000 Forint.

Cole extracted the exact amount from his wallet and passed it over. 'Have a nice day; you look like you need one.' The driver's eyes flashed briefly but he made no reply.

British Embassy

The young man on reception was expecting Cole and invited him to follow him up the stairs to the first-floor. He led Cole along the landing to a plain panelled door bearing the nameplate; Nicola Watson - Ambassador. A single knock brought the invite to enter and Cole was ushered forward into the ambassadorial suite.

Nicola Watson was a forty-something rising star, pencilled in to be the UK's next Ambassador to the United Nations Assembly. In political circles the talk was that she was destined to be the UK's Foreign Secretary. She reminded Cole of a young Margaret Thatcher – striking – confident – waste no time -knows what she wants, kind of woman. She pointed at a magnificent Georgian settee. 'Take a seat and I'll pour us a coffee. How do you like it?'

'Black please, no sugar.'

She poured both cups then returned to her desk on top of which sat a sealed envelope and a longish rectangular sealed box. 'These are yours Mr White. The box is quite heavy, I wouldn't want to guess what it contains.'

'Do call me, Terry.'

'Terry it is. I'm Nikki. I haven't been briefed on why you're here, and don't want to know. I find that secrecy usually has an ulterior motive in my kind of business.'

'I have no intention of telling you, Nikki. And in any case, I won't know why I'm here until I open this envelope.'

'Feel free to open it, Terry, if that's your real name. My guess is you're a secret service operative, MI5 or MI6, probably the latter. You have that look about you.' She smiled and raised an eyebrow.

Cole grinned, 'I'm definitely Terry. I can show you my passport if you don't believe me.'

'Stop the games, Terry; passports are a dime a dozen in your business. I've been told to provide you with an embassy car and I've set aside our oldest, and most dented for your use. It's a nine-years old black Honda Civic, mechanically sound but a bit bashed here and there.'

'Sounds perfect, I didn't want anything flash.'

'I've also been asked to provide accommodation and I've identified…'

Cole cut her off. 'Sorry to interrupt but I'll make my own arrangements for accommodation.'

Watson shrugged. 'Your choice, Terry'

Cole gave an apologetic grimace. 'Sorry Nikki. It would be helpful if someone drove me out of the embassy in the car and found their own way back.'

Watson creased her forehead inviting explanation. Cole offered none. 'Believe me, it's best you know as little as possible, sorry.'

'OK, I'll get Harry to do that, he's the young man you met in Reception. Now, I'm not rushing you, but is there anything else I can help you with?'

'No thanks, I'll get on my way.'

Watson persisted. 'Are you sure? You might want to read what's in that envelope before you leave here.'

Cole sought to be a bit conciliarity. 'That's probably a good idea. By the way, I won't bring the car back here; I'll leave it at the airport when I fly out.'

'No problem. Just let Harry know it's whereabouts when you're finished with it.'

'Will do. I'll need it for a couple of days, three max.'

Watson rose and went over to her desk and sat down. 'Want a letter opener?' She offered one with an expensive silver-handled blade.

'Good idea.' Cole retrieved the envelope and returned to settee where he sliced it open. There were three pages in all. He froze when he read the first sentence. *Christ, there must be some mistake.* He leafed through to the end of the briefing notes to check if Moore's signature was there. If it wasn't he would have phone her for clarification. But it was there. *Fuck it.* There was no mistake, Moore would have checked the letter for accuracy, and so would Sal Galt. They were both were meticulous; they just didn't make mistakes. It was time to go, he needed some fresh air and a stiff drink to recover from the shock.

'I'll go now, Nikki, thanks for your help.'

Watson lifted the phone and buzzed reception. 'Harry, Mr White's on his way down. You're acting as his chauffeur, use the black Honda Civic and take him wherever he wants to go.

When you get there, leave the car with him and get a taxi back. You'll collect the car in a few days when he's finished with it.'

'Understood, Ambassador.'

United States Embassy

Meanwhile, Denard, alias Marcella Gizzi, was finishing up her business in the American Embassy. She had taken less than twenty minutes. There was no brown envelope, no briefcase, just a single automatic pistol to take away. Her contact was briefing her. 'You're booked into the Hilton on Castle Hill; a double room, you'll no doubt be pleased to know.' He smirked. 'I wish you good luck, Toni.' There's a taxi waiting for you at the gate; the driver's been paid, don't even give him a tip. You're OK for local currency I assume?'

'Nope, didn't have time to get any. Leaves a paper trail anyway.'

'Funny, but I expected you to say that.' He passed her an envelope. 'There's 500,000 Forint in there; that should cover you. The hotel and any costs you incur there are being charged to the embassy. Keep me posted.'

Danube riverside park

Harry pulled up near the Szecheny Chain Bridge and handed Cole the ignition key. 'All yours Mr White; enjoy your visit to Budapest.'

'Thanks Harry, see you anon.'

Cole slid over behind the wheel and scanned what he could see of the park for Toni but she was nowhere in sight, so he opted to drive round the perimeter. He was driving slowly and was continuously being honked by irritated local drivers. *Fuck you lot; you think you got problems.* At the bottom of the park, he took a right, ready to go round again when he saw a statue; he was to learn later it was Ferenc Deak. *I bet that's where you are, Toni.* As it turned out, he was right; she was the sole figure admiring the statue.

Cole swerved over and drew another deluge of car horns. Fortunately, the din attracted her attention and she ran over to join him. She slid in beside Cole and gave him a full-on kiss before he could say anything. 'Missed you, darling. How did you get on?'

Cole grimaced. 'Fucking awful, really bad.'

This wasn't like the Cole she knew. 'Oh dear, best save the story for now. We're booked into the Hilton courtesy of Uncle Sam.' She waved a hand, 'It's up there somewhere on top of Castle Hill. We'll eat in tonight, if that's OK with you?'

Cole nodded and pulled away. She looked round at the car's shabby interior and whistled. 'Gosh, you Brits spare no expense. I guess this is what you guys call a vintage motor.'

Cole had to smile; it was time to loosen up.

CHAPTER TWENTY-THREE

Budapest: Day Seven

Cole turned into the Hilton car park and quickly found a space, remembering to make a mental note of the car's number plate for Reception. He felt on the scruffy side, but nobody seemed to care and he began to relax. Denard introduced herself and was given the swipe-card to the room her Embassy had reserved. Cole declined portering assistance and took the lift to the fourth floor. He and Toni were the only passengers and he put his arm around her waist, drawing back in surprise when he felt the unmistakable outline of a gun.

'You're carrying?'

Denard nodded. 'Tell you about it later; you're not the only one on duty, Jos. There was a dispatch waiting for me at the Embassy. It seems like someone has upset the White House.'

'Sorry about that. Hope it doesn't spoil your time in Budapest.'

'It won't, it's a piece of cake if the brief's right. I'm more worried about you.'

The lift slowed to a halt and they followed the signs to room 411; it was comfortable but less plush than the Waldorf suite back in Rome. Denard immediately put her arms around Cole's neck, her lips searching for a passion that wasn't there.

'You gone off me already?'

'Don't be daft, I've got things on my mind that's all.'

'Well get fucking rid of them, Jos, you hear me. I want you and I want you now. We can deal with whatever is troubling you later, but for now my focus is us.' She took his hand and gently pulled him over to the bed. It didn't take long for his resistance to melt away. *Toni's right, live for the moment.*

Their passion spent they lay together recovering; Cole was first to speak. 'I hope I earned a pass mark.' He smiled., wondering how she would respond.

'Only just, I graded you 'must try harder, much harder.' She let out one of her inimitable giggles.

'You're absolutely incorrigible, come here.'

Afterwards, Cole went to the bathroom and retrieved a couple of dressing gowns. He put on the larger of the two and dropped the other on Denard. 'Cover up girl, I'm going to get room service to bring us a pot of coffee and then we'll have a chat.'

Ten minutes later there was a knock at the door and Cole moved across to open it. The attendant was old, short, bald and skinny; his piggy eyes darted round the room and immediately locked onto Denard lying on the bed. Surreptitious glances ensued as he took his time transferring the coffee pot and cups to the table.

'There are some complimentary biscuits for you, Sir.' He looked across to Denard, 'And of course for you Madam.' He held Denard's eyes. 'Please call if I can be of any further assistance.'

When he closed the door behind him, Denard burst into laughter. 'I got the impression he fancied me.'

'Can't say I blame him. Now how about you get out of bed and join me over here. We've got things to discuss.'

Denard slid out of bed and began to tip-toe across to the table. Cole smiled. 'Go back and put the dressing gown on, I don't want any distractions.'

'Only if you insist.'

'This is me insisting.'

Denard put her dressing gown on and made herself comfortable in an armchair. 'OK, you have my undivided attention. The game playing is over, honest. Tell me what's troubling you, honey. I haven't seen you so wound up before.'

'I've never felt this way about a mission before.'

Denard took his hand. 'Go on, tell me.'

'I've been instructed to kill the British Ambassador, right here in Budapest. I can't believe it, Nicola Watson, one of the UK's rising stars, next Ambassador to the United Nations, and tipped to be Foreign Secretary one day.'

Denard pulled her hand away. 'Is that what's causing you so much grief? I don't get it, she's just another hit.'

'I know that, but I met her earlier today, she's charming, I like her. She's …..'

Denard cut in. 'Our business isn't personal, Jos, she's just another target; no better, no worse than any other. You're just doing your job, nothing more, nothing less.' She paused, studying his expression, watching her words sink in.

Cole clenched his lips and shook his head. 'I can't.'

Denard put both hands on his shoulders and shook him several times. 'What is it with you, Jos? Do you know her from the past? Have you taken a shine to her? Did she give you the come on? What the hell is it? Is she married with kids? What is bugging you? Tell me.'

'She's not married and she doesn't have kids and the answers to all your other questions is a resounding no. She doesn't hold any attraction for me whatsoever. Got it, Toni?' There was a touch of annoyance in Cole's voice for the first time. Denard nodded vigorously. 'OK, OK, I get it.' She softened her tone and took his hand again. 'So, what is it, darling? Tell me. Please.'

Cole slumped, searching for words. 'I've never killed a woman, I just can't do it, just can't.'

Denard squeezed his hand. 'I understand, Jos, I really do. I doubt if I could kill a child. But we have to remember, we are in this business because we're good at killing people. The bad guys are usually men, but there are nasty women out there. Look at me for instance.'

Cole let out a weary sigh. 'Thanks, darling. You're right of course, but I just can't do it. '

Denard sat back, shaking her head. 'So, what are you going to do?'

'There's only one thing I can do, Toni. I'll have to resign. I guess that'll please you. We can set up that partnership you spoke about.'

To Cole's surprise she shook her head. 'Sorry, darling; I want you to partner me because you want to, not because you were forced into it. Besides which, when you come to resign, I don't want your reputation to be in tatters. Sleep on it; make your mind up in the morning.'

'OK, but I doubt if I'll change my mind.' Cole meant what he said; he knew he couldn't kill Watson. 'Let's change the subject; tell me about your op.'

Denard's thoughts were racing, worried about Cole's stance, but an idea had occurred to her. 'My orders are to take care of a local scumbag. He runs the local vice rings with blackmail on the side. He imports slaves, kids in their early teens, girls and boys. The word is he's brutal and uses them for his own sadistic pleasure before putting them to work.'

Cole nodded. 'Lucky you, it would be a pleasure pulling the trigger with him in my gunsight.'

Denard nodded. 'Damn right. And, according to our intelligence, he has a big role in the Hydra. He co-ordinates the sex industry across most of Europe. He has access to any illegal migrants that meet his spec. My guess is he's got scores, maybe hundreds of politicians and celebrities on his books.'

'What's this guy's name?'

'Janos Nagy. Ever heard of him?'

'Nope, but he sounds like a nasty piece of work.'

Cole topped up the coffee, reflecting on their conversation. His thoughts were broken when Denard snapped her fingers,

'Got it.'

Cole looked at her puzzled. 'So, tell me what you've got.'

'We swap missions. I take out Watson and you take out Nagy. It's the perfect quid pro quo.'

Cole breathed a sigh of relief. 'Thank you, darling, that'll work. We're way out of line doing this; we'll end up in Guantanamo if our Chiefs ever find out.'

'Who's gonna tell them? You can be sure they won't ask questions if they get what they want. The big boys only hold post mortems when things go wrong and they're looking for someone to take the blame. Have we got a deal?'

'You bet we have. But I would like us to work as a team on both of these ops, cover each other's backs.'

'You betcha. Now let's fill in the detail.'

Cole and Denard studied the briefing notes for the next hour. All options for timing, locality, travel and method were discussed, and decisions made. When both missions were accomplished both guns would have to be returned to their respective embassies. Denard would use Cole's rifle, and he would use her handgun.

'I think we've covered everything, Jos. Just wish I was more familiar with the area.'

'I must remember to check out Signor Armati tomorrow and hopefully get rid of the Novichok.' Cole checked the time. 'Tell you what, it's just coming up to 5pm let's go for a ride in the car and check it out. Just a drive past. Shouldn't take much more than an hour and a half unless the traffic is really bad. That done we can come back here and have a shower. I think you said we could eat in our room but I'm happy with the hotel restaurant if you would prefer.'

'Nope let's eat here in our room. To be honest, I can't be bothered getting dressed up to dine out.'

Reconnaissance

Nagy lived in a detached house near Nepliget. Watson on the outskirts of a small town called Vecses. Both locations were in the same general direction. Traffic wasn't too heavy and by the time forty minutes had passed they had driven past both dwellings and were on their way back to the hotel.

'I reckon I got the best part of the deal, Jos, if the brief is right, Watson is an easy target; same can't be said about Nagy.'

'Agreed, but I have an idea, one I've used before. Sit back, I'm going to hit the accelerator; I'm looking forward to a shower, a bottle of champers, a good meal and special desserts afterwards.'

'Sounds perfect to me, as long as I get to choose the desserts.' As usual she let out one of her giggles

Cole laughed. 'Looks like I'm going to be on duty all evening.'

CHAPTER TWENTY-FOUR

Budapest Day Eight

Next morning Cole and Denard rose early, neither had slept well; no matter how experienced you were, your overnight brain kept processing the next day's op. A series of black coffees served as their breakfast, both seeking the caffeine boost. An early start was necessary due to Nicola Watson's programme for that day.

Cole had removed the rifle components from the cardboard box the previous night and instructed Denard on its assembly. The rifle had been carefully chosen; it was the shortest available; not accurate over a long distance but suitable for its next target. Do you want to have one more go at assembling the rifle?' Cole enquired of Denard. He knew what her answer would be, but felt the need to ask.

'No, I fucking don't,' she snapped back. 'I went through the process half a dozen times last night. It's child's play, Jos; have a bit of respect for me, please.'

Cole nodded and gave her a cuddle. 'I'm sorry, I'm a bit strung up. I do more than respect you, I think you're the best. Let's get moving; we can kill time at the other end if needs be.'

The hotel car park was just coming to life when they pulled out and headed off to Vecses, the small town where the Ambassador resided. Cole had studied her routine and found that Watson had sought to be of some service to the local community. The Ambassador did her best to observe one weekly commitment; one that would bring her life to an end if his plan worked out.

Vecses

Morning traffic was bound to be heavy heading into Budapest but they hoped that there would be no hold-ups travelling in the opposite direction. Their hopes were fulfilled; traffic was fairly light and it took barely forty-five minutes to reach the outskirts of Vecses. Their luck continued when the found that the road they were on took them past the small chapel that was their destination. Cole motored on, noting as he passed that there was zero activity in the vicinity of the chapel. He spotted a small lane ahead where he was able to reverse in and turn back.

Cole pulled up short of the chapel entrance on the opposite side of the road and turned to Denard. 'Good luck, darling.'

'A piece of cake.' Denard got out of the car. 'I'll go check if she's turned up and come back for the rifle if she's there.'

Cole nodded. 'Hold it.' A car was slowing and turning into the drive leading into the churchyard. 'I think that's her now; that car has CD plates.'

Denard got back in and quickly assembled the rifle, then wrapped it in a shawl. 'I brought this along for added effect. She put a black scarf over her head and tied it beneath her chin. 'How's this for the grieving widow?' She put on a sad face and wiped away an imaginary tear. 'I'll give her a minute or two to place the flowers.'

'What if the priest is there?'

Denard shrugged. 'I'll decide on that as and when I need to. The clergy are always saying how good it is on the other side, so who knows I might just do him a favour and give him an early admission ticket.'

Cole shook his head. 'You're wicked, Toni. You're destined for Hell.'

'OK by me. I'll meet up with lots of old friends including yourself. Enough of the chat, I'm off.'

Cole watched as she crossed the road and walked up the short tree-lined drive. He shook his head when she crossed herself before entering the porch where she pushed open the large arched door.

Once inside Denard took a deep breath and walked confidently to the pews; a feigned look of grief on her face. To her surprise she found the chapel was empty and deathly quiet. *Where the fuck are you, Watson.* She was momentarily non-

225

plussed, but immediately rationalised the situation. *Gone to get some vases for the flowers.* She settled into the rearmost pew and bent her head forward as though praying.

The chapel door's hinges squealed and she continued her simulated praying, glancing sideways as the arrival walked past her down the aisle towards the altar. She let a minute pass then looked up, wiping away more imaginary tears from her eyes. A woman was trimming and putting flowers in a vase - it was Nicola Watson. Denard waited until her back was turned then lifted the rifle and took aim. The rifle was silenced but the loud phut of the shot echoed round the ancient stone walls; Watson pitched forward, blood staining the back of her jacket.

'Sorry, darling.' Denard hadn't aimed for Watson's head; she thought that would somehow upset Cole. It meant though that she couldn't be sure her victim was dead. She pondered on dragging her outside. *Hide the body somewhere in the churchyard to delay its discovery.* She dismissed the thought; it ran the risk of being seen by some passerby. Her eyes lit up when she spotted the Confessional.

She hauled Watson over to the Confessional and manhandled her up into sitting position. *There you are darling, make your peace and confess your sins. The priest will be along shortly.* She took hold of Watson's wrist and felt for a pulse; there was none, the Ambassador was dead. *Still, best to be certain, Toni.* She retrieved the rifle from the pew and pressed the barrel into Watson's heart. *Sorry, darling.* She pulled the trigger and without a second glance at her victim wrapped the rifle in the shawl and calmly walked away. On impulse, she opted to leave the churchyard by a side gate and rejoined the road about fifty metres ahead of Cole. He saw her immediately and flashed his lights, then pulled forward to pick her up.

'How did it go?'

'Routine. You'll be pleased to know that I took body shots and didn't mess up that pretty head of hers.'

Cole nodded. 'Thank you, I appreciate the thought. Do you want to grab a bite to eat before we tackle Signor Nagy?'

'I will if you want, but I'd prefer to get that job done and leave our afternoon free for a bit of sightseeing.'

'Agreed.'

Cole lapsed into silence, the fate of Watson weighing heavily on his mind. Life of late seemed to be all about killing. *Get a grip, Jos. What about Toni? You wouldn't have met her if you hadn't been engaged in killing. Give yourself a shake.* It was easier said than done. Denard sensed he was moping and left him to it.

CHAPTER TWENTY-FIVE

Nepliget

They were nearing Nepliget, a residential area on the edge of the huge People's Park; Cole was trying to focus on the job ahead when Toni interrupted his thoughts. 'Not long now, Jos, you've been very quiet. Have got a plan? If you're feeling out of form, I don't mind taking it on.'

'I'm fine, darling, I'll keep my side of our deal. I'm going to park up some distance away and walk round the area.'

'You seem confident he'll be there?'

'You read the briefing notes, this is where his computer set-up is and one of his brothels is just along the way. This isn't his only property; he owns a villa in the Swiss Alps and another in Monte Carlo, but here is where his daytime ops are based. I'll bet it's a mix of business and what he would call pleasure. If he's not there, we'll hang around for a bit. If he doesn't turn up, we'll go and have lunch and come back later.'

'And if he's got company, tooled up or otherwise?'

Cole sighed. 'I'll take it as it comes.'

'I'm happy to tag along, cover your back.'

'Leave it to me for now, OK?'

Denard recognised the finality in his voice tone and just shrugged. Five minutes later, Cole pulled over. 'I'll walk from here; best you get behind the wheel. If I'm not back in thirty minutes, go back to the hotel. Or better still get the first flight out of Budapest.'

'Shut up, Jos, you're scaring me.'

Cole leaned over and kissed her. 'Things go wrong sometimes, darling.' He kissed her again and got out of the car.

Nagy's place was located two lanes ahead on the left and he would get there in a few minutes. Cole strolled along trying to look like a visitor; from time to time eyeing the tourist guide he'd brought with him. He passed an old guy gazing out of a ground floor window and looked away, hiding his face from view. Some distance ahead two mothers with prams were engaged in a conversation and didn't seem to notice him.

Despite its sought-after position near the People's Park, the housing stock was modest; a mix of brick-built terraced and semi-detached. Number thirty-eight however, was detached and surrounded by high hedges which largely obstructed the view of neighbours across the road. It had a narrow parking strip running along its left side where two vehicles were parked nose to tail; a green Audi and a black Mercedes. His briefing notes had Nagy on record as owning a number of vehicles including a black Mercedes. *Bingo, there it was.*

Satisfied no-one was watching Cole crossed over and strode quickly past the cars giving each a healthy nudge. Both alarms went off and their howling tones filled the air shattering the piece of the neighbourhood. Cole carried on to the end of the building and waited for the cars' owners to appear from the front door. It was an old trick, but it had served him well in the past. Without warning, he was taken by surprise by a sound of a door being opened behind him and he swivelled, gun in hand, ready to kill - but it wasn't Nagy. *Shit* The man caught sight of the intruder holding a gun and raised his hands in surrender just as Cole pulled the trigger. The guy pitched forward clutching his midriff, groaning in agony. A second shot to the head put him out of his misery.

Where the fuck are you, Nagy? The car alarms continued to wail as Cole inched forward to the rear doorway and looked into the room, an empty office. Cole was in a dilemma, enter the building or wait for Nagy to appear. *Come on Nagy.*

'Mario. Mario.' The voice came from upstairs. Cole smiled when he heard the sounds of footsteps thumping down the stairs. *Not long now, Jos.* 'Mario.' A string of Hungarian expletives followed.

Cole ran across the room and stationed himself behind the open door; the footsteps had reached the hall. *Please be Nagy.* A man dressed in shorts entered the room, hesitating when he saw the door to the outside was open.

'Hello, can I be of assistance, Janos?

Nagy swung round and died immediately, a bullet hole in his forehead, another in his chest. The look of surprise on his face didn't leave him as he fell to the floor.

Cole acted quickly; he needed to silence those damn car alarms. Back outside he retrieved the keys which had fallen from the hand of Nagy's late departed lieutenant then pressed both fobs. The car lights flashed once and silence was restored. Cole took a few seconds to enjoy the peace then dragged Mario into the room.

He was keen to get out of the area, but there were things he had to do; not least to make sure the house was empty. He pulled on the latex gloves he always carried when he was on a mission, then closed and locked the outside door. Next, he drew the curtains and stood listening for a minute, but there wasn't a sound.

Cole tiptoed quietly along the hall and slowly, carefully, ascended the stairs to the landing. There were four doors, all partially open, one a bathroom clearly empty, next to it an office, also empty. He turned left and started to gently push one of the other doors slowly open, stopping when he saw a young girl lying on the bed face down. She was naked and sobbing, awaiting whatever fate awaited her. Cole drew back. *Sorry darling, I can't help you.*

He turned to the other door and found another young woman lying naked and unconscious on a bed, her body and face bruised. Cole felt sick, but there was nothing he could do. He hurried back downstairs and exited by the front door. *Rest in Hell, Nagy.*

The two mothers were still chatting as he walked away - the old man had fallen asleep - a couple of schoolgirls were laughing at their mobiles – no-one gave him a second glance. With a sense of relief, Cole slid into the passenger seat. Denard kissed him on the cheek. 'Job done?'

'Job done; chief rat and his henchman exterminated.'

'Twenty-five minutes, what took you so long?' She smiled and winked at him. 'I hope you weren't spending time with one of Nagy's young ladies?'

'At this moment in time, that's not the best question to ask.' Cole explained about the girls.

'Sorry, Jos, not nice. I'll get us on our way.'

'Ignore me, it's OK, you weren't to know. Pull in when you see somewhere quiet; I want to change these plates and get onto the Embassy about collecting the car.'

Budapest

Back in the city, Denard turned into the Mester multi-storey car park and drove all the way up to the top floor Pleased to see it was deserted, Cole quickly changed the number plates and phoned the Embassy. His call was answered on the fourth ring. 'British Embassy, how can I be of assistance?'

'Can I speak to Harry please?'

'Might I say who's calling?'

'Tell him, it's Terry White.'

'Hold the line; I'll put you through, Mr White.'

'Harry speaking, Mr White. How can I help?'

'I no longer require the car. I've left it on the top level of the Mester multi-storey. The plates have been changed and the ignition key is on the ground behind the front driver's side wheel. The parking ticket is on the seat.'

'No problem, I'll see to it as soon as possible.'

'Thanks Harry. Oh, please pass my regards onto the Ambassador, a charming lady.' Cole's stomach churned momentarily but he had to continue with the subterfuge.

'Will do, Mr White. She hasn't shown up yet but I'll pass on your regards on when I see her.'

'Thanks, bye. Maybe see you another time.'

Cole rang off, his thoughts with Nicola Watson.

They ignored the lifts and decided to walk down the stairs, Denard was first to speak. 'So, what plans do you have, Jos? Are we flying out today?'

'Nope, I want to get the past few hours out of my system. We're going to spend the rest of the day taking in the sights of Budapest. I'll fly back to London tomorrow. I've decided I've had enough of obeying orders; I'm going to hand in my resignation. I hope you'll come with me.' To his surprise she didn't react as he'd anticipated.

'I need time to think what's best, Jos. We'll discuss it tonight. We are going to form a partnership, darling, that's for sure, but there are some details I have to work on.' Cole gave her a querying look but she didn't respond and he knew better than to pursue further.

They exited the multi-story and followed signposting to the Danube. At Cole's suggestion, Denard agreed to go for a walk along the riverside. He felt the need to clear his head and reset his mood. They had been walking for nearly an hour; spent taking in the views and sharing gentle conversation, when he squeezed Denard's hand.

'Let's get a taxi back to the Hotel, shower, change and go out on the town.'

Denard smiled at him. 'Now you're talking, count me in.'

CHAPTER TWENTY-SIX

Budapest: Day Eight

Back at the Hilton, they stuck to the agenda; both showered and dressed up smart-casual; their usual diversions were put on hold for the present. Cole announced that he was going to book them flights to London, flying out late tomorrow afternoon.

Denard protested gently. 'I said I wanted to think over my plans, Jos; I haven't had the opportunity. I thought I'd talk through the options with you this evening over dinner.'

'No problem. darling. I can cancel a flight if needs be; look on it as our fall-back position. Now here's my plan for the rest of the day and tomorrow morning; top of my agenda, I want to get rid of the rifle; the Danube seems the best bet if we can find somewhere quiet. Next up if we get news that Armati has succumbed to the Novichok I want to get rid of it too.'

Denard nodded. 'Best done when we go out this evening, it'll be quieter. So how are we spending the day?'

'Wait and see. First up, I'm starving, let's find a local eatery.'

The pair began their outing by taking in the view from Castle Hill, gaining a fuller appreciation of the whole Budapest vista. Next, they took the Siklo funicular railway down to the riverside, and from there crossed the nearest bridge to the other side of the Danube. It wasn't long till they ended up in the Café Miro.

Over coffee, at the end of a hearty lunch, Denard dropped a bit of a bombshell. 'You know, Jos, I've been thinking a lot about our partnership, if we ever get it off the ground., that is.'

'We will get it off the ground, I promise.'

'I believe we will too, but…'

A frown flashed across Cole's face. 'But? But what?'

Denard licked her lips, trying to choose the right words. 'I can't see it making us rich for a long time, if ever. I know that might sound shallow, but I want to be rich, very rich. We're only on this Earth once and I want to make the best of it.'

It was Cole's turn to search for words. 'I've no objection to being rich, but it's easier said than done. Getting rich is difficult.'

'There are ways difficulties can be overcome, Jos. In our line of work, we go about killing people to order and the reward for the risks we take is a very modest salary.'

'Are you suggesting we go private, and sell our services? Kill people for money?'

Denard nodded. 'That's exactly what I'm suggesting. The big difference is we would be able to choose what we take on and not have it dumped on us.'

Cole was astounded. 'You're serious, aren't you? '

'What's to stop us?'

'Killing people is illegal, Toni.'

'The CIA does it, MI6 does it, soldiers do it, policemen do it; they are working for their governments. So why not us?'

'They only take out bad guys.'

'Mostly.' Denard shrugged her shoulders. 'So, we could be picky and only kill bad guys. Maybe even sell our services to the CIA or your lot?'

Cole had to nod his agreement, *She's right.* 'Hmm, you've got a point, Toni. I guess it's my turn to think about it. How about we park it for now and get on with our tour of the city; it's 2.30, we need to get a move on.'

They continued their walk along the bank of the Danube, then through the park to the Gellert Baths. Denard was notably quiet, barely responding to Cole. 'So much for the famous thermal baths, darling, and unless you want a dip, I'm going to hail a taxi and head for the Hungarian Parliament.'

'Whatever you say, Jos.' Her response was polite but cool. *Something's not right, Jos, you've upset her.*

Taxis were plentiful in the area and they were on their way within minutes. Again, silence ruled; her hand limp when he took hold of it. Ten minutes later they were dropped off at

Hungary's centre of politics, which was located in the Pest side of Budapest. It was a truly magnificent neo-gothic building, constructed towards the end of the 19th century and believed to have been inspired by the British Houses of Parliament.

'Magnificent building, don't you think?' Cole enquired.

'OK I guess.'

The almost surly response irritated Cole, and he swung her round to face him. 'It knocks spots off the White House, that's for sure. Look here Toni, you're behaving like a naughty fucking schoolgirl who hasn't got her own way. I told you I'd think about your proposal and I will. I'm not going to cave into every idea you come up with. If that's what you're hoping for, we had best go our own ways now.'

A flash of anger in her eyes left as quickly as it came and she threw her arms around his neck and pressed into him.

'Sorry, you're right. I am being unreasonable; I just want us to be together and in control of our lives. But dammit, I do want to be rich, and that's not negotiable.'

'I haven't said no.'

'You haven't said yes either, and I want to know where I stand.'

'Of course you do, I understand that. But I'm at a crossroads in my life and I need time to choose which path to follow. Let's leave this for now, darling, and take a tour round this wonderful piece of architecture. Please?'

'Lead the way, **darling.**'

The tour took just under two hours and although they were starting to tire, Cole took Denard's hand and led her through the streets to the Basilica of St Stephen.

'I'm getting tired, Jos, can we keep this tour short?'

'I'm with you on that one.'

Once inside the Basilica, they both marvelled at its magnificent dome, although generally the interior proved to be somewhat dark and gloomy.

'We're nearly done; just a quick look around the Holy Chapel and we'll be on her way back to the hotel. OK?'

Denard sighed. 'As you wish, **darling,** I'll follow your lead.'

The tour of the chapel was perfunctory and ten minutes later they were seated in a taxi on their way back to the Hilton. Back in the room, Denard threw herself on the bed, 'I'm knackered, I think I need to sleep.'

'Me too.' He checked his watch. 'It's just gone six o'clock, let's relax for an hour before we go out to dinner.'

'Maybe an hour and a half.'

Denard fell asleep almost immediately. Cole lay beside her, thinking about her proposal and what it would entail. *Resigning from the service. Killing to order, bad people only including those who had placed themselves outside the reach of the law. They would be in control of their lives and there would be rich rewards. In some ways, it was a no-brainer*

The more he thought about it, the more the idea appealed, being rich would have its benefits. But there was one major obstacle. and it wasn't a moral dilemma it was a practical one. *How the hell did you advertise that you were a killing machine for hire and the forces of law and order not find out? And if they advertised their services to the criminal fraternity, why would that lot believe they weren't still working for the CIA or MI6?*

He was minded to take up Toni's offer, but could she answer that crucial question. He let her sleep for the full hour and a half then kissed her on the forehead. 'Waken up sleepy head.'

Denard stirred and rubbed her eyes. 'Hmmm, I feel so much better.'

Cole kissed her full and long on the lips, and felt her respond. 'Just how much better do you feel, honey.'

'There's only one way to find out.'

They made love passionately, their desire for each other reborn. *You can't let her go, Jos.* Their lovemaking over, they showered separately, then dressed and made their way down to the hotel's restaurant where Cole ordered a bottle of Bollinger. Denard's eyes lit up. 'Celebrating, darling?'

'It's a double celebration. First up, we've completed our Budapest mission and second, wait for it, I'm going to join that partnership you proposed.' He paused briefly, 'But there is one proviso and it's not negotiable.'

Denard's brow creased. 'Proviso?'

'Yes, and it's a toughie. The idea of being a modern-day Robin Hood appeals to me, but I need to know how we advertise our services without the cops and others getting to know?'

'News gets around, Jos'

'That's what I'm afraid of Toni - the wrong people getting to know.'

'I've got connections, Jos, good connections.'

'How good?'

'The best in the business.'

Cole was starting to get frustrated. 'We're partners, remember; spell it out with me.'

Denard hesitated for a long time. 'This is strictly between you and me, right?'

Cole nodded, starting to get wary. 'OK.'

'Promise?'

'I swear, now out with it, or do you want me to get a fucking bible.'

At that moment the waiter arrived with the champagne, and with a flourish removed the cork, then poured a taster into Cole's flute. He wasn't one of the connoisseur types but he had a sniff and took a sip. 'Yes, it's definitely champagne, please pour.'

The bemused waiter filled both flutes and moved away, quickly sensing the atmosphere and knowing that his presence wasn't welcome. Denard raised a glass for a toast which Cole ignored. 'First things first, you were about to enlighten me about your connections.'

Denard sighed, looked around, then bent forward over the table. 'I've got a connection inside the Hydra.'

Cole's eyes widened and he sat back in his chair. Alarm bells were ringing. 'You're joking, aren't you?'

She shook her head, very slowly, her face serious.

'My God, one day we're killing them off, next day you tell me you've got a mate works for them. I don't believe what I'm hearing. Do you really want us to work for the Hydra?'

'We would only take on contracts that involved the bad guys, remember? I bet they pay well and when we've built up our bank balance we could stop doing business with them. Maybe even pass on, or even sell, all we've learned to the Intelligence agencies.'

Cole was thinking fast. *Toni had a point; the Hydra would always find someone to do a job. If he or Toni didn't take it on, someone else would. But working directly for the Hydra was a step too far - or was it.? Fuck it.* He smiled at Denard, then raised his glass and chinked. 'We have a deal, darling, with one little condition.'

Denard took another mouthful of champagne and eyed Cole warily. 'What little condition are we talking about, Jos.'

'For the first twelve months of our partnership, you do all the negotiating with whosoever is your contact. I operate undercover.'

Denard smiled broadly. 'I'll drink to that; we have a deal. We'll sign the contract in triplicate in bed tonight.'

CHAPTER TWENTY-SEVEN

Budapest: Day Nine

Around 7am next morning, Cole woke to the sound of Denard singing in the shower. Minutes later she came out towelling herself, smiling when she saw he was awake.

'Good morning, sleepyhead. What are our plans for today.'

Cole patted the bed, come here and I'll tell you.' She giggled and stepped away to get dressed. 'No time for that, I want to see a bit more of Budapest before we fly out this afternoon. And on that subject, I was thinking maybe it's best that I fly straight back to Washington. We'll get lots of opportunities to spend time in London together when we're free agents. I'm sure you'll have lots to clear up after you hand in your resignation. I'll certainly have lots of loose ends to tie up. And who knows, I might even get us our first contract.'

Cole was taken aback, but on reflection, it wasn't a bad idea. 'I guess so, though I'm a little disappointed that you're not travelling back with me.'

'Me too, I hate the thought of parting but I think it's for the best. Now get showered and dressed, and I'll order us our usual breakfast. You can think about what we're going to do for the rest of the morning.'

Cole punched his head. 'Fuck it, I forgot to get rid of the rifle last night. And I've still got that fucking Novichok. We'll need to check the newspapers when we're out, see if we've made the headlines.'

Denard put a hand over her mouth. 'Shit. We'll have to get rid of that stuff in broad daylight.'

Over breakfast they agreed to stay on the Castle Hill side of the Danube and use their time to cram in visits to the Hungarian National Gallery, the Royal Palace and the Castle Museum. It would be a whistlestop tour, their time was limited. They didn't linger over breakfast, keen to get packed and on their way. Cole broke the rifle down into its three sections and wrapped them it in a pullover ready for disposal.

They left by the rear of the hotel smiling and nodding politely at the guests who were sitting around enjoying the morning sun. Some wanted to chat, but they made their excuses and kept conversation to a minimum.

Arriving at the riverside, they headed towards the famous Chain Bridge where they waited for an opportunity to dispose of the rifle. 'I don't think we can't risk being seen throwing it into the middle of the river from the bridge, Jos. We would be bound to be seen by someone. We'll need to dump it fairly close to the riverbank.'

'Agreed, and we'll leave a bit of space between the bits. You can be lookout.'

Whether they were seen chucking the stuff in, they would never know but job done, they opted to go to the furthest attraction on Cole's list and work their way back to the hotel. They ended up at a bazaar in the Castle gardens where Denard wanted to browse, but in view of the time pressures, Cole gently steered her past most of the line of stalls. Along the way they stopped to scan a couple of newspapers which carried the headlines they had hoped for. They couldn't translate Hungarian but there were accompanying photographs and it was clear what the headlines referred to.

BRITISH AMBASSADOR MURDERED.
GANGLAND BOSS ASSASSINATED.

Cole's guilt about Nicola Watson flared up again. 'Let's go, we can buy a newspaper at the airport and read it on the plane. We need to get moving. On the way back Cole discharged the Novichok into a quite grassed area and threw the canister into the Danube.

Budapest Airport

Two hours later Cole and Denard stood hugging each other at the airport saying their goodbyes.

'I'm going to miss you, Toni. I feel like I've known you a lifetime.'

She hugged him tightly. 'It won't be for long, I promise.' Her plane was scheduled to depart thirty minutes before Cole's, and he watched with sense of loss when the moment came for her to turn her back on him and walk away.

In the time he had available Cole's thoughts dwelt on how he would explain his resignation to Moore, she was bound to ask why. He also thought about the future, about being on the wrong side of the law and what kind of future it would bring.

CHAPTER TWENTY-EIGHT

London

As soon as he was clear of Border control and Customs, Cole texted Moore, seeking an early meeting. He wasn't looking forward to telling her he was resigning; there was still an underlying reluctance in the recesses of his mind. But he cast his doubts aside, being with Toni was his priority. *The grass is always greener on the other side, Jos, at least until you step on it. Stop dithering, Jos, your heart is with Toni, get used to it.* Moore replied whilst he was in the taxi heading back to his flat. *Tomorrow morning 9am sharp, don't be late.*

Back in the flat, he gathered up the pile of mail that had gathered dust in his absence; the usual mix of adverts and bills, some things never change. There was one personal letter; an invite to a residents' committee meeting. It joined the adverts in the rubbish bin. Cole made himself a coffee and sat down to reflect on the events of the past few weeks and yet again how he would explain his sudden resignation to Moore.

The evening passed slowly but eventually bedtime arrived and he slid into bed, longing for Toni's company; life was so much better when she was around. Allowing for the time difference she ought to have landed in Washington and he was tempted to phone, but in the end just sent a simple text. *Missing you xxx*

The warbling ringtone of his mobile woke him up very early next morning; it was Toni and he grabbed at it, eager to accept the call before she rang off. 'Deception.'

'Deception bollocks! How are you, darling? I hope I've got the time right and haven't woken you up.'

Cole smiled and lied. 'Not at all, I've been up for ages.'

'I just phoned to say I love you, and to wish you luck when you meet Moore this morning.'

'That won't be a problem, I've rehearsed my storyline. Love you too, missed having you at my side last night.'

'Me too. Sorry, Jos, but I'm flaked out. I had a load of stuff waiting for me when I got back and I've and got a busy day ahead. I need to get some shuteye. Just wanted to say I love you. We'll speak later. Look forward to hearing all about your meeting with Moore this morning.'

MI6 Headquarters

Cole got to MI6 Headquarters fifteen minutes early, making sure his meeting with Moore didn't start with a rebuke.

Sal Galt greeted him in the outer office. 'Welcome back, Jos. I've missed seeing you around.'

Normally he would have pressed his luck and sought a date but things had changed; Toni was his world now. 'It's good to be back, Sal. How is Gerry these days?'

Galt rolled her eyes. 'She's got a lot on her plate.'

The intercom buzzed. 'Send him in.'

Galt smiled and motioned him forward. 'Your inquisition awaits.' she whispered.

Moore made no time for niceties. 'Take a seat Jos, fill me in on your adventures.' *Good to see you too, Chief.*

Cole took a deep breath. 'Before I report back on my mission, I've got an announcement to make.'

Moore leaned back in her chair. 'Sounds ominous; let's have it.'

'I'm tendering my resignation, as of today.'

Moore blinked, her jaw dropped, 'Might I ask what's brought this on?

'I met someone whilst I was away and we're going to start a new life together as soon as I wind up here.'

Moore looked genuinely dismayed. 'I'll be sorry to lose you, Jos. You were someone I could rely on.' Momentarily she sounded sad, but the old Moore quickly resurfaced. 'You'll have to work your three months' notice, less any outstanding leave. What plans do you and your new found interest have for the future? Tell me a bit about her, if you will.'

Cole hesitated; he didn't want to reveal that Toni was CIA and his opposite number, but he had to say something. She's

American, we share common interests, and we're going to set up a detective agency; advise on security, and such like.'

'I suppose there's a tenuous connection to what you do now. I hope she knows what's involved and doesn't think it's a TV scenario.'

Cole shook his head. 'She knows the score; she's had military experience.'

Moore sighed. 'Whatever, I wish you both well; maybe you'll introduce me to her someday. Now let's hear about your missions.'

Cole nodded. 'Not much to add to what I suspect you already know. All the hits went according to plan and I don't think I attracted any attention; I certainly wasn't questioned at any time. All the Embassies co-operated, to a greater or lesser extent.'

'I see you did your usual and gave the local gangland a kick in the balls. How did the Nagy killing go on the day?

Cole had a dilemma. *Shit, she knows about Nagy. Toni must have reported back to Rosetti and he's been in touch with Moore.*

'No problem really, though one of his henchmen got in the way and I had to take him out. I researched the guy and it was a pleasure giving him a bullet in his guts.' Cole went on to explain what had taken place and the state of the two girls.

'Nagy was a real bastard; I wish I'd had time to make him suffer.'

'Best set emotions aside in your line of work, Jos. A sad coincidence that Nicola Watson was assassinated when you were in Budapest. She is a big loss.''

Cole's heart missed a beat. *What did Moore mean? Was she playing some kind of game? Had circumstances changed or had the intelligence on Watson proved to be wrong? Was Moore distancing herself from the operation before the shit hit the fan? It didn't make sense. Something was wrong; alarm bells were ringing, and ringing loudly. The situation was mad but he was too confused to challenge the statement.* 'Yes, I remember reading that she was destined for greater things, perhaps even Foreign Secretary.'

Moore nodded. 'That was certainly a possibility in the longer term. Very few knew that she worked very closely with us, especially regarding the Hydra scenario. She had contacts all over the world and her appointment as Ambassador to the United Nations would have been invaluable. A big loss.'

Cole was grappling to come to terms with what he was hearing. *Watson was his target, what was going on? There could only be one explanation.* He reached across Moore's desk for a notepad and biro and began to write.

I need to see you in private. Not in this building, somewhere away from here. He put his fingers to his lips and passed the note over. He had to say something innocuous to fill the silence. 'Was Watson married?'

Moore was puzzled but played along. 'Let me think? I don't think she had a partner.' She finished reading Cole's note and raised her eyebrows, then scribbled a reply. *What the fuck are you up to? I have a very full day, can you come to my flat 7pm tonight?'*

'I guess that's a small blessing. Are her parents still alive?' Cole took back the notepad. *Not your flat, nor my flat; we might be bugged. Somewhere neutral of your choice.*

'Yes, they're both alive and live in Surrey. They're devastated, Nicola was their world.'

Moore raised her eyebrows again, her expression sceptical. *OK, the Oleander Club, Bond Street, 7pm. I'll book a private room and dinner.* 'I think we've covered everything, Cole. I'll be in touch if needs be.'

Cole nodded and reached for the notepad again. *Ideal. Not a word to ANYONE. It's important this remains between you and me.* 'Thank you, Chief, I'll go now. I'll let you have my resignation letter before the end of the week. Oh, I should have mentioned, I had to ditch the rifle I used in Budapest. It's at the bottom of the Danube, sorry.'

'And so you should be, Cole. A waste of resources that I'll have to account for; my budget is already overspent. And you treated yourself rather well when you were in Budapest, all at the public's expense.'

Cole smiled; things were back to normal. 'I did, didn't I? Goodbye for now.'

252

'Before you go, you don't happen to have a photo of your lady, just in case I don't get to meet her? I'd like to see the woman whose stolen Jos Cole's heart.'

Cole paused, and was going to decline, but had second thoughts. He fished out his mobile and brought up his photo album. 'This is her, her name's Toni. What do you think?'

Moore whistled. 'You've certainly picked yourself a gorgeous-looking young woman. I hope she knows what she's getting into; you're a difficult sod at times. Would you mind forwarding me a copy of that photo.'

Cole went to red alert, 'Why would you want a photo of Toni? You're not thinking of checking up on her?'

'Of course not.' Moore sounded adamant. 'Sal, or one of your colleagues, is bound to ask why you're resigning and I want to show them why. They'll understand when they see Toni's photo, she's stunning.'

Cole was still suspicious of Moore's motive but forwarded a copy. He leaned over her desk and whispered. 'I don't trust you, Gerry.' He winked. 'Let me know what you find out.'

Moore scribbled a few more words. *Better safe than sorry.* She tore out the used pages of the notepad and passed them to Cole. signalling they were for disposal. 'Goodbye.'

Cole did want to explain his resignation to Sal Galt in person, but as it happened, she wasn't in the outer office when he left. *Damn, I'll have to phone her this evening. I just hope Gerry doesn't tell you in the meantime.*

CHAPTER TWENTY-NINE

Oleander Club; later that day.

Cole got to the Oleander Cub at five minutes to seven and was greeted by the doorman. 'Good evening, sir. Can I see your membership card please.'

'I'm not a member, I'm a guest of Ms Moore.'

'And your name, sir?'

'Cole, Jos Cole.'

The doorman scrutinised his notepad. 'Ah yes, Mr Cole. Please go straight in, Ms Moore arrived a few minutes ago. You'll probably find her in the main lounge, second door on the left.'

The Oleander Club was open to a select few: Government and Shadow Cabinet Ministers, Chief Executives of the finance, commerce and industrial worlds and successful entrepreneurs. Celebs and media were extremely unlikely to be given membership.

Moore rose from her comfortable armchair and moved across the carpeted lounge to greet Cole as soon as he entered. To his surprise she embraced and touched his cheek with hers.

Her expression seemed solemn; her voice lacked its usual sharpness. *She's sorry you're leaving, Jos.*

'They're ready for us, let's go straight to the room I've booked, unless of course you want to have an aperitif in here?' Cole looked around and thought he recognised one or two of the faces. 'I think I'd prefer if we went somewhere private.'

Moore retrieved a briefcase from beside her chair and led Cole back to the foyer and from there along a corridor to room number seven where a table was set for two. The carpeting, wallcovering and furniture shouted opulence.

'Quite a set-up. Do they charge members for breathing?'

Moore smiled. 'Only at weekends.' She pointed at the menus. 'I suggest you make your choice and I'll ring for service.'

'I'm not a gourmet, Gerry, I hope the meals are simple.'

'I'm not either, Jos, I like good plain food. There is some fancy fare, but I suggest you make your choices from the fixed menu.'

Cole smiled inwardly when he saw the choices; he was ravenous and his need would be met in full.

'Ready, Jos?'

Cole nodded and Moore buzzed the waiter who put in an appearance almost immediately. He looked enquiringly at Moore who pointed at Cole. 'Chestnut pate, Gourmet burger with chips, and to finish, Apple and Blackberry crumble with custard.'

Moore gave him a thumbs up. 'Make that for two please, David, though I'll skip the burger roll.'

'Certainly, Madam. And will you partake of wine?'

Moore glanced at Cole who shook his head. 'Just a jug of chilled water please.'

The waiter nodded and cleared the wine glasses from the table and put them on a nearby serving table. 'I'll be back in a few minutes, Madam '

When David had gone, Cole made to speak but Moore raised a restraining hand. 'I would prefer to have our meal before we get down to business.'

Cole nodded willingly, 'I'm starving, so that gets my vote.'

'In the meantime, let's compare our views of the Eternal City. I'd like to know your likes and dislikes. And, as it happens, I've never been to Budapest, so look forward to hearing what you thought of it.'

The meal ended just under an hour and a half later. Coffee was served and Moore opened the discussion. 'So, why are we here, Jos? What is so secret you wanted to meet in neutral territory?'

Cole replied with misplaced humour. 'I just fancied a free meal.'

Moore's eyes glinted. 'Not funny in the circumstances, Jos. Cut to the chase. Why are we here?'

Cole licked his lips, apprehension gripped every nerve and sinew in his body, 'You know you said Nicola Watson was one of us? Well, I have to confess that it was me who killed her.' It was a lie but one he felt he had to tell.

Moore slapped her cup down on its saucer, almost spluttering to get her words out. 'You killed Nikki? Was it an accident? How the fuck did that happen?'

Cole shook his head. 'It's not my fault she's dead, it's yours. Your brief clearly instructed me to assassinate her.'

'Don't be fucking ridiculous, Cole. Your brief was to kill Janos Nagy and you did that. You can't have it both ways. One brief - one victim - Janos Nagy. Explain.'

Cole was knocked back on his heels; this couldn't be happening. He was in trouble, big time. 'I don't have all the answers, but you're right, I've fucked up big time and I'm devastated. But before I explain; please, please believe me your brief identified Nikki Watson as my target. It was definitely your signature on the letter.'

Moore's anger didn't subside. 'You've made that claim, several times. It's undiluted rubbish. Now get on with it and explain yourself.'

Cole nodded and decided to come clean about the series of events leading up to Watson's death. He told how, Toni had contacted him, identifying herself as a CIA agent and joined him in Rome. 'She knew the Deception code; I had no reason to believe she wasn't genuine.'

Moore snorted. 'Oh yeah, and added to that you allowed yourself to get romantically involved.'

'I fell in love with her and I can't deny it. She's brave, she's skilled and she helped me in Rome. She's the real deal, I swear it. I still love her.'

Moore wasn't impressed and didn't hide it. 'Yeah sure, blah, blah, blah. Carry on.'

Cole bit on his tongue but recounted how he had collected Moore's instructions from the embassy telling him to kill Watson and, by chance how Toni had received instructions from her people to kill Nagy. I met with Ambassador Watson and I liked the woman. I confess I didn't like the idea of killing her, nor any woman for that matter. So, and I know it was completely out of line, I agreed to a swap. Toni would kill Watson and I would kill Nagy.'

Moore shook her head in frustration. 'And you didn't think it was too much of a co-incidence that she got briefed to go to Budapest on exactly the same date as you? Got briefed to kill in the same city as you? Are you really that naive? Blinded by fucking love, that's what went wrong.'

Cole had a little burst of anger. 'Listen here, Gerry, I had clear written instructions from you to kill Watson. The brief was signed by you; I know your signature well. What was I supposed to do? Challenge your instructions? Ignore them completely? Coincidences happen whether we like them or not.'

Moore was rubbing her brow, stroking her chin. Her eyes opened wide, her expression one of horror, 'Oh my God, I know what's gone on. I've got something to show you, something you're not going to like.' She opened her brief case and removed an A4 sheet of paper and a number of photographs,

'Take a look at these.'

Cole pulled them towards him, his heart sinking when he saw several showing Toni romantically embracing another man. *It's nothing, Jos, she's bound to have had other admirers in the past; they're old photos, history. Tony loves you.*

He looked at Moore for an explanation. She waved the A4 sheet at him. 'As you know, Mitch Rosett is the Director of the CIA. What you don't seem to know is that Toni Denard is his daughter by a former lover. The woman, Catherine Denard, died from a drug overdose when Toni was a child. He's looked after her ever since. She was brought up as Toni Rosetti and kept that name until she left university; after that we have no record of her.'

Cole shook his head, bewildered. 'She's never mentioned that she's Rosetti's daughter.'

'The man in the photo is her fiancé, Chuck Kingsley. A very successful business man. He's currently under investigation for big time tax evasion and not for the first time. Somehow, he's always managed to escape the net.'

Cole was bewildered, devastated, his guts wrenched, his dreams were fading. 'Toni never mentioned being engaged. Maybe she's gone back to America to break it off.'

Moore shrugged. 'It's tough, Jos, believe me I can understand how you feel. But stick with what we know - she didn't tell you who her father was - she killed Watson, one of our best sources - she phoned you out of the blue and pulled you into her open arms.'

Cole was struggling to come to terms with what he was hearing but slowly began to think more clearly. 'And she's asked me to go rogue - go into partnership with her – even take on commissions from the Hydra. But none of that explains your signature on the brief to kill Watson.'

Moore's expression was downcast. 'It's clear that my brief was tampered with after I passed it on for transmission to you. We knew we had a leak in our set-up and now we know who it is.'

Anguish gripped Cole's face. 'Oh my God, not Sal Galt? I can't believe she'd betray us.'

Moore was crestfallen. 'I can scarcely believe it, but it has to be her. There's no other explanation. She's our leak, no doubt about it.'

Cole snapped his fingers. 'I've just recalled a conversation I had with Toni after she landed back in the States. She wished me well when I met you **this morning**. The thing is, I hadn't told her that I had arranged to meet you **this morning**. She could only have learned about it from Sal.'

Moore looked thoughtful. 'Added to that Mitch Rosetti gave me all that info about the Hydra command. Quite a trio - Mitch giving me info - Sal the insider - Toni corralling you. We've both wondered how Mitch came by his inside info about the Hydra; my guess is he's in league with them.'

Cole shrugged.'It might be bigger than that; maybe he's an executive member of the Hydra and is killing off the opposition.'

Moore gasped. 'My God, you've hit the nail on the fucking head - Mitch Rosetti is setting himself up to take over the Hydra. We've all been used – you – me -Sal Galt, all lambs to the fucking slaughter. I suspect they knew we'd rumble Galt this time round and were prepared to ditch her.'

Cole's heart sank further. 'Toni told me she had a source inside the Hydra and I'll bet that source is her father. It's all beginning to add up.'

Moore nodded. 'This is dynamite. I need time to think through all the implications.'

Cole muttered. 'I've got some thinking of my own to do. I'm a fucking idiot, I've been duped big time. I reckon Toni knew all along how this would pan out, or at least Mitch Rosetti did. He's got rid of his opposition in the Hydra, he's got rid of Nicola Watson and made me the fall guy. I go along with your thinking about Sal Galt; she's just another sacrifice. And dammit, he's probably confident that you'll hush it all up to safeguard MI6's reputation. What a fucking mess, how the hell do we deal with this?'

Moore grimaced. 'It's a fucking disaster but we can't solve it here and now; we need time to think this through. Not a word to anybody, Jos, nobody. I'll be in touch tomorrow. We need to meet again. Keep yourself available at short notice.'

CHAPTER THIRTY

CIA Headquarters: Langley, Virginia.

A father and a daughter stood hugging each other, Mitch and Toni Rosetti, both pleased to see the other. Rosetti had given instructions that he wasn't to be disturbed for any reason; the President excepted.

'Great to have you back Toni. I've missed you; it's been a while.'

'Good to see you too, Dad. Sadly, being parted goes with the territory in our line of work.'

'I guess so.' Mitch Rosetti was genuinely wistful; he loved his daughter. 'You've been to Rome. You've been to Budapest. You've taken out Ambassador Watson. And you've got Jos Cole under your spell. A very successful trip all round.'

Toni smiled. 'It's been a great trip and I have to confess I am feeling rather pleased with myself. But there was one outcome I hadn't planned on.'

Concern crossed her father's face. 'Oh. And what was that exactly?'

'I've fallen in love with Jos Cole. Head over heels in fact. I never thought it could happen to me.'

Rosetti was astounded. 'Cole? The British MI6 Agent? No, no, tell me you're joking. I hadn't planned for you and he to become an item; I saw him as a holiday romance, nothing more than that.'

His daughter smiled. 'It is true, Dad; you had better believe it. Jos has probably tendered his resignation by now and we're going to set up as partners in a detective agency. We'll still do work for you and the Hydra on the side. We're going to be the best contract killers ever.'

'You haven't told him about me, have you?'

Toni shook her head. 'Of course not. I used my mother's name; Jos knows me as Toni Denard.'

''That's fine, it's best he doesn't know that I'm your father.' *Damn it Toni, you've really fucked up my plans. I had a job in mind for Cole, and, your fiance knows too much about my off-shore accounts. God knows how he'll react if you break off your engagement.*

'He'll have to know sooner or later; we're public knowledge here in the USA. I intend to come clean next time we meet up. I'm proud of you and I want to introduce Jos to you when the circumstances are right.'

Rosetti wasn't pleased, he could tell his daughter was serious and knew he would have to tread carefully. 'I knew you had Cole in the bag and I had plans for him. I wasn't sure he'd accept but I was going to offer him an important role if he played ball.'

Toni tensed. 'He will have an important role; he's going to be my husband. What did you have in mind for him, bearing in mind we want to be free agents? We don't want to be at anybody'd beck and call. And I'm sorry Dad but that includes you.'

'That's a shame, I was going to arrange for him to be Head of MI6. Gerry Moore is a bit of an obstacle to my plans for Europe; I thought it was time she met with an accident. I was going to fix for Cole to replace her, but if he doesn't want to join us, then…' *This is becoming a bit of a disaster; I'll have to play my cards carefully. Looks like Mr Cole is going to have to meet with an accident.*

Toni shook her head in disbelief, 'I can't see how you could guarantee he'd get that job, assuming he wanted it. I'm not sure he would join the Hydra even for me. And before you get any ideas, Dad, I'd take it very badly if he turns down the offer and something bad happened to him. I know how you deal with people who get in your way. Please don't make an enemy of me. I don't want to have to put you on my hit list.'

Rosetti was shocked at the threat but he smiled. He could see the conflict of interest and needed to placate his daughter 'Of course not, you'll always be number one in my life, Toni, you know that.' *Hmm, if it comes to it, I'm going to have to very careful when I deal with you Mr Cole.* 'When we explain our ultimate goal, I'm sure he'll come on board. You've already persuaded him to resign; he's eating out of the palm of your hand. And for your ears only, the Chief of MI6 is appointed by the UK Foreign Secretary and let's just say he is sympathetic to the Hydra. The job can be Cole's, if he wants it, but I wouldn't want him to know it was a fix. It would be nice for him to think he got it on merit. So that's my vision for the future.'

Toni was worried, bigtime. 'We'll see what he says if and when the job is offered to him, but I don't think it'll work. MI6 is based in London and I do a lot of my work over here. I love Jos and want to be with him; he's my vision of the future. You might have to seek an alternative solution.'

Rosetti nodded. 'I'll work something out. Maybe you could head up the Hydra in Europe, then you would both be based in Europe. How would that suit?'

'You're just not getting it, Dad. We want to be free agents and that wouldn't be the case with the kind of commitments you're proposing. And who knows, when we get married, in due course I might want to have kids.'

Rosetti was struggling to work out what was best for him, best for the Hydra; the immediate outlook was fraught with risk. *Buy some time, Mitch. You need to give the situation a lot of thought.* 'Let's leave that subject for now, darling. What are you going to do about Chuck Kingsley?'

'I'm going to break off our engagement when we meet up in Florida this weekend. I like him well enough, but not in the way I love Jos.'

Rosetti scratched his head. 'I won't stand in the way of your happiness, Toni; you mean the world to me. But I need a favour.'

'Name it, I'll help in any way I can, Dad. You know that. Just tell me what you want me to do.'

'I want you to hold off ditching Chuck until I give the word. Carry on as you've always done when you're with him. There are some off-shore tax arrangements I need him to sign off this weekend; personal tax matters. Once he's done that, you can give him the bad news.'

His daughter smiled. 'OK, a day or two breaking off our engagement won't matter either way.'

Rosetti smiled. 'Thanks, darling, you're a gem. Thinking about it, Chuck knows more than he should about my tax affairs, maybe he should have an accident. Maybe even a boating accident this weekend.'

Toni shook her head in a panic. 'No Dad, that wouldn't work for me. Jos doesn't know about my engagement and I don't want Chuck's demise making the headlines in any way associated with me. You're famous, it would make headlines everywhere if the Head of CIA's prospective son-in-law lost his life on your boat. I would inevitably be part of the media storyline – heart-broken daughter and all that crap. It wouldn't do your image any good either.'

'Yeah, I guess you're right. This has as all come as a bit of a shock, let me think about it. I'll go along with you for now. Poor old Chuck. He lives to fight another day but not much longer. It sure is a pity; I kinda like the guy. Now, if there's nothing else to discuss, I need to start taking calls again?'

The two rose and gave each other a parting hug and Toni Rosetti left her father's office smiling. *As the song says, Toni, 'Everything is coming up roses.'*

CHAPTER THIRTY-ONE

London

Back in her flat Moore poured herself a large gin and tonic and sat back on a sofa, feet up and Bruch's violin concerto playing softly in the background. She had to come up with a way to clear up the mess she was in. It would be easy to arrest Sal Galt and easy to convict her. But even if her trial was held behind closed doors the news would get out. *The Head of MI6's personal assistant is a spy.* She gulped at the imaginary headlines the media would serve up. Sadly, they would be deserved. How could this have happened? She had recruited Galt three years previously from the Home Office pool, and had trusted her implicitly ever since.

Galt had a flat in London's Mayfair that she claimed she had inherited from her parents, but was that true? Moore opened up her departmental laptop and entered her code; there was nothing she couldn't access. The Land Registry recorded that Galt had been the owner of the flat for the past five years. The previous owner was a company known as Galt Enterprises. Further digging into the records showed Galt as the solitary shareholder.

Fuck it, why had this not been picked up? Moore went further back in the registration history and found that prior to that it had been owned by Rosseti Industries, a company based in the Seychelles. And there it was, an apparent link to Mitch Rosetti, or a very unlikely coincidence. With time she could possibly get access to the Seychelles equivalent to Companies House, but that might end up being reported to Mitch Rosetti. *No, Gerry, that's not what you want. At least not in the immediate future.*

The Bruch violin concerto was now well into the second movement and she had a self-imposed deadline - to have a resolution in her head before it ended. *How do I deal with you, Sal - assistant – friend – traitor? You have to make an exit. But how? That was the question.*

Next Morning

Moore arrived at her office at her usual time; as always Galt was already at her desk in the outer office.

'Good morning, Gerry. Did you have a good evening?'

Moore smiled broadly. 'I had a relaxing evening, thank you. A couple of G&Ts with my favourite music playing in the background; sheer bliss. What about you?'

Galt shrugged. 'Just read a book and watched a bit of TV. Nothing too exciting I'm afraid.'

'A good-looking young woman like you ought to have a man in your life; or a woman, if that's your choice.'

'The right man, or woman, hasn't come along.'

Moore smiled. 'What about Jos Cole? He's footloose and fancy-free, and I'm sure he fancies you?'

Galt nodded. 'Well, he has suggested we go out for dinner, and we probably will one of these days. But he just wants to get me into bed.'

Moore shrugged. 'There's nothing wrong in going to bed with a man if you fancy him.'

Galt nodded. 'Maybe someday. But you can't talk. You don't have a man in your life.'

Moore smiled. 'And how would you know that, Sal? Have you been checking up on me? Listening in on my calls?'

'Of course not! I'd never do that.'

'Only kidding, must get on.'

Moore turned away and made her way into her office, a smile on her lips, she had a call to make. 'Bill, can you spare a minute?'

'Sure, I'll come up now.'

'Tell you what, I skipped breakfast; I'll meet you in the canteen, for a coffee and a slice of toast.'

Galt was busy on her keyboard when she walked past. 'Meeting Bill Tanner, down in the canteen for a cuppa; I shouldn't be long unless he has something on his agenda.'

Her Chief of Staff, Bill Tanner, was sitting in the far corner, well away from prying eyes, when Moore walked into the canteen. He waved her over.

'I've ordered, they'll bring it to the table. Not often we meet here, Gerry. What's the score?'

'I know who our leak is!'

Tanner's eyes widened. 'You know more than I do. Out with it; who the hell is it?'

Before Moore could reply, a plate was put on the table with two slices of crinkled nearly-burned toast and two black coffees. Tanner frowned and pointed at the toast. 'I said toast, not roast. Take that away and tell the cook he'll find himself looking for another job if that's the best he can do.'

The poor girl looked flustered. 'Yes, Mr Tanner. Sorry Mr Tanner, Sir.' She quickly gathered up the plate and scurried away.

'So, who's our leak?'

Moore grimaced. 'Sal Galt.'

Tanner slumped back in his chair, mouth gaping. 'No! That's so sad, I liked the girl. You're absolutely sure? Don't answer that, of course you're sure or we wouldn't be sitting here. How are we going to deal with this, Gerry? If it got out, the publicity would be highly embarrassing to say the least.'

'Absolutely, I've given it a lot of thought and this is what I have in mind for our precious Sal.......'

CHAPTER THIRTY -TWO

Oleander Club

Gerry Moore was seated, waiting for her lunch guest to arrive, her eyes lighting up when Professor Sir Clarence Miller was ushered into the room. Sir Clarence was a surgeon, university lecturer and one of London's coroners. He and Moore had known each other since they met at university many years ago. Moore met him half-way across the lounge and embraced him warmly with a kiss on the cheek 'You're looking more handsome and distinguished than ever Clarence; life is obviously treating you well. How is Lisa these days?'

'Can't complain, Gerry. Lisa is expecting our third child and enjoying everything motherhood throws at her'

'Congratulations. Do give Lisa my best and let me know when number three arrives. Follow me, I've booked a private room for lunch.'

Miller nodded, linked arms with Moore and was led to the same room she had met Cole in just twenty-four hours ago.

'I do have a bit of a deadline, Gerry, so I can't have a leisurely lunch I'm afraid. And nothing too substantial please; I usually skip lunch.' He patted his tummy. 'Helps keep my weigh down.'

A waiter arrived and Moore ordered a sharing platter of mixed tapas. 'There you are, you can eat as little or as much as you want, Clarence. What shall we have to drink?'

'A glass of iced water will do for me.'

Moore glanced at the waiter. 'Ditto, and our time's limited.'

The waiter smiled. 'I'll see that your order is given priority madam'

'So how are things in the world of deception and intrigue, Gerry?'

'Not good at the moment. In fact, they're on a knife edge which is why I have urgent need of your services.'

Miller's eyes hardened. 'I'm listening.'

Moore explained the Sal Gault situation in detail and had just completed her discourse when the waiter returned with their lunch and a jug of iced water. Miller forked a selection of Tapas onto his side plate and looked at Moore thoughtfully. 'Sounds like you have to change your PA, Gerry, and do it quickly. I'm sure MI6 could make that happen. Lots of people go missing or commit suicide.'

'I don't want either of those options, Clarence. I want her to die suddenly of natural causes, then the department can indulge itself in an outpouring of grief. It's vital that no-one in my department or my political masters find out Galt is a spy.'

A smile flickered on Miller's lips. 'Of course, Gerry. That way there will be no adverse media headlines and no calls for your resignation.'

Moore nodded. 'I confess that's a big driving force, but of more importance, no damage to our country's reputation. Added to that we'll be better placed to further our fight against the criminal organisation Galt is working for.'

'Count me in, Gerry. I'll help if I can; I hate traitors. What is it you want from me?'

'Thank you, Clarence. I knew you would help if you could. What I want is for you to carry out the post mortem on Galt and produce a report that results in the conclusion that she died of natural causes. Galt has no known relatives and hasn't seen her GP for years.'

'And just how will the young lady meet her end?'

Moore smiled wickedly. 'Something she ate; something that's virtually untraceable.'

Miller rolled his eyes. 'I hope you've got a good poison in mind? It really must be untraceable. I'll do the post mortem of course, but it will have to fit in with my schedule.' Miller took out his mobile and perused his calendar. 'Assuming this is urgent, the earliest I could intervene would be the day after tomorrow. That's when I get first choice of bodies to work on for teaching purposes. So, reporting her demise late tomorrow night will enable me to select her for post mortem the day after.

I'll deal with the paperwork. I think that concludes our business, let's deal with these exquisite tapas. You owe me one, Gerry.'

'I did assist in getting you a knighthood, remember? Anyway, rest assured, if ever I get the call, Clarence, I'll return the favour.'

Thames House

Moore was starting to feel relaxed by the time she got back to Thames House, and headed straight to Bill Tanner's office. She walked in without knocking, a finger pressed to her lips and pointed outside to the corridor. Tanner followed her out and she explained her plan in a whisper as they walked along to the lift. Tanner nodded, 'Sounds perfect, I'll wait to hear from you Gerry.'

Moore ignored the lift and walked up the stairs to the floor above where Galt greeted her. 'You're back early. Not your usual leisurely lunch?'

Moore smiled sweetly. 'Sadly no. My lunch date had another meeting to go to. Could you get in touch with Jos Cole and book a meeting with me first thing tomorrow morning.'

'Will do.'

Cole's Flat

Cole had drunk the best part of a bottle of whisky the previous night and was paying the price, a blinding headache and an aching tummy. His world had fallen apart and alcohol was his only comforter. His headache heightened when his phone rang.

'Yeah, who is it.'

'You sound like shit, Jos.'

'Oh, hello Sal. I feel like shit. What do you want?'

Galt's bridled at Cole's terse tone. 'The Chief wants to see you, tomorrow morning, nine o'clock.'

'I'll be there. Sorry if I'm a bit offish. How about I apologise over dinner?'

'No thank you, Jos.' Galt rang off.

'Cow.'

Next Morning.

Cole had showered and dressed and was watching early morning news when his doorbell rang. He was taken aback when he saw Gerry Moore standing on his doorstep.

'Chief, I thought we were meeting at your office?'

'We are but I wanted to fill you in on the situation beforehand.'

'Come in and grab a seat. Coffee?'

Moore shook her head. 'Just wanted to let you know what is happening regarding Galt.'

Cole nodded. 'I hope you're not going to ask me to…?'

'Just sit back and listen.'

When she finished, Cole gave her a thumbs up. 'I like it, cunning stuff. What about Rosetti and his daughter?'

'I thought you might like to handle that. I'm giving you two weeks leave, starting the day after tomorrow.' She stood up. 'See you at nine, and don't be late, I've got a busy schedule.'

Thames House

Cole walked into the outer office, and immediately knelt in front of Galt's desk. 'Forgive me, fair lady I was very rude when you phoned me yesterday. Pray let me make it up to you.'

Galt laughed. 'Get up you idiot! You sounded like you had a hangover.'

'Guilty as charged. Now how about we have dinner tonight and I make it up to you.'

'OK, I'm persuaded. Pick me up at 7.30, there's a new Thai Restaurant I'd like to try out.'

Before he could reply, Galt's intercom buzzed. 'Send Cole in please.' Galt motioned Cole to Moore's office. 'Prepare to meet thy doom. See you at 7.30 and don't be late.'

Moore, as always, was seated behind her desk. Sit down, Jos. I'm embarking on a series of staff reviews and I've been looking through your file. You haven't had time off this year and I think it's time you had. How do you feel about that?'

'I'm not likely to turn down leave, am I? And anyway, it's your fault I haven't taken time off. You keep giving me assignments. Seriously, I'll be very happy to take a break and enjoy life without having a mission in the background.'

'Good, you're on fourteen days leave, starting today. We're done here. Enjoy your leave and come back refreshed. You're going to be busy.'

'Don't you want me to complete my assignment? The General is still unaccounted for.'

'I'm deferring that till you get back. We're in the process of feeding him some duff info, which hopefully, he'll pass onto his contacts. See you when you get back from leave.'

Galt looked up from her keyboard. 'That was quick.'

'I've just been told I'm on leave for two weeks. How about you come on holiday with me?'

'Let's see how tonight works out.'

Cole put his hands together in mock prayer. 'Whatever you say, milady. See you at 7.30 and I promise not to be late.'

CHAPTER THIRTY-THREE

Galt's Mayfair apartment

Cole arrived at Galt's swish two-bedroom Mayfair apartment on the dot of 7.30, his breath taken away when his eyes took in her appearance. This was the glammed up drop-dead gorgeous version of his office colleague; not the woman he encountered regularly in Thames House.

Her make-up was subtle and her hair transformed. Her pale-blue dress was figure-hugging, low-cut and off the shoulder. He could only find one word. 'Wow! Is this the same Sal Galt I've worked alongside for nigh on three years?'

'Somehow, I don't think Gerry would approve if I turned up looking like this in the morning. Come on in Jos, and pour us both a glass of wine. I've decided to cook us a meal, Thai inspired. I hope that's OK?'

'My favourite eastern cuisine, though truth to tell I like them all.'

Their meal finished, they sat opposite each other in the small lounge, each secretly appraising the other and liking what they saw.

'What made you decide to eat in? Not that I'm complaining; that really was a scrumptious flavoursome meal'

She caught his eye and held his gaze. 'Simple really, I want find out what you're like in bed and tonight presented the best opportunity. It's strictly a one-night stand, Jos; you can spare me the lovey-dovey stuff.'

Cole nearly choked; this was unexpected, blatant. *Why now? What's your game, Sal?* 'I can't believe what I'm hearing; you've steadfastly resisted my advances for the past three years. What's brought this on?'

'Guys aren't the only ones who get horny, Jos. Are you up for it? she winked at him, 'Or are you turning me down?

Cole's thoughts were in turmoil, as Toni came into his thoughts. *Is this some kind of a trap to test my loyalty? Is this part of Rosetti's strategy? What a fucking mess I'm in.*

Galt shook her head, 'Looks like I've misjudged you Jos. I thought you fancied me?'

Colt smiled; he had made his decision. 'Put on some romantic music and let's have a smooch. I promise, you'll very quickly find out what my feelings are. I just can't believe that you're giving me the come-on for the first time in three years.'

'Let's find out about those feelings.' She moved away to put on a CD. Seconds later the unmistakeable voice of Rod Stewart singing the dreamy For the First Time filled the air. Cole took the opportunity to turn off the main light, leaving only the low-level lighting of a couple of table lamps. Galt smiled and moved over to join him, putting her arms round his neck.

Cole pulled her close. *If this is some kind of a trap, I'm a more than willing victim.* Her lips brushed his. Her body was pressing into him. His thoughts momentarily travelled to Toni and the expressions of love they had shared, but his body was responding to Sal Galt. Whatever he had shared with Toni, whatever he still felt for her, was losing to the here and now. He couldn't help but wonder what the reality was? *Maybe Toni still wanted him as a partner-in-crime but had committed herself to her fiancé? In spite of everything he still had feelings for her. Fuck it, why does life have to be so complicated?*

Galt voiced what they both wanted. 'Let's go to bed, Jos, we both know where this is heading.'

In bed, both naked, nuzzling gave way to kissing, kisses gave way to duelling tongues, their bodies welded together. *She was leading the way, and yet she must be aware of his relationship to Toni. Or maybe she didn't.*

'I'm all yours, Sal, this is a dream come true.' His words were hollow but suited the moment

She laughed at him. 'I bet I'm not first woman you've said those words to, Jos, and I suspect I won't be the last. Now let's get this show on the road, I'm already in top gear.'

Afterwards they lay side by side in bed, letting their heartbeats get back to normal. 'That was good, Sal. Worth being rebuffed these past few years. I felt unleashed, I hope I didn't hurt you?'

Galt burst out laughing. 'What do you think I am, some naïve little virgin who's been lusting for her hero to come along?'

'Of course not.'

'What then?'

'Well, I've never known you to have a man in your life.'

'Nope and don't want one. When I want a guy, it's on my terms.'

Cole sighed. 'Fair enough. Glad I made the grade tonight.'

Galt laughed out loud, and rolled over on top of him. 'I'm not finished with you Jos. Lie back and enjoy the ride.'

'I've got no answer to that.'

Their love-making, their sex-taking finally over, they lay together, talking aimlessly about past, present and future. In the back of his mind, Cole was still wondering if it was all some kind of set-up. *I wonder how much you're getting paid, Sal?*

Galt broke into his thoughts. 'It's nearly eleven, time you were going, Jos.'

Cole protested. 'I'm happy to stay the night and give a repeat performance in the morning.'

She shook her head. 'Maybe another time. It's been good, more than good, but tomorrow morning it's work as usual.'

Cole felt guilty; he knew there wouldn't be another time.

'Don't forget about my offer of a holiday.' Cole felt himself cringe as he said the words. He quickly dressed and Galt gently led him to the door.

'See you in the office, Jos. Sleep well.'

CHAPTER THIRTY-FOUR

Thames House

As usual, Galt was at her desk when Moore arrived. 'Good morning, Chief.'

'Good morning, Sal. You're looking a little shadowy under the eyes this morning?'

'Yeah, it was a bit of a disturbed night.'

Moore nodded, 'I know what you mean.'

Galt smiled. *I wonder if you do?*

'Oh Sal, as you know I'm carrying out staff reviews. Would my office, say 4.30 suit you? Shouldn't take long, half an hour at most.'

Galt was still puzzled; there had been no mention of performance reviews during the three years she'd been Moore's PA. 'Sure. Look forward to it' *Must be a Human Resources thing.*

Moore nodded. 'Good, you can bring yourself a coffee, or join me in a G and T.'

Galt smiled. 'I think I've gone off coffee.'

Cole's Apartment

Cole hadn't slept well; his brain had taken a long time to switch off. He knew what he wanted to do but just didn't know how to do it. One thing was clear though, he couldn't sort things out on this side of the Atlantic. Moore had given him two weeks leave, but then told him to be readily available. What did she have in mind? Until he heard from her, he was stuck in his flat. The least he could do was use the time to book a flight to America and go through his selection of passports. But first priority was to contact his old friend Jethro Watkins to check on his availability.

'Hello, Jethro, it's Jos. How goes the day in sunny Bateman's Bay.'

'It's pissing down and blowing a gale, if you've really phoned to enquire about the weather. It's good to hear from you man. How's life treating you?'

'I'm good thanks, and I've got some leave to use up. I was wondering what your plans were for the next couple of weeks?'

Watkin's brow furrowed, this wasn't like Cole, but he played along. 'I've got no commitments for the rest of the month, so I'm busy doing nothing the whole day through, as the song tells us. You're welcome to spend some time with us, if that's why you've phoned. I'm certain Billy would second that. What have you got in mind?'

'I've not made my mind up yet, but would definitely want to meet up with you and Billy if I possibly can. It'll depend on where my itinerary takes me. I'll check out flights and get back to you later today.'

'Go to it, man. Speak soon.'

Cole spent the next hour sorting out his travel plans; he wanted to be able to answer any questions Moore might ask when he saw her. His thoughts were sombre when they dwelt on the background and what lay head. He would need to cover his tracks and part of that would be to see places he'd never been to. After many deliberations he came to a decision - tomorrow, he planned to fly out of Heathrow to the Bahamas and from there to Miami. His return journey to the would take in Ottawa and Montreal before heading back home to Heathrow.

This was all on the assumption that his plan came to fruition. What would happen between Miami and Ottawa was up in the air, but flights in America were plentiful and wouldn't pose a problem.

His mobile rang and he was pleased to see it was Moore; he wanted to get that meeting over with.

'Hi Jos, I'd like to see you in the next hour or so. I've a meeting with Sal at 4.30.'

Mention of Galt brought images of the previous night's escapade flooding into his mind's eye. 'Hi Chief. If it suits you, I can come now.'

'Your choice, see you soon.'

Thames House

Cole felt a bit awkward when he walked into the outer office, but Galt on the other hand showed no sign of discomfort. Her smile was broad and there was a gleam in her eye. 'Hi Jos, the Chief told me to expect you; she's ready when you are. You're looking a little tired.'

'Yeah, I had quite a demanding physical workout yesterday evening, so I'm a bit worse for wear. By the way, I've spent the morning sorting out flights for my holiday.'

'So where are you going?'

'The Bahamas, Miami. Ottawa and Montreal. I still have to fill in some of the detail and book hotels. My offer is still open, you're more than welcome to join me.' Cole felt a surge of guilt making such an ingenuous offer. It doubled when she nodded.

'I've been thinking about it, and I would like to join you. I'll ask Gerry for some time off and phone you tonight.'

Cole continued the deception by bending over the desk and kissing her. 'That's great, speak later.'

Galt buzzed Moore. 'Jos is on his way in.'

It might have been his imagination, but he thought Moore looked disapproving when he entered. 'Sit down Jos. This won't take long; I know you're on leave but I want to know your plans.'

'I haven't finalised my itinerary yet but it will start in the Bahamas and end up in Montreal.'

'So, you'll be on the other side of the pond if something crops up and I need you? Hmm.'

'Fingers crossed you won't need me, Chief.'

'To be honest, Jos, I don't know what the immediate future holds. I know that we and other enforcement agencies are gearing up for a major offensive against the Hydra; your recent experiences might prove useful.'

Cole shrugged. 'I'll help out if I can but I am serious about retiring from the Service. I'll be using this holiday to think through how Toni and I will set up our business venture.' *If you're listening in Sal, I wonder what you're thinking about our holiday?* He winked at Moore and touched his nose.

'I don't want to lose you, Jos, you know that. Please reconsider. Give the matter careful thought. I won't press you further now, but we'll get together as soon as you get back from your holiday. You've obviously got things to do so I won't keep you.'

Back in the outer office he took a long hard look at Galt, who was standing at a cabinet engaged in filing. *Why do you have to be a traitor?* She turned to face him, smiling, hand on her hip. 'Well now, have I passed the scrutiny test?'

'Oops sorry, was just thinking of last night. We'll speak later.' Traitor or not, he pulled her to him and gave her what was destined to be a farewell kiss.

Moore's Office.

'Grab a pew, Sal. I'll pour you a gin, you can add your own tonic.'

Galt settled down on the nearest sofa, smiling when Moore handed her a generous gin, still wondering about the purpose of the review. 'Thank you.'

Moore handed her an open bottle of tonic. 'Help yourself.'

'I'll use most of it; this is a generous measure of gin.'

Moore took a large sip of her drink and smacked her lips. 'Nice to relax at the end of the day. Got any plans for the week ahead?'

Galt shook her head. 'No firm plans. Maybe a long walk around the parks. Maybe go to the theatre. I'll see how the mood takes me. There is always something to do in London.' She took a generous mouthful of her G & T. 'Hmm, an interesting flavour.' She lifted the tonic bottle and looked at the label, didn't recognise it and shrugged. She took another large sip. 'This is OK but wouldn't be my first choice.'

Moore smiled. 'Me neither. Any holiday plans in the coming months?' Galt was starting to get puzzled; these were social questions. *When would Moore make a start on her performance review?*

'Talking about plans, by co-incidence Jos has just invited me to join him on holiday. I told him I'd ask you if I could have some time off.'

'I should be careful, Sal; Jos is a bit of a womaniser.'

Galt laughed. 'Suits me, I guess you could refer to me as a man-iser, if there is such a thing.'

Suddenly she started to feel dizzy, the room was beginning to spin. She put down her glass and looked at Moore, her life ebbing away. 'You... you...'

'Afraid so Sal; we found out that you have been passing on State secrets to a criminal organisation, known as the Hydra. I believe it's run by Mitch Rosetti.'

Galt clenched her fists in anger, or maybe pain; she died before she could say anything further.

Moore gathered up the glasses and the tonic bottle and moved across to her ensuite where she washed them thoroughly. She dried them on a hand towel before returning to her desk and putting them in her handbag for disposal later. Just to be sure Galt was dead, she felt for a pulse and held a mirror to her mouth to check for exhalation. Satisfied, she took a last look at Galt, muttering 'Traitor.'

That done she buzzed Bill Tanner. 'Bill, I need your assistance, could you come up now please?'

Tanner joined her in minutes and together they carried Galt into the outer office, eased her into her office chair and left her slumped over her desk.

'Thanks for that Bill. Prof Miller has assured me that her body will be taken to Guy's mortuary tonight unless there's an unexpected change in the rota. He has a Post Mortem teaching session tomorrow and knows what's required. Clarence is reliable, I've got no concerns in that direction. He'll write up a favourable report; a sudden unexplained cardiac arrest or such like. The poison I used is virtually untraceable by the usual blood tests. I think that's everything, I'm off now. Call me at home, Bill, when you get to hear of the sad passing of Ms Galt. Follow normal procedures.'

Tanner nodded. 'I'll hang around until the cleaners arrive; one of them will discover the body and will be sure to come straight to me. I'll phone 999 for an ambulance and take it from there. I'll call you later to give you the bad news.'

'Final thought, Bill. Maybe best to check with the ambulance paramedics which hospital they are taking her to, just in case there are any changes to the rota. If there are, I'll have to alert Clarence.'

'Will do, Gerry. Have a relaxing evening if you can and definitely steer clear of those gin and tonics.'

CHAPTER THIRTY-FIVE

Next morning

Cole was dithering, he was still missing Toni and wanted to speak to her, test her, hear what she had to say - no matter the outcome. He tried her mobile, ready to use the old password Deception, but the phone rang a couple of times then went to call log. *At least you haven't blocked me or discarded your Sim.*

He decided to go through his fitness regime then try again. An hour and a shower later he tried again with the same result. *Fuck it, I give up.* Galt would be in the mortuary and, sooner or later, Toni or whosoever would be wondering why she hadn't been in touch. It was time he moved things along.

He went on-line and booked a flight with Air Canada for the next day to Nassau, the capital of the Bahamas. Take off was 8am and, adjusting for the time difference, he would land between noon and 1pm which was perfect. Next, he booked himself into the British Colonial Hotel, mildly surprised that they hadn't changed the name which was a clear reflection of its colonial past. He had to decide what passport to use on this occasion, travelling as Jos Cole was out of the question. He rummaged through his pile of fake documentation and found a passport with matching driving licence and credit card - he was now Charles Gibb, born in Glasgow thirty-two years ago.

He wasn't good at hanging around and he had a long day ahead. *Come on Jos, get your act together.* After much thought, interspersed with packing his suitcase in fits and starts, he went for a walk. He'd eat out, then fill the rest of the evening surfing TV before going to bed; he would have to be up at 5am.

Later

'Hello, Jethro, it's Jos. I'm flying into Nassau tomorrow, midday, and will plan the rest of my trip when I get there. In the meantime, I need a favour, a mega favour; one I hope Billy can help with. I'll tell you the whole story when we meet up; it's dynamite.'

'I thought you had something on the burner when you last phoned; sounds like it's a big deal. Look forward to hearing all about it, Bro. What's this favour you have in mind.?'

'I need to know Mitch Rosetti's movements over the next ten days.'

Jethro took a deep breath. 'Am I hearing you right, man? Mitch Rosetti, the CIA Chief? That might not be easy, I'm not sure Billy has access to Rosetti's movements. I'll get him on the case as soon as we ring off.'

'It's important Jethro, mega-important.'

'What the fuck are you up to, Bro?'

'I'll tell you when I see you. As I said, it's dynamite. I'll get in touch with you from Nassau.'

Next day. Heathrow

Cole's plane took off on time; he didn't have a MI6 blank cheque this time so he travelled economy. It wasn't as comfortable and there weren't the same perks as First or Business, but it was adequate and the films showing were the same.

Guy's Hospital

Professor Sir Clarence Miller was scanning the list of the mortuary's latest arrivals, looking for those requiring a post mortem. His programme for the day required four bodies; two male, two female, one young, one old for each gender. Sal Galt was his first pick, the others he chose at random. His selection made, he phoned the Chief Mortician and asked for Galt's body to be prepared immediately. The lecture would begin at 9.30 am with half a dozen students in attendance.

'Good morning, everyone.' Miller began with his usual spiel. 'Believe it or not, cutting open bodies isn't my favourite preoccupation, but there are many instances where it is the only way to find out how the deceased came to die. Sal Galt is 32, she died suddenly in her office yesterday. An ambulance was called, and she was pronounced dead at the scene. There is no obvious cause of death. Samples of Ms. Galt's blood have been sent to pathology. Samples of the organs we remove today will also be sent for analysis. Any questions?' Miller looked around the room. The first-year students in front of him looked apprehensive; this was their first autopsy.

'Very well, I'll begin.'

An hour later, Miller addressed the students again. 'That completes the initial stages of the autopsy. We have found that Ms Galt was in good physical condition and there is no obvious cause of death at this stage. Subject to anything the test results reveal, her death appears to be the result of sudden cardiac failure, cause as yet unknown. A conclusive causation will not be known until all the test results are forthcoming. Any questions? None? Right, take a break and assemble back here in thirty minutes.'

Grand Colonial Hotel, Nassau Day One

Cole was settling into his room when a text came through from Bill Tanner. *Hi Jos, thought you might like to know that Sal Galt died suddenly yesterday in the office. She was found by one of the cleaners. Cause of death unknown, autopsy today. I'll share the findings of the autopsy report with you in due course. A very sad day for us all.*

Cole bit on his lips. *What a waste, at least you had a good send off, Sal.* He decided to text a reply. *'My God, that's devasting news, Bill, such a lovely woman. She'll be missed by us all. Gerry must be heartbroken.'*

Cole had call to make. 'Jethro, it's me. I've landed in Nassau. Just thought I'd let you know.'

'Hi Bro, ain't got nothing for you yet. Billy is working on it and he's pretty sure he'll get the info you've requested. It just takes time.'

'It's early days, Jethro. I won't book a flight to the States until I have something definite. I might need your help with some bits and pieces.'

'Care to be more specific, bro?'

'Can't say until we hear from Billy.'

'Understood, Jos. Let's go silent until I phone you.'

'Agreed.'

Later

Having showered and changed into something comfortable Cole went for a walk along the pristine stretch of white sand beach that bordered the historic hotel. It was one of the best hotels he had ever stayed in and benefitted from being centrally located. Most of Nassau's tourist attractions were within walking distance but, attractive as they were, touring around didn't appeal.

He was still missing Toni and struggling to accept that she had betrayed him. *Get over her, Jos, there's no way back. She suckered you, good and proper. Maybe one last phone call.* The signal strength on his phone looked good and he dialled her number. After a few rings it went to voice mail again. 'Shit.'

But she still hasn't blocked me, maybe I'll try again tomorrow. Get out of cloud cuckoo land, Jos.

He walked for around forty minutes, enjoying the sound of the waves and the cries of the various seabirds, then began his return to the hotel. By the time he got back, he was feeling both tired and hungry, added to which the time zone effect was starting to kick in. He opted for the Red Pearl Grille, the hotel's eatery on the beach, and ordered a rum punch and fish tacos. By the time he'd cleared his plate he was fighting sleep and headed back to his room.

Cole was in the deepest of sleeps when his phone awakened him; the caller display showed him it was Jethro.

'Hello.'

'Hey, that's none too welcoming, man.'

'Sorry Jethro, truly. It's 5am here and I was in a deep sleep. I'm with you now.'

'I've got good news for you; you're a lucky sonofabitch. Your man is taking a week's leave and is headed for a place he owns near Jacksonville, north Florida but not a million miles from Miami. He has a pale blue waterfront house with its own dock on Jacksonville Beach. We're pretty sure he's on his way there now. Seems he owns a flash motor boat, sleeps ten comfortably; spends a lot of time on it. I guess he can escape the Press when he's out on the sea. So, there you have it; is there anything else I can help you with, Bro?'

297

'Given what you've told me, I reckon I can handle things from here on. How about you remain on standby though, whilst I work out a plan? Pass on my thanks to Billy; I'm in his debt again. I look forward to seeing you guys soon. I'll be destroying this burner phone Sim. We never had these conversations.'

'What conversations? You go careful bro. Sorry I ain't got your back this time, but I'm here if you need me.'

The call ended and Cole lay back, he had a lot of thinking to do.

CHAPTER THIRTY-SIX

Nassau: Day Two

Cole got up early the following morning and booked the first available flight to Miami; scheduled to take-off at 7.30am. He made himself a coffee but food would have to wait. The next steps could prove difficult; it was so much easier when arrangements were made through the Embassy, but this mission was under the radar.

Miami

The flight was pleasant and took just over an hour. The usual arrival formalities followed, then Cole headed to the car hire area. He chose a white Ford F-150 with the facility to drop it off in Jacksonville if necessary. The 350mile journey to Jacksonville would take about five hours; the route was straightforward and fast. First up, the Florida turnpike then the 1-95 N; the Americans certainly knew how to build roads. He drove carefully and within the speed limit, not wanting to attract the attention of the Traffic police.

Arriving in the centre of Jacksonville shortly after 2.30pm, Cole parked up and went in search of a Newsagents, where he bought a copy of the current edition of the Gun Advertiser. That done he headed for a small café he'd spotted near the local bus station. He ordered a hearty American-style breakfast, and scanned the Gun Advertiser whilst he ate.

Buying a gun in the USA wasn't out of the ordinary and gun laws were fairly relaxed in Florida, but it carried some risk and he wanted to avoid a main dealer. After ten minutes searching, he found what he was looking for; a smallish back street dealer in second-hand guns of all descriptions.

Cole knew that cash would open most doors, and had brought nearly $20,000 with him. He asked his waitress how to find the gun shop street, settled his bill and went back out to the car. It was time to change his appearance and practice his best US southern drawl. Cole reverted to his favoured disguise; a near shoulder-length blond wig and a matching horseshoe moustache. *Not bad, Jos.*

A five-minute drive took him to a long, quiet street, mostly houses. He parked up halfway along the street about a hundred metres from the shop in the hope that its owner wouldn't be able to make out the car's registration number should he be interested. The gun dealer operated out of a small red-painted tired looking shop. A bell rang as he entered and a fat slob of a man appeared behind the counter. Even from a distance Cole could smell liquor on his breath. 'How can I help you, Buddy?'

Cole summoned up his southern twang. 'I'm looking to buy an assault rifle.'

The guy appraised Cole. 'You got identity, papers?'

Cole shook his head. 'Nope, the only paper I'm carrying is the dollar kind.'

Another appraisal followed. 'There's rules I have to follow, you understand.'

Cole shrugged. 'If you can't help, I'll be on my way.' He half-turned, ready to leave.

'Hold on there. I didn't say I couldn't help you. I'm just being careful, that's all. Now what kind of assault weapon do you want, exactly?'

'One that has a magazine of say 30 rounds; the more compact it is the better.'

Another appraisal followed. 'You with the media or some do-gooding lot?'

Cole smiled. 'Wouldn't tell you if I was; now are we doing business or not? You were recommended by a friend of mine.'

'And, who would that be exactly?'

'He didn't want to be named. Now, last time of asking, are we doing business or not?'

The guy nodded. 'Follow me.'

He led Cole through a smelly untidy office to a poorly constructed, but secure, windowless annexe. An array of second-hand guns of every description was on display. A large iron safe standing in the corner attracted Cole's attention.

'Plenty to choose from, that's for sure.' Cole sustained his drawl, hoping the guy wouldn't ask him where he hailed from.

'Whatcha got in the safe?'

'None of your business.'

'Just asking. I organise some training exercises and you might have something I could use. No matter.'

Cole received another appraising stare. 'You choose your gun and, if we do a deal, I might show you what's in there.'

Cole moved round the shelving and picked up a GMMC Banshee 300; it was compact and the magazine held twenty-five rounds, ideal for his purpose. To cover all emergencies, he picked up a SIG Sauer M17 - a handgun might prove useful. 'If the price is right, I'll take these and a spare magazine for each. And remember I pay cash.'

After a five-minute haggle they settled on a price. 'Now let's see what you have in that safe of yours.'

'Have to open it up anyways; that's where I store the ammo.'

As well as the ammo, there was a small selection of military material including two hand grenades. Cole lifted them. 'I'll take these.'

'You sure you know how to handle them?'

Cole laughed. 'I'm a qualified instructor; I told you I organise exercises, and I've seen active service. How about you?'

The dealer ducked Cole's question. 'They're a hundred bucks each.'

'I'll give you fifty for the pair, max.'

The guy took them back and Cole shrugged. 'Suit yourself, man.'

'A hundred and fifty for the pair and I'm not making any profit on that price.'

Cole raised an eyebrow. 'Throw in those binoculars and we have a deal. What do you say?' He extended his hand and the guy slapped it. 'You drive a hard bargain, mister.'

'And you ain't no soft touch either; stick this lot in a sack and I'm outta here.'

Jacksonville Beach

It was late afternoon when Cole got back in the car, and headed for Jacksonville Beach. He was gambling on recognising Rosetti's place when he saw it, smiling around thirty minutes later when the pale-blue painted villa came into view. He drove straight past, scouting the area as he went.

The villa sat at the foot of a small hill, on the far end of a private stretch of beach. Three expensive looking cars were parked to the side of the house but there was no-one in view as he drove by. He noted that there was no boat tied up in the dock. *Looks like you're out for a sail.*

Cole took the first turning left, hoping it would take him to the other side of the hill. His luck was in; the road led to a large parking area, presumably for walkers and climbers. The hill was less than sixty feet high and the slope undemanding. Cole made his way to the top and sat down, focussing the binoculars on the bay. There were a few yachts under sail, and a solitary motor launch that seemed to be at anchor about half a mile off shore. The binoculars were powerful and he felt like he could reach out and touch the boat. There were three men, rods extended, fishing off the bow, one with his back to him. He panned to the stern; his heart missing a beat when he saw Toni. She was wearing a white bikini and lying on a lounger reading.

One of the men was Mitch Rosetti, another he recognised from the photo Moore had shown him - Toni's fiancé, Chuck Kingsley. The third man still had his back to him. As he watched, Toni got up and walked forward to the bow and put her arms round her boyfriend's waist. Cole felt pangs of jealousy consume him. She was saying something to the men and they all began to wind in their fishing lines. Kingsley was first to finish and he and Toni wandered off towards the stern.

At that point, the third man turned round. Cole gasped; another dream had been shattered. It was none other than his ex-commanding officer, General Tiger Wilson. He swore out loud. 'Fuck it, fuck it, can nobody be trusted?' The men finished clearing up the fishing gear and Rosetti started up the engine. The launch moved forward, gathering speed as he steered towards the dock. *This might prove easier than you thought, Jos.*

On board the yacht

Wilson nodded at the couple. 'How long have they been engaged, Mitch?'

'Best part of a year.'

'Any sign of them getting hitched? Not that it's necessary nowadays.'

Rosseti wanted to get off the subject. 'No date set as yet; I leave them to it. Whilst we've got a minute, Tiger, I've never pinned you down on something I want to know. Why did you decide to throw your lot in with the Hydra?'

'That's an easy one to answer. Firstly, the pay's good; secondly, I'm fed up working for politicians. We in the West have a big stick and don't know how to use it. We seem to bow the knee to every Tom, Dick and Harry. I don't like everything the Hydra does but at least it knows where it's headed and doesn't let anything get in its way. Heading up the European end of the organisation appeals to me.'

Rosetti smiled. 'That's the kind of attitude the Hydra's looking for.' *Where the hell is this going? If Toni sticks with Cole, she might be persuaded to take on Europe, then you'll get the bullet, Wilson. What a fucking mess you're getting me into, Toni.*

'I've a question for you Mitch; just what is your connection to the Hydra? I know you're involved but what exactly is your role?'

305

Rosetti thought quickly to come up with a believable reply; only Toni knew that he was Hydra's Leader. 'Me? I am their main covert intelligence source, I co-ordinate intelligence from all round the world. Nearly there, we'll talk more later.'

Cole watched in thoughtful silence as Toni jumped off the launch and tied up forward; Kingsley attended to the stern mooring. That done, the four of them walked along the dock towards the villa, chatting and laughing, Kingsley with his arm around Toni's waist. *That should be you, Jos.* Jealous anger returned briefly.

Rosetti's residence

Toni Denard had been thinking hard about how to break the news to Kingsley about breaking off the engagement and for that matter, his night time expectations. 'Chuck, I've been thinking about us.'

Kingsley immediately stopped on the boardwalk and turned to face her, worried about what was coming. 'Thinking what about us, darling? You're not about to give me bad news I hope?'

'Of course not, I was thinking we ought to set a date for getting married. And I'm not wanting a fancy wedding, something simple will do me. And, I'd like it to be sooner rather than later.'

Kingsley's eyes widened and he glanced down at her midriff.

'You're not... you know...?'

Denard giggled. 'Don't be silly. Let's look at a calendar when we get back and announce it tonight, over dinner.'

Kingsley leaned forward and kissed her. 'You're on.'

Cole watched as the foursome filed into the house. After a few minutes, lights came on downstairs and upstairs; preparations were taking place, but for what? *Oh gosh, I hope they're not going out for a meal.* He caught a brief sight of Toni and Kingsley at an upstairs window; both in their underwear.

Toni's bedroom

'How's about a quickie, whilst your dad and Wilson are having a shower? You're giving me the hots walking about in your underwear.' Kingsley kissed and groped her but stopped when she shook her head.

'No Chuck, I've come to a decision that there will be no sex hereon until we get married. That way our honeymoon really will be something to look forward to. And please don't argue, my mind's made up.'

Kingsley sighed. 'That's a toughie, Toni; if that's the case I'm going to insist on the earliest possible date for our wedding.'

Toni Denard smiled. *Success! You're OK in bed Chuck but you're not like Jos, and anyway, I don't love you anymore.*

'Suit's me, Chuck. We'll talk about it later.'

Cole was watching the exchange and swore under his breath; he wanted to end it all right then. *Please don't have sex; I'll kill you now.* But now wasn't the right moment; it would be easier,

307

and safer, if they were all off guard and in the same room. *Don't underestimate Toni, Jos, she's a killer, just like you.*

CHAPTER THIRTY-SEVEN

Later

Cole returned to the car and drove back along the way he came, parking a hundred yards or so from the villa. He replaced his blonde wig with a bald skull cap and a bushy black beard. Toni would recognise him if she paid close attention, but if things went to plan it wasn't going to matter either way.

It was evening and dusk was beginning to settle in when he stationed himself back up on the hill; his armoury in a bag beside him. He raised his binoculars and made the pretence of watching the plentiful seabirds but every now and then stealing a look into the ground floor rooms. The dining room was on the left of the building and the lounge on the right. Rosetti and Tiger Wilson were engaged in conversation in the latter.

Toni and Kingsley were setting the table in the dining room. Cole smiled; it was all going his way. *Not long now, Jos.* Kingsley finished what he was doing and joined the men in the lounge. Toni headed to the kitchen presumably to prepare the evening meal. At one point, she joined the men and Rosetti popped a bottle of champagne and filled everyone's glass.

Whatever was said, Toni burst out laughing, the others joining in. Drinking and conversing ensued for ten minutes or so, at which point Toni left the room.

Five minutes later she started carrying lidded silver salvers into the dining room. *Great! You're dining in. Little do you know it's your last meal. Eat up. Enjoy! You don't have much time left.* It was time to go. Cole rose and made his way down to the beach, his stomach knotting as he thought about what lay ahead. He walked along the silvery sand and studied the sea for a few minutes. The lights at the rear of the house were off; presumably they were assembling in the dining room. Cole pulled on a pair of latex gloves; he wouldn't be leaving any trace of his visit.

The sun was moving downwards to set on the horizon as Cole climbed up onto the dock and tip-toed along it to the villa's rear garden. He pushed open the gate and moved swiftly to the rear door where he slowly tried the handle. The door inched open and he could hear voices coming from a door on the right beyond the kitchen. Cole primed his handgun and stuck it in his waistband, then reached into the sack and took out the Banshee assault rifle.

His relationship with Toni broke into his thoughts momentarily and his eyes moistened. At that minute he hated Toni, hated Kingsley, in fact he hated the whole fucking world. He gathered himself and set it aside; Jos Cole the lover was history and had to be forgotten. The moment he dreaded had come; Jos Cole the killer was back in charge. He was now reliant on the guns; they were loaded and ready; he wished he'd had the opportunity to test them. *Too late now, Jos.*

The dining room door was wide open; Cole strode forward on his toes, quickly but quietly, the voices getting ever louder as he approached. Drink was flowing, everybody was noisy and happy but not for much longer. He stepped through the dining room door, his finger on the trigger. 'Good evening, all.'

Four heads swung round in unison as Cole pulled the trigger; Toni and Kingsley pitched forward and slumped onto the table. Rosetti and Tiger Wilson, were knocked backwards off their chairs onto the floor. Silence followed the outburst of gunfire; his mission was complete.

Cole dropped the rifle, pulled the Sig Sauer from his waistband and walked to the table; he had to finish the job. Toni, Conroy, Wilson and Rosetti were all dead, but even so they all suffered the same fate; a single bullet to the head. Cole inwardly thanked his lucky stars that Toni had fallen facing downwards and he didn't have to see her lifeless face.

He picked up the rifle and laid it on the table, its job was done. Next, he headed out into the garden, and over to a shed he'd spotted earlier. His lucky stars had been working overtime; he found what he'd hoped he would – a ten gallon can of diesel. Most motor boat owners had a can for emergencies.

Cole had decided to complicate matters for the scene of crimes people; he rolled Rosetti onto a rug and dragged him by the heels out of the room, through the kitchen and out into the garden. Rosetti was bleeding from his head and chest but with luck the rug would ensure there would be no trail of blood for the investigators to follow. That done, he returned to collect the boat ignition key from a hook next to the back door; he had recognised it by its cork float when he first arrived.

The sun had set and darkness was taking hold as he dragged Rosetti's body to the motor launch and tumbled it onto to the deck. Cole jumped on board and started up the engine and left it idling as he ran back to the house.

Back in the dining room he stripped down to his boxers, discarding his clothes along with his false beard and skull cap. That done, he poured diesel over each body and around the dining room, followed by the living room and kitchen and finally up the stairs. With one last dispassionate look at Toni's lifeless form, any lingering feelings of love were gone. He struck a match and threw it onto her boyfriend's body – revenge of a sort – the vapour ignited immediately.

Cole grabbed the rifle from the table and raced from the house back to the dock and Rosetti's boat. He threw the rifle and hand gun onto the deck alongside Rosetti's body then untied both mooring lines and stepped on board. He used the boat's stern control set-up to manoeuvre the launch round and set its course for the horizon. The launch was sailing slowly away from the dock; Cole was feeling good, everything had gone to plan.

The boat was a hundred or so metres from the dock when Cole carried out his final actions. He lifted both guns and threw them in opposite directions into the sea then pulled the pins from both grenades and lobbed them forward down the steps onto the lower deck and well away from the engine. In the seconds before the explosions, he pushed the speed lever to Full Speed Ahead and leapt overboard. He remained under water until the grenades exploded. As he had hoped, the boat sped away towards the horizon, slowly sinking as it took in water via its ruptured hull.

Cole swam to the beach, walking when he reached the shallows and smiling with satisfaction when he saw the flames beginning to spread through the villa. Within minutes, he was back in the Ford and on his way to a quiet area where he dressed in shorts and a tee-shirt.

He needed overnight accommodation and stopped at a cheap motel on the outskirts of Jacksonville where he booked in for the night. He was starving but crisps, cola and chocolate bars were the only fare available from a slot machine in reception, none of which appealed.

A disturbed night followed, one filled with conflicting dreams of Tony; pictures of her in good times, others of her body going up in flames.

CHAPTER THIRTY-EIGHT

Next day

Early next morning he got up early and drove to Jacksonville airport to return the car and catch the first available flight to New York. The flight took under three hours and he felt completely relaxed by the time the plane touched down at JFK airport around half-past ten. During the flight he partook of a light breakfast and the all-important caffeine-boosting coffee and enjoyed his first nap without harrowing dreams. Life was already starting to feel better.

He told himself he was feeling good having reached the conclusion that his personal vendetta had been justified. But his thoughts had other ideas, they weren't ready to rewrite history. *Toni was a mirage, Jos, just a mirage, forget her. No she wasn't Jos; she was the woman you loved, the woman who you planned to spend your life with. Fuck it Toni, why did you have to come into my life?*

Cole was tempted to fly back to the UK, but all hell would break loose when the authorities began their investigation. He concluded it was best to stick with his original plan and fly to

Ottawa, another two-hour flight, and then drive 200 kilometres along the Trans-Canada Highway to Montreal airport. If he did by chance get on law enforcement's radar it would be a difficult trail to follow.

There was one other complication; he would have to use his false United States passport and driving licence to get out of the States and into Canada, but it would be risky to use it to get back into the UK. That problem would have to wait for now.

The plane landed in Ottawa around 4pm and he hired a car for the two-hour drive to Montreal. The Highway was busy, but the journey went smoothly and he arrived at Pierre Elliot Trudeau Airport around 6pm. The adrenaline had drained away and tiredness was taking hold. It was too late to catch the last flight to Heathrow; he would have to stay overnight in one of the airport hotels and he chose the Marriot.

The check in procedure at the Marriot went routinely until the Reception Clerk asked him where he was from. Cole looked at her blankly. 'Where are you from Mr Reilly, sir?'

'Sorry I was miles away. Boston, my home town is Boston, though I live in Washington now.'

'I love Boston, but you don't really have their accent. You don't sound Irish either, though with a name like Reilly you should.'

Cole smiled and put the slightest inflection of southern Irish into his accent. 'Sure, I've lost all my accent over the years.'

She eyed him curiously. 'A pity, I love an Irish accent. I've put you in room 202, second floor; the elevator is behind you. Do you require any assistance?'

Cole shook his head. 'I'll be fine.'

He felt mentally exhausted, bed was calling him and his tummy was rumbling, but a long soak in a hot bath was his first priority. He spent an hour and a half luxuriating in a bathtub, regularly topping up with hot water as it cooled down. It was time to resolve his one outstanding problem. He had exited the States and entered Canada using his false American passport and that meant he would have to fly back to the UK using the same passport. Doing that would require an entry visa for the UK which he didn't possess. That would present difficulties when he landed at Heathrow and generate attention he wanted to avoid.

He phoned Gerry Moore on her personal mobile. 'Hi Chief, I need your assistance.'

'Now, why am I not surprised?' He noted that Moore didn't sound annoyed; it was almost as though she had been expecting his call.

'I'm in the Marriot Hotel in Montreal airport, travelling under the name Liam Reilly. I'm using an American passport but don't have a visa. Getting back into the UK will prove problematic.'

'Hold on, I'm going have to make notes. OK, let's have your date of birth, your passport details and your US driving licence number just in case I need it, though I doubt if I will.'

Cole gave her the info and then pushed his luck. 'I haven't had time to book a ticket but I'd like a morning flight out. It's short notice but I'm wondering if it's something you could arrange. I'll refund the department of course.'

'Leave it with me. I'll do the necessary and call you back later.'

'Thanks, Chief. I'm looking forward to getting home.'

Moore chuckled. 'I'll bet you are.'

Cole decided to eat in his room to avoid dining in the restaurant and perhaps have to face up to more inquisitive questions. *Where are you from? Are you on holiday? Where have you been? What did you think of ...* As he ate, he watched CNN. Predictably the headline story was about Rosetti's villa burning to the ground and three charred unidentified bodies being found in the house. The Police and CIA were investigating.

Moore phoned him two hours later. 'Hello, Jos, or should I say Liam? You're booked on Air Canada flight, 9.05 am to Heathrow, Business Class. You'll land around 3pm and I'll be there to meet you.'

'Thank you, Chief. Business Class, that's great, aren't I the lucky boy. Look forward to catching up.'

317

CHAPTER THIRTY-NINE

Heathrow

Cole's flight touched down fifteen minutes early and he was among the first to walk across the air bridge. His eyes lit up when he saw Moore standing with a Senior Immigration Officer at the entrance to the terminal. She smiled broadly when their eyes met. He was introduced to the Immigration Officer, Lynda Jones, who accompanied them and took care of the Border Control and customs formalities. Cole gave her his thanks for her assistance and Moore led him outside to her waiting car.

'Whilst I remember, Jos. Give me the US passport and driving licence you've been using. I'll deal with those.'

They settled into the rear seat of her chauffeured Jaguar and she instructed her driver to take them to Cole's flat.

'Tell me about your trip, Jos.'

'What do you want to know?'

'Everything.'

Cole glanced at the driver. Moore shook her head, 'He can't hear us unless I switch on the mic.'

'I don't know if you'll like what you're going to hear but here goes.......' Cole went through the details of his latest exploits; he knew Moore would have worked out most of his expedition. When he finished, he sat back and drew a deep breath. 'I don't suppose you approve of my exploits. Am I still with the Service or are you giving me the boot?

To his relief, Moore smiled. 'On the contrary I'm proud of you; the CIA are chasing their tails trying to figure out what's gone on. I think the way you disposed of Mitch Rosetti was shear genius. It'll be a long time, if ever, before they find his boat. And my guess is, that when they finally get round to searching Rosetti's main residence, they'll find all sorts of incriminating evidence related to money laundering and criminal acts. I'm not sure if it will reveal that he was the head of the Hydra, or whether they would ever admit it, even if they found out he was.'

Cole nodded. 'I doubt if we'll ever get to know everything about the Hydra.'

Moore nodded.'I agree but we know enough to inflict severe damage, especially now that its main sources of intelligence have been taken out of the game. By the way, that reminds me. There are reports of three bodies in Rosetti's house and I guess Toni and her fiancé account for two, Rosetti was at the bottom of the sea, so who was the third unfortunate.?

Cole grimaced. 'Sadly, it was another traitor. It was my ex-commander, General Tiger Wilson.'

Moore punched the air. 'Bugger me! We knew he'd gone off on holiday to the States, but he went off our radar soon after he landed. I'm not sure how his disappearance will be explained; thankfully that's a problem I'll leave to the MoD spin merchants. Sadly, he leaves a wife and three teenagers behind. I know you admired him, and with good reason, but in the end there's no escaping the fact that he let his country down. Good riddance, I say.'

'I guess so.' Cole still felt bad.

Moore smiled. 'Cheer up, I have a bit of news for you, good news, I think. I'm pleased to tell you, that not only are you still with us, Jos, but you've also gained a promotion and a large salary increase. You'll have to earn it though; we have a task to finish. You'll be heading up MI6's involvement in Operation Extinction with the objective of wiping out the Hydra in Europe.'

Cole was stunned. 'Gosh! Really? I can hardly believe my luck. And do I have a new title?'

'It's not luck, Jos, you've earned it big time. As for your title, formally you'll still be addressed as Commander but you'll be on the books as Senior Agent; Special Services Europe. And, more good news, the PM has guaranteed a generous ring-fenced budget which will cover the appointment of two Agents under you direct command.'

Cole shook his head his thoughts were spinning. 'I think I'll stick with my Commander title, but two Agents reporting to me, that's more than I could ever have wished for. As for the Hydra operation – bring it on.'

The car pulled up outside Cole's apartment block.

'Take the rest of the week off and report to my office next Monday, 9am sharp. I want you to bring some ideas along as to how you'll manage Operation Extinction. It'll involve liaison with our counterparts in Europe, Interpol etc.'

Cole saluted. 'Yes Chief, I'll be there on the dot. It really is good to be back.'

'By the way, I've got a new PA. I hope she'll meet with your approval.'

Cole smiled. 'I'm sure she will, make sure you tell her good things about me.'

He waved goodbye then made his way into the apartment block, singing random lines from songs as the lift rose. His apartment door was a welcome sight and he was still singing when he let himself in; even the scattering of junk mail on the floor didn't irritate him. He gathered it up and was heading for the waste bin when a handwritten envelope from the USA caught his eye. It was sealed and stamped Special Delivery; Diplomatic Post. Cole's stomach knotted – it could only be from Toni. For a split second he was minded to throw it away but he knew that if he did, he would forever wonder what the envelope contained.

Cole tore open the envelope, his heart catching when he saw it was indeed from Toni. His first thought was to crumple it up and throw it way. *Read it Jos, surely that's the least she deserves.* Her handwriting was easy to read.

My Dearest Darling Jos,

I've got a few confessions to make and should really be making them face to face but I've taken the coward's way out, hence this letter.

When you've read this, you might not want to have anything more to do with me and if that is the case I'll understand. But just know that whatever happens I'll go on loving you and hope that in time you'll come back to me - we were meant for each other.

So, here it is Darling, as you read on just remember I love you.

There's no easy way to say this – Mitch Rosetti is my father – he is high up in the Hydra – he sent me to Europe to entrap you. To make matters worse, I'm engaged to a guy called Chuck Kingsley but I promise that will have ended by the time you get this letter.

There it is - I've confessed, I'm so sorry our story began the way it did. We were just two agents of the system set against each other – we weren't meant to fall in love.

But fall in love we did and you're my ideal; we are 100% meant for each other. I've told my father everything and that you are my priority above all else. He says he understands, though I'm not entirely convinced. I've told him if he tries any funny business regarding you, I'll kill him, and I mean it. I love you and nothing is going to change that.

I haven't taken your calls because I wanted to clear the air before we made arrangements to meet – maybe I'm not as brave as I like to believe.

Speak soon, all my love always

Toni xxx

Cole dropped the letter and cradled his face in his hands, tears ran down his cheeks. *Life can be pure shit at times.*